MOURNING

EMBER

MOURNING EMBER

BOOK TWO

ODIN V OXTHORN

ISBN: 978-0-9998349-2-3 (Ebook)
ISBN: 978-0-9998349-3-0 (Paperback

Edited by: Valorie Clifton
Cover Art by: Karolina Jędrzejak (RinRinDaishi)
https://www.facebook.com/rinrindaishi
Formatting by Erica Alexander
https://www.facebook.com/SerendipityFormatting/

A NOTE FROM THE AUTHOR

This work was inspired by a severe lack in representation in fiction. I wanted to create a world that is not so focused on what society pressures us to be. A language that focuses more on what the individual can accomplish, not predetermined by status or biology. Consent and consequence are the primary ideals of this place. While this is an alien world, I wrote this to be accessible, and to make it seem not so far-fetched that we could take from it as humans.

But all in all, it is still a piece of fiction. A story that takes the reader on a trip through the imagination.

No matter your take, my ultimate goal is to entertain, and I hope you get something a little more than just enjoyment.

-Odin

PROLOGUE

##0.1##

The pathetic sea of misguided creatures ambled toward her, stumbling as they pawed at their hollow eye sockets, demanding answers. Demanding penance. She refused to face them, their wails and moans berating her defiance.

One by one their forms sparked, igniting the forest with an ethereal crimson glow. The legion of burning forms carved a trail through the trees, a jagged path stretching toward oblivion.

Hot, breathy air danced around her slurred stride. The warmth seared her spine, her withdrawal halted, her aching bones creaking with the strained effort. Their pleading voices tore through her ears, pain flicking across her brain with flashes of light. She cursed her syrup-laden joints, pushing her protesting body forward.

The drove lurched on with arms outstretched, clawing their way up the mound of earth she stood upon. "*Peacekeeper.*" The arid murmur of the host eroded her nerves. "Nara."

Her voice evaporated as her jaw clamped shut. Cracks echoed through the trees as she ground her teeth to dust. A trickle of fragmented bone spilled over her lips as she fought to gain control of her insolent limbs.

A bellow resonated from her throat, shuddering the leaves as she manifested her wrath with a torrent of wind. Her force beat back the advancing flames, splicing the blaze at the neck. But her efforts only provoked their ire. Their enkindled forms intensified, swallowing the foliage with voracious light.

"Nara…"

The creatures raised their ashen hands to the flickering sky, their ember-studded digits unfurling into serrated points. A web of sharpened tendrils cast a shadow over her, piercing the air with a rending shriek as the snare plunged toward the earth.

She challenged the crowd as they latched onto her, claws ripping through her soft flesh. A scowl radiated through the inferno. Her skin burned as her own fire churned inside, threatening to break free of her control as the blades snaked up her arms. The collective pulled at her, tearing out sinew and flesh in streaming banners. Her throat cinched shut as she endured the rite, her resentment exploding inside her.

Plumes of smoke expelled from her wounds, choking out the air with her spite. Billowing clouds surrounded her form in blackness, impeding the advance of the discontented crowd. Hisses coaxed her ears as the fingers corroded away from her skin, their liquid metal forms dripping onto the soil.

"Nara!" Louder the cacophony shrieked. Her suffering was not enough to satisfy them.

She refused to acknowledge, casting the noise out of her head as she imbibed the featureless smog. Silence approached as she sank into the ground, watching intently as she embraced the darkness.

***

##0.2##

"HEY, NARA!" Garrett's voice burst through the murk of her consciousness.

"Fucking… *What?*" She leered at the meek human leaning over her.

"Sorry." He promptly retracted his hand from her shoulder. "We're approaching Ara'yulthr territory, and we need you at the front before they blast us out of the solar system."

"Nrgh." She groaned, laboriously rolling off the bed. *And again with this bullshit. What in nine hells could Xannat want from me now?*

"How's your leg?" Garrett gently prodded.

Nara wiped the grime from her face as she ambled toward the cockpit. "I'll live."

Both Nara and Cain had spent the flight in solitude, each drowning in the quandaries of their personal despair. The tension made awkward company for Garrett, who had to find other creative means to amuse himself through the journey. Refreshing the signal of the market trade boards in search of the fleeting trends in antiquities quickly grew tedious. It was only a meager distraction from the brevity of the situation, and while he was relieved the trip had finally come to an end, he was worried for the one person he tentatively considered a friend.

Despite its modest size, Cain's ship had proven comfortable enough to call base camp for the duration of their travel. While the craft was legally classified as a light cargo freighter to curb GaPFed's suspicious dock foreman, it was more accurately described as a heavy attack vessel that occasionally ran as a courier. Though considerably larger than a fighter, it had the speed and maneuverability to surpass overconfident pirate flyboys who might attempt to harass them. And more than triple the teeth.

The three spent most of their time in the modest living quarters, with enough space for the troubled passenger to have a reasonably sized pacing lap. Furnishing was sparse, composed of two bunk beds that doubled as medical units, utilitarian shower facilities, and a small storage unit for prepackaged food and sundries. The rugged interior décor left little to the imagination, its brushed gunmetal paneling serving its purpose to reinforce the hull, and nothing more.

An emergency airlock divided the quarters from the cargo hold, the border of the blast door emblazoned with glaring yellow and black stripes. The entryway extended into a chrome-railed balcony, opening into the adequately-sized hold containing a few parcels of supplies and spare hardware for ship repairs.

The control deck sat on the opposite side of the lodgings, accessible by a short ladder climb upward. Cain rarely occupied the lonely command seat during the trip, depending on AI piloting while only periodically checking on its status to ensure no hostiles tailed their ship.

Nara pulled herself into the cockpit, firmly leaning against the pilot seat as Cain coordinated their flight path. She begrudgingly pried her eyes from the glittering controls, braving a glance through the viewscreen at the space she had once called home.

The horizon was engulfed by a giant orb of swirling cerulean blue, the planet's orbit flecked with the magnificent presence of the Ara'yulthr vanguard fleet. Metal bone-plated draconic beasts soared across the viewport, their plumes of bright blue fire pushing them along. The resplendent battleships led the brood around the nest, sensory wings outstretched as their hatchlings accompanied them, remaining vigilant for intruders encroaching their hunting grounds.

"So that's what a full-scale navy looks like," Garrett breathed, pulling himself on deck as his eyes remained transfixed to the screen. "It's beautiful."

Before Nara could decide whether to dignify his observation with a reply, a fledgling cruiser broke formation and swooped around, homing in on the visitors with a wing of fanged interceptor drones in tow.

A sharp chirp jittered the flight deck as a notification flashed on the panel, accompanied by a shallow hum of warning from the targeting sensors. Cain reached for the strobing blue light, flicking the switch to acknowledge the hailing ship.

"You are approaching Ara'yulthr territory. Our borders are closed to trade," an authoritarian voice stated in Galactic Trade. "Please revert your heading and we will direct you to the nearest inhabited port in this system."

Cain looked up at Nara, who nodded in defeated approval.

"I have a high-priority shipment to be delivered planetside," Cain responded. "I was directed to ask for Commander Tosk of the *Armored Wake*."

The communication line quieted, leaving the three simmering in apprehension.

"They don't seem pleased," Garrett vocalized.

"Don't expect swift results around here." Nara scoffed. "It takes a century to decide who has the authority to take a piss."

The drones darted in agitated loops, their sharpened wings flitting violently as they adjusted trajectory, impatiently awaiting orders from their elder while its commander deliberated over the fate of their quarry.

"Patching you through to the *Armored Wake* now," the cruiser finally conceded, closing off the communication line. The ship remained still, maintaining their imposing presence and keeping Cain within range of their weaponry.

"Tosk here," a new voice announced from a separate channel. "State your business."

"Priority cargo for qu'ol Fariem of Pa'arthex clan," Cain obliged.

Another biting silence replied to the declaration, leaving Garrett squirming in discomfort. He glanced between his two companions, but neither was willing to acknowledge his concern. Reading a stone would be more productive than searching Cain's face for a reaction, and Nara was far too distracted to acknowledge him.

"A squadron has been deployed to meet you. They will take you to the *Wake*," Tosk flatly announced. "And don't test me, mercenary. I have no patience for deceit."

Four of the drones broke away from the cruiser, speeding toward their position. They situated themselves around Cain's ship, one at each cardinal point. The sensor screens on the control deck flickered acknowledgement as the drones transmitted homing beacons to his navigation computer, broadcasting their position and heading.

Cain matched speed to let the fighters guide him toward the battleship, the *Wake's* monstrous form surpassing the limits of the computer display. The drones ushered them over the starboard side, guiding them along an orderly row of weapons batteries projecting from the ship's jagged plating.

They stopped at a break in the spikes, edging toward the gaping maw of one of the *Wake's* numerous fighter bays. Crackling pink energy sealed the expanse, protecting the crew from the external elements while they worked on the deck. As the entourage centered over the bay opening, the drones removed themselves from Cain's bow, lining up at his exposed side while keeping their weapons focused.

"You have been cleared for landing," the *Wake's* control officer declared. "Please lower your shields and divert your energy to accept the docking tracker."

The command deck wound down as Cain complied with the order, permitting the *Wake* to take control. A ray of vibrant fuchsia light ejected from a fanged protrusion overlooking the bay opening, feeling over the diminutive morsel of Cain's ship with its energetic forked tongue.

Garrett leaned in, a rush of excitement flooding his skin as the ship eased into the mouth of the *Wake*. Ever since watching the starports on Arcadia, the nuances of space travel had always fascinated him. Because of his cursed heritage, he never dreamed he would be able to witness the inner workings firsthand.

He strained to contain a smile, staring in fascination while the craft breached the force field, its energy swallowing the hull within its embrace. When the *Wake* engulfed them completely, Cain initiated his landing procedures, gently planting the ship on the shining floor of the deck.

The engine murmured a last acknowledgement before drowning the cockpit with an eerie silence. The lights on the control display slipped into a gentle slumber as the power diminished, leaving the trio inside a muted smolder of emergency lighting.

"You okay?" Garrett watched Nara's dour face intently.

"Ask me after I've left this rock," she rebuked as she headed down the ladder. *I should have just run to another planet.*

##0.3##

A RAPID SUCCESSION of terse clangs battered against the cargo door. Cain hit the hatch control, concealing his annoyance as the pneumatic hinges slowly peeled the entrance open in a hiss of mist.

The towering frame of Commander Tosk greeted him from below. An uncertainty with a hint of displeasure flickered through their stony features. They exchanged glances with Cain as they stepped on board, speaking wordless warnings through garnet eyes. Cain met their expression with similar mistrust, letting disdain warp his expression.

"Not what I was expecting," Tosk declared, scrutinizing the mechanics of the modest ship. Cain pointed to the front, directing the dignitary to the living quarters. They gave an affirming nod before making their way across the deck, taking no notice of Cain's scornful glare as they climbed the stairs to where Nara awaited.

"Warlord," Tosk flatly greeted the cold figure leaning against the bunk, scanning her up and down.

She scowled, exposing her fangs. "That is not my title."

"Half the Council seems to disagree." Tosk sneered.

"And you?" Nara challenged. "Where does your loyalty stand?"

"I do not have all the facts regarding your situation, so I have no opinion." The commander looked down at their nails. "But I couldn't care less who holds power as long as I can have full control of my ship back."

"I will bear that in mind."

Garrett compacted his presence as he lay on the floor of the cockpit, inching over the edge to watch the conversation below. Unable to understand the language, Garrett tried to gauge the tone of the conversation, bouncing his vision between their guarded postures as their brusque words assaulted the walls.

Commander Tosk's regal aura commanded authority. Every movement was succinct and calculated, even as they raised an arm to brush back their impeccably groomed slate-colored hair. They stood taller than Nara by a few inches and appeared considerably older. Their imposing frame was sharply trimmed by a modest dark-hued uniform, their build concealed by a skilled tailor. No insignia or other extraneous decoration adorned their chest, as if the garment was meant to be practical instead of showy.

"Do you think you can fix this nonsense?" Tosk folded their arms.

"No." Nara hid a sneer as she shook her head firmly. She watched the commander intently, sensing the concern in their features at her admittance. Though she possessed no context to the games the Council had played in her absence, Tosk was concealing something from her. The scale of the conflict was far greater than they were attempting to play off.

"I see." Tosk glanced up at the nosy human. "I suppose there is nothing more to discuss. I will take you to my transport personally and send you to qu'ol Fariem immediately."

"Fine." She summoned a twinkling light from her pocket, raising a small circular badge to her throat. In a flash, her body was engulfed in a silvery liquid metal, morphing and adjusting to fit her form. When the strange intelligent material completed its task, it hardened to a suit of sleek plated armor, concealing her face in a ghoulish featureless mask.

"My crew will not bother you," Tosk pointed out. "Disguise is not necessary."

"That remains to be seen," Nara retorted as the helmet snapped over her features.

"As you wish." They gave a small nod before exiting the living quarters.

Nara followed behind, letting her expression display her full ire beneath her mask. Her angst amplified as she heard the patterning of Garrett's boots darting for their position.

Ugh. She stopped halfway across the deck and abruptly turned to the human. "Cain will drop you off to wherever you need to go."

"Oh. Uh, well, I don't exactly know where that would be." Garrett glanced over at the man attempting to look nonchalant while organizing the sparse pile of cargo crates. "I don't have a place to call home now."

"Cain is well-traveled," she replied. "He can recommend anywhere you like."

"I…" He suppressed a chill as he scanned the quiet man. Her cold dismissal baffled him. After all they went through in Arcadia, was she going to cut him off so quickly? "I… I still have questions. About our previous associations."

Now is not the time, human. Nara sighed, resting a palm on her visor. "You will be waiting a long time for answers."

"I am patient."

That's a bold claim, Nara internally scoffed. "War isn't a tourist experience, kid. You'll find nothing here worth your amusement. And you'll probably get killed in the crossfire."

"That isn't fair of you to judge me like that." The firmness in his voice caught him off guard, and he quickly cleared away the hostility from his throat.

Oh, for fuck's sake. Nara ground her teeth. She examined the human's face, detecting irritation and uncertainty in his features laced with a heavy dose of dread that he was desperately trying to hide from her. *Why the hell am I still entertaining this creature?*

Despite his clumsiness, the human could take care of himself just fine. His insistence on staying in her company confounded her. He was amicable enough, more than capable of making contacts of his own accord. It wouldn't be long until he could establish a business elsewhere. He just needed time to explore matters for himself.

Her pessimism began to color her search for his reasoning. What would happen if Galavantier got wind of his whereabouts during his travels? The Biotech's name was affluent enough to pull strings in GaPFed parliament. That was all she needed, another fleet of GaPFed ships trying to hurl their weight around an argument they have no voice in. She already had to quiet one planet-sized war. She wasn't about to deal with another one on the galactic scale.

But one thing was for certain—the human was a living omen. One she needed to keep a watchful eye on.

"Fine. Come along," Nara conceded. "Keep covered and stay out of my way."

Cain approached them with a small metal container, offering a cache of spare mechanical parts to maintain the guise of a delivery. She met his vibrant odd eyes as she accepted the box, troubled by the concern radiating from the flickering augmented light. The ghostly man never used his voice if he could avoid it, but his language expressed more in these few moments than the entire time she knew him.

But choices had to be made.

"Three words, Cain." Nara turned away and stepped off the ship.

##0.4##

A HOLLOW SURGE of air droned through the abyss of the fighter bay, forbidding the echoes of their footsteps from touching the unreachable ceiling. The hold was cleansed with blinding white light reflecting off polished chrome walls and floors. Rows of stalwart fighter drones amplified the unsettling ambience. Their flickering red status lights glared warily at the diminutive intruders as they lined the path.

Tosk marched Nara and Garrett toward a small winged beast gently purring in idle slumber. The creature stirred as they approached, stretching open its jaws with a labored yawn. In a sharp about-face, the commander motioned for their guests to climb aboard. They watched Garrett cautiously as he stepped inside the ship, casting a side-eye at the human's ingenuous wonder radiating from his aura.

The beast lazily pulled its mouth shut, awaiting orders while the passengers settled inside. Tosk seated themself into the pilot chair and executed a concise cycle of takeoff checks, pitting the air with a terse flurry of clicks and beeps. A throaty rumble acknowledged their actions, its call elevated to a rushing tumult as the engines engaged, wind pushing against the deck. The beast gradually lifted upward, stretching out the fatigue from its wings in a flowing arc.

Tosk maneuvered the ship above the legion of drones, gravity pawing at the cabin as they glided toward the opening of the *Wake*. The energetic membrane of the atmospheric shield warped around the hull as they eased through the force field, pursing back together as the ship left the safety of the hold. When they were clear of the *Wake's* jagged perimeter, Tosk ramped speed to join the brood out in space.

Garrett gripped the arm of his seat, his nervousness combating with his unrelenting excitement for the journey. He made a conscious effort to avert his attention from the cockpit, looking up at Nara for guidance. But she was unnervingly still, her featureless helmet burning a hole through the floor. He squeezed out a soft exhale, trying not to disturb her meditation with the noise.

A gentle mechanical whirr startled his concentration, and a panel slithered down the ceiling across from him. The screen flickered to life, projecting the viewport of the cockpit. Garrett glanced over to Tosk, just missing their eyes as they turned their head back to the controls.

"Thank you," Garrett attempted, but only silence replied. He focused on the screen, shaking off the discomfort clawing at his skin.

The gas giant swallowed the view as they approached, revealing whirls of currents defining its pillowy surface. Gaps broke apart the striated patterns as thorny ships emerged from the body, the engines stirring and blending the shades in a foamy celestial concoction.

Tosk's ship slowed to a gentle coast as they pierced through the clouds, the blue mist curling around the beast in fibrous plumes. Scores of mechanical winged insects danced inside the fluff, excitedly scanning the area with rays of probing light. The antics of the swarm abruptly halted as the creatures spotted the intrusion, darting for the ship in aggravated droves. A wave passed their feelers over the hull, gleefully transmitting their approval with chattering bleeps. They scattered as quickly as they arrived, whizzing through the cloud to find another shiny object to harass.

The ship emerged through the barrier into a layer of empty space, revealing the cosmic candy center of a terrestrial planet, considerably smaller than what the cloud implied. Lilac clouds wisped lacework over green-blue seas, the landmasses an attractive gradient of teals and greys. From behind the earth, the gas cloud revealed its illusory magic, its ephemeral form bending light to its will, displaying an unobstructed backdrop of the fleet haloed by the searing rays of a lonely star.

I haven't seen the sun in thirty years, Nara lamented, her gaze tracing around the light of the celestial body. *Even Arcadia forbade me that luxury.*

The jewel-toned planet claimed their focus as they neared, showcasing the facets of the continents that adorned the surface. Tongues of warmth lapped the hull as Tosk edged the ship into the glittering atmosphere, the interior shuddering as they contested with physics.

The environmental shields proved a worthy opponent, warping the forces of gravity around them to provide a gentle descent for the passengers.

Buildings began to take shape as they hovered near the surface, clusters of metallic columns that barely reached above the trees. They blended seamlessly with the foliage, the synthetic structures imitating the surrounding wood, overtaken by the waves of greenery stretching over the land.

Tosk steered toward the outer reaches of a populated zone, aiming for a clearing near a warehouse facility. The ship groaned in compliance as it gently lowered to the docking pad, rustling the trees with a swirl of its exhaust. The creature quieted down with Tosk's firm assurance, filling the cabin with a compliant murmur.

Garrett immediately forgot how to breathe as the hatch opened, awestruck by the mystical world of greenery unfolding before him. The trees appeared more like minerals than plant life, their crystalline foliage of teals and pale blues scintillating in the radiant sunshine. Each towering structure was armored with a rocky chrysalis, the legions forming a variegated spectrum of maroons and plums.

Nara snapped him back to reality with a jab at his shoulder. He cleared his throat and rose from his seat, shaking out the travel fatigue from his arguing limbs as he headed for the door. Frigid air pricked his neck as he edged forward, flicking his nerves with a shudder. He absentmindedly shook the sensation away, engrossed by the splendid alien world.

"Elam," Tosk called to Nara, their expression softened. "You have my direct line."

"Is that a fact?" Her eyebrow raised. She didn't know the commander personally, much less their affiliation with Fariem. As a foreigner on her own planet, she was hesitant to entertain the notion of allies from the other forces.

"*Xannat's* favor, Warlord." Their evasive confirmation pierced her suspicion.

"I'd prefer to depend on yours," Nara retorted as she disembarked. Luck was an adversary that she refused to acknowledge.

CHAPTER 1

##1.0##

Nara left Garrett to his own devices, heading straight for the warehouse. She stepped under the simulated leafed canopy draped over the frame of the loading door, shedding her mask as she examined the maze of laboratory equipment and computers.

Everything is where it always was. She steeled herself as she approached an aged individual hunched over a console screen. Their expression focused as they vehemently combed a stylus through ashen jade hair.

"The rumors were true, serr'kahn," the figure replied, looking up from their work. "Words cannot express your presence appropriately."

"It's nice to see you too, Fariem." Nara's lips twitched as she tried to force a smile, bringing her gaze down as their eyes passed over her. She remained still as the petite figure paced around, discordant emotions impeding her ability to discern their reaction to her presence.

"Ki'nit, Syf, look who is here." Fariem beckoned a pair of individuals cleaning a stack of sample trays. The associates' faces lit up as they noticed Nara, gliding over to her with relief and fascination.

Though the duo hailed from different clans, they were united by a far-reaching thread of fate. They shared a unique psychic bond, their pointed features carved from the same stone. Even their movements were in synch as they curiously circled Nara like a gentle flow of water.

"Greetings, Warlord," Ki'nit said. "We thought we had lost you."

They were both much younger than Fariem, yet at least five centuries older than her. Their physical appearance was the key to distinguishing them, their differences reflecting in their mannerisms. Ki'nit's cool, calculated ocean blue eyes sought order from the world, their sight unhindered by their gleaming raven hair forcibly restrained in a tight pleat.

"My, how you have grown since last we met," Syf added with a head tilt. "It was not even that long ago."

Syf viewed the world differently, mirroring their counterpart with a void of blackened eyes that divined secrets from otherworldly realms. Their roguish streak was amplified by the cerulean flyaway strands of hair encircling their blithe expression, deserters that broke free from the halfhearted bonds of the loose tail playfully brushing against their shoulders. Together they were an equalized force, each counteracting the extreme of the other to maintain a peaceful balance in their relationship.

Though the duo had always projected a soft demeanor, Nara broadcast her discomfort at the scrutiny. Fariem and their two assistants were her caretakers, the closest semblance to family. They were safe people, or at least they were before her exile. She was unable to witness their reaction to her downfall, and Fariem's role in the Council injected her with apprehension.

"You must be exhausted. Come along inside." Fariem took the box from her hands, then projected disapproval when she spotted Garrett quietly marveling at the faux tree bark coating the warehouse's exterior. "Who's the meat bag?"

"Ow, Fariem." Nara scowled. "Contractor with a mutual enemy."

"I see." They scanned the human up and down.

"Garrett, this is Fariem," Nara introduced in Trade. "A developer of experimental medicine by profession."

"Pleased to meet you…" His voice trailed off as Fariem sharply turned their back to him.

"You're injured." They jabbed Nara in the armored abdomen with a scolding finger. "Off with it, immediately!"

"It's not that bad." Nara gave off a rumble as she raised a palm to her forehead.

"Do not stab me with your impertinence." Fariem scowled. "You're a terrible liar. I know exactly what 'not that bad' means to you."

"Ugh." Nara peeled back the armor to reveal the ichorous medical patches sticking to her flesh. After the altercation with the security droids during their escape, Cain's medbots kept her together enough for her natural healing to take over. But Fariem was a stickler for efficiency and would not have her depending on substandard technology.

Fariem tsked at the sight and waved at their minions. "Serr, help Elam out."

"Yes, Serr'Maht." The duo bowed and flanked Nara, slipping their arms around hers.

I guess nothing has changed. Nara groaned, submitting to her captors as they ushered her deeper into the complex.

Garrett jogged to keep up with the brisk stride of the group, following them down a charcoal-walled hallway. The aesthetic of the facility was pleasantly clean with bold streaks of martial order. It was not stiflingly uncomfortable like a makeshift Undercity hospital, and certainly not as luxurious as Upper, but the rigid bellicose structure of shapes and forms cast an imposing shadow over him.

Nara was led into a room appearing more like an apartment than a medical station, complete with a living room and kitchen facilities. The furnishings matched the blend of militaristic yet bizarrely reassuring atmosphere of the building. Their solidly built boxy structures displayed limited artistic expression.

The duo practically hoisted her onto the bed, echoing sympathetic hums as they scrutinized the patches plastered over her shin. Blood trimmed the edges of the material with a crusted barrier, flaking away as she was jostled. Her abdominal plating began to protrude through the bandages, peeling back the spongy material from her skin in shredded tatters.

"Ouch, would you look at that ineffective garbage?" Fariem shook their head admonishingly as they began to pluck back the bandages. "You're in good hands now."

"I'm sure." Nara rolled her eyes. "What's the situation in the Council?"

"You have barely just arrived and you ask a loaded question like that?" Fariem chastised, pawing through their tools. "I bet you want to march off to meetings immediately. You certainly haven't changed a bit."

"The pain, the grief, Fariem," Nara cursed.

Fariem planted a hearty shove on her chest, pushing her back against the bed. "Relax first, then you can talk filth. I'm sure Ren will visit you tomorrow anyway to discuss it."

Nara stifled a grumble as the duo began work on her. *Good to know Loremaster returned without incident.*

"Now let us see what you have been up to." Fariem waved a scanner over her, uttering an escalating chorus of disgust as they uncovered Nara's battle history through an infinitely scrolling list. "Whoever worked on you had no idea what they were doing. Leaving all this behind, I can see every hole and scar. Rusted knives, that's what they are."

Nara couldn't help but smirk. Back on Arcadia, Declan had more than the capability, but he always made sure she *felt* the consequences of her actions, doing the bare minimum to try to teach her a lesson about caution. It never worked, and he stopped trying. Eventually.

Fariem snapped their eyes up. "And can you please explain to me why your left arm is approximately two-and-a-half decades younger than the rest of you?"

Nara clicked her tongue and averted her gaze, focusing on the work of their assistants. *Yeah, that wasn't a fun ride.*

"I see." Fariem grumbled more curses. "I can fix it all later with a few sessions in a biotherapy tank, but seeing as it's mostly cosmetic, I *suppose* the priority isn't high. Still, what an infuriating lack of professionalism."

Nara didn't acknowledge the ranting, instead observing the sorcery unfolding on the talon wound in her shin she'd endured from the security bots upon her exodus from Arcadia. Though she could see the incisions and the jabs the pair of assistants drove into her muscle, her nerves remained calm, devoid of pain. She had forgotten how gentle medical procedures were here and how much care was taken to ensure the comfort of the patient. It was a nice change to the dire conditions of Undercity, but she was almost guilty for not experiencing her mistakes on a visceral level.

"I have your house, by the way," Fariem added. "They certainly took no time with decommissioning it. You can probably find a nice discreet field to settle in."

Her living arrangements were far from Nara's immediate concerns. It would be unwise to let others find her by building her residence exactly where it was. But traversing through the forests sent a sickening revulsion coursing through her guts.

"I'd rather stay somewhere familiar." Nara flexed her fingers uncomfortably.

"Suit yourself. You can make an extension on the lab in the meantime," Fariem said.

Nara rumbled in acknowledgement, half hearing the offer. The web of political intrigue began to wrap itself around her brain. Her knowledge of the current power structures was a blank slate, uncertainty and suspicion coloring her previous affiliations. How many knew of her coming, and how many were as helpful as they claimed?

"Tosk, huh?" Nara raised an eye at Fariem.

"The humans overstretch your vocal chords too?" The medic ignored her venomous glare. "Qu'ol is a good friend. And owes me quite a lot. They'll do you no harm."

Nara considered their admission in silence. Fariem was not forthcoming with the extent of their emotions toward her arrival. She could sense their relief, yet an underlying conflict teased around their presence. But they habitually guarded their concern from the outside observer. Perhaps that's where she learned it from.

"I appreciate you, Fariem." Nara attempted to provoke a reaction. "I thought I should tell you since I haven't before and was granted this second chance to do so."

"Quiet. I'll have no sentimental pains gnawing on my skull while you are here." Fariem dodged her attack, storming off to wash their hands. They then shattered the air with a sharp clap to summon the attention of their minions, who wordlessly bowed and skirted toward the door. "Now rest."

"Yes, Fariem," Nara sighed as her oppressors departed, poking at the film coating her skin, now a perfect match to her skin tone.

Garrett disguised his uneasiness and slinked into a chair, finding it astoundingly comfortable and form fitting despite its harsh appearance. Watching the interaction gave him a swift reminder of how far out of water he was. The intimate familial connection was an outlandish concept, given his upbringing by blood relatives.

He had prided himself on being an expert on etiquette, deftly navigating through distasteful interactions while remaining the epitome of respectful toward offending engagements. But the few people he had met here were as cold and distant as Nara when he first met her and experts in all forms of intimidation.

Perhaps all it took was a shift in mindset, learning what it takes to crack the chill in new exchanges. And given what he knew of the terms of her departure from her home planet, he resolved to remain patient with his curiosity.

"You're unusually quiet," Nara commented.

"I—" Garrett was startled by her prompt. "It's a lot to process."

"This world is considerably different from Arcadia. Complete with its own set of problems."

"I'm sure I can adapt." Garrett broadcast a nervous smile. *I'm going to have to if I'm a fugitive.*

"Mmm." Nara stared up at the ceiling. *Why the fuck am I here?*

To stop a civil war, or at least that's what she convinced herself. But she was absolved of that responsibility the day of her exile. The most reclusive civilized planet in the galaxy could settle their issues with cataclysmic fire, and not a single mote of dust would reach her if she had remained where she was.

Abberon... Her jaw clenched as the name bore through her ears.

Was that it? Nothing more than a personal vendetta? The rotten creature was just a childish annoyance that did everything in his power to provide opposition. The issue was resolved, and he had been removed from the Council even before her trial took place. But apparently, half the planet followed his lead, and there was no telling how deep his poison ran through the waters of the legislature.

Unanswered questions she painstakingly buried so long ago began to claw their way into her mind. The search for closure was not enough justification to shatter the traditions of a culture over twenty millennia old.

"Fuck this. I want to sleep in my own damn bed." Nara stomped to the floor and dusted herself off.

"Won't Fariem have an issue with your moving around?" Garrett watched her agitated march to the door.

"They haven't stopped me before. They won't now," she said. "C'mon, you'll probably want to see this."

##1.1##

NARA SCANNED the area behind the warehouse, escorting a torso-sized gunmetal crate. Its engines warbled happily as it tagged along behind her, the compact jet playfully stirring the grass beneath it. She ordered the curiosity to land at the far corner of the back wall, then prodded at the screen on its top face, nudging the system awake.

>> *INITIALIZING SETUP. WELCOME WARLORD ELAM'-MUTAVREH.*

Ugh, that name. Nara scowled as she wove through the grid of the last saved floor plan in the device's memory. She slid her fingers around the display, examining the modest accommodation. Kitchen, facilities, bedroom, all the minimum regulated size. Her office space took up nearly all of the area, as it was where she spent the most time on the rare occasions she visited home. If she decided to sleep, it was on the patio floor, where she could enjoy nature and pretend the world wasn't a blazing inferno of policy and duty.

She dragged a square of floor from the selection menu and snapped it to the grid, attaching an additional bedroom to the second floor. With pinched fingers, she stretched out the dimensions, attempting to make the space more comfortable for her unaccustomed aristocratic roommate.

>> *YOU HAVE UTILIZED 75 OF 500 ALLOCATED CREDITS. PROCEED?*

Her status had perks, but she never had the desire to take advantage of them. Work was her main priority, never taking a breath in case the race in her mind caught up to her.

She shook her head at her predicament and accepted the configuration. What was good enough then was good enough now.

>> *ACKNOWLEDGED. SCANNING ENVIRONMENT.*

"Hey, hold still for a bit," she called to Garrett.

He was about to question her intent when the panels of the box burst into a lotus of metal, revealing menacing needle-like protrusions aiming toward him. The pincers stabbed the air with an orb of lasers, flourishing in a precise choreography as the emerald feelers passed over the surrounding area. He blinked as the intrusion assaulted his eyes, sending clouds of green billowing across his vision.

The box continued its luminous assault, collecting information on every inch of the ground, from each leaf in the shrubbery, every blade of grass, and even the collection of jagged rocks that littered the surface of the earth. After a final explosion of white, the damnable contraption quieted down, offering its findings to Nara on the screen.

>> *SCAN COMPLETE. INITIALIZING CONSTRUCTION PROTOCOL. PLEASE REMAIN STATIONARY DURING PROCEDURE.*

The sides of the box rhythmically unfolded into snakes of square tiles, slithering over the grass in systematic steps to coat the ground it in their cold embrace. Garrett jumped back as the metal snakes snapped toward him, threatening to surround him with their sharpened scaled plating.

"Relax," Nara rebuked, remaining in her patch of grass as she checked the status of the machine. The screen provided information as it resumed construction, highlighting the active areas with a white glow.

Garrett forced his flight response to still as the paneling crawled around him, shrinking to a rigid stick to keep as far away from the mechanical menace as he could.

The metal grid began to unfold and march up toward the sky, constructing the walls in precise stitches. When the shelter reached half completion, the onslaught of metal began to creep into the building, dividing its cells to form rooms within the borders.

As a barrier neared a pair of trees inside the perimeter of the house, the metal slipped around the trunks, leaving the green guests in peace as it formed a cocoon around them. From there, the wall continued its mission, carving out the living room and the kitchen access.

A thin slab of metal extruded from the wall, branching out until it formed a sturdy tabletop. Two legs stretched down from the far edge of the surface, latching to the floor with a confirming click.

Another piece of furniture began to cut itself out of the floor, the seams of a side of a chair etching into a panel. It slowly raised from the ground until it stood upright, stretching into a seat and a back frame. The floor produced the other face of the house, bringing it toward the first with a gradual arc. The procedure repeated three times to form an orderly row of perfectly congruent pieces.

The floor began to carve a stairway into a second level, stepping up in jagged motions until it reached its destination on the programmed second level. From there, the ceiling began to unfurl, stretching to start construction on the bedroom spaces.

While it completed its tasks on the second floor, the side wall split open to reveal a modest patio self-contained with transparent barriers. The center of the deck dipped into a cushioned pit, a cozy respite for meditative contemplation.

>> CONSTRUCTING ENERGY AND RESOURCE COLLECTION UNITS.

The screen desaturated the floor plan, shifting through menus as it initialized the outer workings of the maintenance channels. The earth below rumbled as the machination bore sensors into the soil.

Pipes slithered over the screen, connecting the kitchen and facilities to water collectors and filtration units. Panels spread out on top of the ceiling, spitting out information on the status of the sky. As the drills and collection units injected themselves into the ground, information on material collection joined the revelry on screen, filling up colorful bar graphs in an attractive display.

>> *INITIALIZING GROWBED PRODUCTION AND RATION SYNTHESIZER. PLEASE STAND BY.*

Noises erupted through the kitchen as a curious tray stretched from out of the wall, gradually filling with moist soil. Display screens emerged from the trays, broadcasting pH levels and nutrient conditions and a selection of vegetation options to choose from. The trays were divided into quadrants, each set up in a distinctive environment that was ideal for plant life in separate locations from across the globe.

>> *CONSTRUCTION COMPLETE. PLEASE STEP ON TO INTERIOR PLATFORM.*

"Come on up," Nara said. As she examined the results of the assembly, the central computer melted into the building, the screen sliding across the floor until it reached the wall next to the front door. She raised a finger and waited for the device to meet her at eye level.

"Whoa. Is everything built like this?" He watched the floor slide over the patch of grass he had abandoned, poking at the tile with his toe.

"Everything apart from the few relics they preserved from before we had this tech." She walked over and kicked at a chair to dislodge it from the perforated metal flooring. "Most have been deconstructed for environmental reasons."

"What does it run on?" He pressed a palm against the cold metal wall.

Nara emphatically shrugged as she poked orders into the screen. "Science."

She swiped through the decoration configurations until the wall displayed a soothing muted blue. With a drag of a fingertip, she bifurcated the walls waist high from the ground. She pawed through the selection of patterns on display until the lower half projected a cozy lumber motif. The wood shifted colors as she cycled through choices, stopping when the grains were tinted a deep mahogany.

After another flurry of swipes and prods, the ceilings shifted transparent, displaying an unaltered glimpse of the sky and forest above.

Though the camera views weren't intended for security, the ability to see above her offered a mild sense of comfort.

"Step over here and stick your arms out," Nara beckoned. Garrett silently complied, forcing his eyes shut as another scanner snapped a ray at his body, feeling over his proportions with invasive digital fingers. "New clothes will be in your closet shortly. Hungry?"

"Yeah, sure," he breathed, his thoughts vanishing from the sight of the technology surrounding him.

Nara walked toward the kitchen and poked through the screen sitting above a curious alcove. "It'll be prepackaged instant meals until the plant beds produce something fresh."

"Ah, that makes sense," he tried to convince himself.

She swiped until a carton of distilled liquor came into view and pressed a confirmation. With an obliging beep, the dumbwaiter snapped shut. After a burst of green light and a jarring ping, the door opened again, revealing the same carton inside the device. "If you want meat, you go out and get it. I certainly don't feel like hunting."

>> SCANNING PROVISION STORAGE, the room announced.

Zips of electronic noises whined through the orderly row of cabinets, sensors searching the void inside with grids of glowing beams. With a flurry of whirrs and clicks, the kitchen resolved to act upon the barren storage.

>> DISPENSING VITAL LEVEL ARTICLES. PLEASE STAND BY.

A series of thunks exploded across the room, settling down as an innumerable legion of objects dropped to the bottom of the cabinets. Nara opened a compartment and dug through the newly spawned collection of grey labeled parcels, selecting one and unwrapping the contents.

She took the tray of desiccated nutrients and shoved it back into the alcove, poking through cooking configurations until the meal she chose came into view. After confirming her selection, the alcove slid shut, chanting acknowledgement with a sizzling expletive. Within an instant, the door popped open, filling the air with a delightful savory aroma of earthy notes and herbal bitterness. She removed the steaming plate from the alcove and slid it before Garrett.

He pulled at the utensil attached to the dish, dislodging the device with a satisfying series of clicks. The meal was a hearty stew that looked about as appetizing as expected, a mass of unknown lumps surrounded by a reddish-brown goo. He poked at a morsel, selecting an ivory lump he thought was a starch. He decided to trust the smell rather than the appearance and put the food in his face without question.

Despite being instantly prepared, the textures of the contents appeared fresh and full of nutrients. Vegetables were crunchy and the meat-like proteins were juicy, a contrast to the barely edible rations he'd found himself eating back in Under. Pangs in his stomach churned a chorus of approval, and he proceeded to devour the meal

"Everything's just… ready? No cost?" Garrett said through a mouthful. The notion was curious to him, having been raised in the capitalist domination controlling every resource back in Arcadia.

She shoved the packaging into a hole in the countertop, which was received with satisfied munches. "Yeah. You want something fancier, you'll have to trade with the farm scientists or find a soldier with a green thumb."

"Trade?"

"There's no money here, Upworlder. Offer something nice, you get nice things back." She cracked open the seal of the carton of liquor, then proceeded to down the entire contents, embracing the familiar berry and citrus-laced fire coursing down her throat. *Oh, fuck yes, I miss this. Not that watered-down shit humanity passes off as booze.*

"Huh." His mind was failing to process, the new environment barely registering.

"This button switches to Galactic Trade." Nara pointed at the computer. "But stick to these categories for food until I get you a translator from the scribes to explain all this shit. They'll have all the time in the world to inform you of the fine details of hybrid onion breeds. I don't."

"Oh, sure." He collected his thoughts and attempted to stand from his seat, swaying abruptly to the side as his body argued with the sudden movements.

"Go to sleep if you're tired. Your room's upstairs and to the right."

She pointed with her drink hand. "Nightfall isn't for another twenty hours or so, so it'll still be light out when you get up."

"Huh?" He blinked.

"64-hour days, human." She ordered another drink from the computer. "They operate under three work phases here. Do what you need to adjust."

"Oh, uh. Sure. Yeah." He wanted her to expound upon that, but travel fatigue was setting in his muscles, and Nara was already midway through the second carton of whatever liquid she took part in. "Goodnight, in that case."

Garrett managed his way up the jagged stairs, drifting toward the room Nara had built for him. It was almost as large as the lower floor, the limited furnishings making the place appear an oppressive void.

He wandered over to the bathroom, finding the facilities as to be expected. But as he became aware of the grime coating his skin, he was faced with the greatest challenge a guest at a new home could face.

Wait, how the fuck does the shower work? He could not find a spigot. Nothing, as a matter of fact, except for another computer screen at the far wall. He poked at the console, already forgetting the command Nara had shown him to switch to Trade. He was too shy to ask again, letting his brain be assaulted by a barrage of foreign symbols and pictures.

Agitation began to manifest beyond his mental barriers, and a garbled string of syllables exited his mouth as he scrubbed at his face. The strange world he would call home for the unforeseeable future daunted him. Where to go and what not to say, he would have to re-learn it all over again. Nara would not be forthcoming with advice, having her own world of problems to deal with. Loneliness began to creep over his thoughts, the futility of his situation pressing hard against his spirits.

Fuck it. I'm just going to go to sleep. His eyes wandered over to the unwelcome-looking bed, a self-contained box that nearly reached his ribcage. The mattress was massive, fit to accommodate the colossal statures of the people here. He poked at the plush material, finding it surprisingly springy.

He groaned as he pulled himself up into the box, rolling over face first into the cushiony pool. *Holy shit!*

The mattress welcomed him with the most comforting embrace, the gentle device swallowing him with warmth. He didn't bother to pull himself toward the pillows, the thought of the effort draining him as the soreness in his bones began to melt away. It was not long before his rampant mind was calmed, pulling him toward a gentle sleep.

##1.2##

NARA RESTRAINED the inebriated fog teasing her brain as she scrolled through the narratives of the last decade. Names she was barely familiar with flipped across the screen, references to events she had never witnessed. She mapped out the shift in power, the figures she once knew and where they currently resided.

Though not many years have passed, everything had moved as if generations had elapsed. Eons of political patterns from an army of nations had been crammed into her skull from years of training. The conflict was clear before her, but what was she expected to do about it?

A soft chime prodded her. A presence outside her home demanded her attention. With a groan, she flicked a switch on her desk, the front door sliding open to reveal the venerable *Loremaster* Khuul'Ren seeking her audience.

"Managed to get past Fariem's defenses?" she called down.

"It was difficult, yes." They smiled as they made their way up the stairs. "But knowing you, I figured you would still be active."

Nara chewed on the side of her mouth, disquieted by her mentor's analysis. She averted her eyes as they entered her office, trying to pull herself back underneath the waves of documents.

"Straight to work, I see." *Loremaster* regarded her weary expression illuminated by the screens, moving their gaze to the small collection of cartons on her desk. "Haven't slept?"

"The sooner I fix this, the sooner I leave."

"I see." They looked across the hall. "The human with you?"

"Unfortunately." She released a sigh. "Would you please find someone to entertain them? I can't handle the invasive curiosity. And keep them out of trouble. The Council doesn't need to know of their existence."

"I'm sure I can find someone appropriate." *Loremaster* folded their arms, watching her intently. Her mentor's presence derailed her thoughts, the scrutiny sending her skin crawling. She couldn't help but feel disdain. His lack of action upon the crumbling council had sealed the tensions, and she was expected to clean it up. It simply wasn't fair, but she could read the signs. This was a long time coming.

"The Council isn't going to listen to me." Nara scowled. "How do you expect this to turn out?"

"There is *one* thing that will force them to at least hear your words," *Loremaster* softly suggested.

She snapped her gaze up, her lip curled into a snarl. "That solution is much more permanent than what we had agreed upon."

He raised his hands defensively. "You can always step down later."

"No one in recorded history has ever stepped down." Nara leaned on a hand. "And you know it."

Loremaster hefted a shrug. "Recorded history is also riddled with firsts. Many of which you have personally chiseled into their volumes."

She inhaled a deep drought of bitter air as she considered his words. Her mentor's constant interference in her position had always baffled her, and what irritated her most was his insistence that it was always a choice. "You sound so certain."

"If I were certain about everything I believed, I would not have withdrawn from the Council."

"I'm surprised Bellanar isn't behind you, trying to force my decision." Nara scoffed. The squirrelly man was a major part of why she'd ended up home. Their persistent hunt through the grimy jungles of Undercity was almost amusing to her, though she could not fathom being enough to convince her to entertain their pleas.

"They're in jail," *Loremaster* revealed.

She blinked in astonishment. "What?"

"After I returned, they went immediately back out. No idea why."

They rubbed their chin pensively. "Either way, their luck apparently ran out and whoever they relied on stopped covering for them."

"Wonderful." Nara scrubbed her face. *Another problem to resolve.*

"Your former commanding officer has been asking about you," *Loremaster* pointed out. "I think you should talk to them about Bellanar's predicament."

"I see." Silence had settled in the room, but words continued to flow through the air. *Loremaster's* enigmatic proclamations danced around her mind, slinging mud over the puzzle she was bestowed. Their neutrality on the subject was a formidable front to another motivation quietly biding its time. Weariness shadowed her mentor's form, but patience forced it still.

"I see that you are busy. I just wanted to see how you were doing and perhaps welcome you back," *Loremaster* said. "Stop by the capital archives when you are ready. I'm sure I can fill you in on a summarized report of current events and save you the trouble of navigating through the insurmountable archives."

"I am sure of it." Nara glanced through the screen, boring a hole into the wall across from her.

Loremaster paused as he turned away, leaning a hand on the doorframe. "Your instincts are sharp. You should rely on them more often. Probability will only get you so far."

Where have I heard that one before? Nara scowled.

CHAPTER 2

##2.0##

Gentle echoes of casual banter bounced around the dimly lit blackened walls of the capital's conference hall. The ambience was devoid of the glimmer of the publicized broadcasting systems, mandated to be switched offline due to concerns of global security. A ring of balconies bordered the arena, overlooking the barren floor of the orator's pit. The rows of seating were divided into a trio of segments, each sparsely occupied by the remnants of the active representatives of the world council, those who cared about procedure after the dissension.

To the east sat the Council of the Future, the diplomats of science that maintained the guidelines on research and production. And to the west the Council of the Present, composed of the most influential warlords from each of the thirteen clans, in addition to their key subordinates.

Silence radiated from the North, which had once held the voice of the Council of the Past, *Loremaster's* official seating, along with a selection of chief scribes and their assistants. It was now deserted, save for one tenacious constituent.

Bellanar fretted with the creases in his clothing, having had to rush to make it to the meeting on time. He poked through his reports, quietly talking through his arguments in preparation for the inevitable questioning.

"Before we proceed," the Head Councilor of Science, the acting moderator, ordered the host of voices to a hush. "Does anyone have issues to be immediately addressed?"

"Oh, yes," Bellanar began, eagerly raising his hand. "I do. I—"

"What are *you* doing here?" The councilor narrowed their eyes at the disruption.

"Oh, well, I was promptly, and thoroughly, reprimanded for my misconduct and then dismissed," Bellanar affirmed with a nervous nod.

"Who authorized k'vai's dismissal?" The councilor scoured the room.

"I did." A voice from the Present piped in. An aged warlord stood to address the crowd, their menacing posture softened by the dash of whimsy tracing over their creased features. "It's not fair to be waiting for so long to try them. I had nothing better to do, anyway."

"Warlord Jav'ril, k'vai is not in your clan, much less your jurisdiction."

"No, they are under mine." The silence from the Past crackled apart as a hologram burst through the darkness, projecting Nara's rigid crossed arms and disapproving glare. A tumult of murmuring washed over the stadium, questioning whispers seeking an explanation for the unscheduled interruption.

"On the subject of jurisdiction," she continued, her scowl deepening, "K'vai is a citizen of the Past that stole Future property. Can anyone please explain to me why they were taken to a Present detention center?"

"Citizen, your status in this convention is clear," The Councilor of Science challenged. "You have been stripped of your title. You have no voice here."

"Wrong." A strobe of documentation assaulted the assembly, slowly sliding across the screen to await the Council's examination. Words drifted past the central hoverscreen, moving down to the signature lines, marked by *Loremaster* and witnessed by a handful of the chief scribes, dated only a few hours ago. Her own mark smoldered beneath, a resentful flourish that slashed through the lines. "I am the Scion of Lore. And no one but *Loremaster* themselves may revoke this title."

Bitterness and anger forced the words from Nara's throat, causing the declaration to resonate in sharp notes across the chamber. Her fists clenched as she adjusted her stance, her unyielding posture firm. The chatter in the room amplified, disquieted uncertainty foaming through the air.

"K'vai's actions impact the entire world. We had more pressing—"

"I'm not interested in the excuses," Nara cut the councilor off. "Nor am I surprised that you disregarded regulations. Regardless of the situation, *Loremaster* should have been contacted."

"There were other matters to attend to."

Nara drafted a message via subliminal NetCom to the ear of the anxious ally looking up at her.

>> *Bellanar, you are excused.*

>> *But I have something vitally important to discuss about security...*

>> *And I think you should be *very* careful who you discuss that with. I will meet with you later. Leave.*

>> *Yes, Savant, my mistake. Welcome back.*

>> *Do not test my patience, Scribe.*

>> *Wouldn't dream of it.*

Bellanar bashfully smiled at the projection, offering a placating bow before backing from the stage.

"Then consider this matter attended to," Nara hissed.

"I object to this movement." A warlord stood up, a figure she did not recognize. "It is not appropriate to elect one who has been tried as a criminal, and of questionable motivation, to a position of such importance."

"I concur." Another snapped to their feet to join the discussion. "Establishing contact with the Separatists has been difficult, and this action requires delicacy. Given your history with their leader, I do not think you have the world's best interests in mind."

The room murmured in agreement, the noises battering her brain. A swirl of dizziness began to tug at her senses as the accusations flogged her memory. She shifted her stance, beating back the sensation as she honed the daggers sliding up the inside of her throat.

"The Present agrees. This citizen's presence is a detriment to productivity if we are aiming for a peaceful resolution."

"I don't recall my opinion being asked." Jav'ril raised a finger matter-of-factly.

"Considering your previous affiliation with this Citizen, your biases may be too considerable to weigh in."

"What sharp nonsense you're stabbing me with." Jav'ril snorted. "*Savant* has not been under my command in over sixty years. And even so, they were hardly in my ranks for any significant time before they advanced beyond my jurisdiction."

"And you were solely responsible for that advancement," another countered. "This also does not explain why they have returned unannounced after having vanished for thirty years."

"*VANISHED?*" Her bellow cut the quarrel in half, rippling through the chamber. Pangs began to shatter through her fists as her skin flooded with fire, her muscles twitching against her bones. *Vanished.*

But she could read the blank pages over their faces. She had been Unwritten, pushed out of the eye of the public. Never to be mentioned again. Even if someone desired to search for the answers, they were unavailable, the only shreds of the occurrence under *Loremaster's* lock and key.

"Your opinions are noted, Councilors." Nara unhinged her jaw, forcing a stillness inside her searing throat. "Take it up with *Loremaster*, but as the records stand, I am the one who shall preside over this matter."

"While your position remains to be verified," the Councilor of Science interjected, "there is no time to brief you on the current situation."

"Half of the Present has split and have made encampments in the gaming arenas." She reduced the potency of the venom through her words. "The majority of the Future is currently drydocked in space, while the scant few who remain on the planet are deciding what to do with the ships. Everyone has decided to ignore

Loremaster, so the Past has never been present in negotiations. Have I got it all?"

She paused, finding it increasingly difficult to stand still. She cracked through the kinks in her neck as the storm inside her brain magnified. Nausea played with her senses, creating a discordant rhythm with the dizziness hammering at her balance. *Keep it together.*

The audience discussed her observations in hushed tones, voices hesitating as they processed the summary of current affairs. But she was not finished, their conclusions inconsequential.

"The Present wants their claims on the new fleet, but the Future is not forthcoming on this due to the conflict with the Separatists. No successful contact attempts have been made to the estranged parties, and no one has any idea what their agenda entails." She paused to take a step, widening her stance to refrain from the temptation to lean. "In addition, many fields of the Future have no interest in negotiating with the Present, namely the Engineering and Materials Development factions, and they desire to leave Homeworld to explore their own motives elsewhere. So, enlighten me. What has been done to resolve this pervasive conflict?"

"Given the track record of the Separatist leader's performance on duty," a warlord explained, "many are unwilling to be proactive in the situation for fear of antagonizing them."

"And the longer you wait, the more devastating their actions will be," she pointed out.

"We have considered that as well, yes," the officer retorted.

"Have you, now?"

"Councilors," the Future representative interrupted, "I recommend an extended recess to process the information put before us and perhaps assess our emotions on the matter."

The assembly rumbled in agreement, not wanting to discuss their matters in the presence of the new arrival.

"Fine." Nara released the air from her nose. "But I cannot guarantee I will not continue to seek solutions myself."

"Your work is your prerogative, Savant." The hesitant acceptance of her new title laced the councilor's tone with resentment.

The tension weighed heavily over the arena as the congregation slowly departed, uneasy hushed whispers drowned out by the fluttering and shifting of moving bodies. Nara met each of the cautious glances in her direction, making sure they knew she was aware of them.

When the air cleared of the noxious atmosphere, she typed out another summons.

>> *Jav'ril, a moment of your time, please.*
>> *Of course, anything.*

##2.1##

THE PROJECTION of Warlord Jav'ril manifested in Nara's office, a warm smile radiating across their features.

Considered somewhat of an eccentric amid the governing warlords, Jav'ril was brimming with eternal patience. They governed with an informal, almost familial bond with their subordinate units, which was most likely why Nara was commissioned to serve beneath them, having no relatives to speak for her.

Jav'ril could never comprehend why it was standard procedure to take every little detail so seriously, preferring to give everyone beneath their command the benefit of the doubt. Failure was just a learning process, and consequence was part of life. The sooner one accepted this, the easier it was to make educated decisions.

"You are right in front of me and I still don't believe it." They tilted their head, creases tracing around their concerned frown. "What a dark aura you cast."

Nara ignored the comment. "Thank you for releasing k'vai."

"It was hardly any trouble, despite the Council's opinion of me."

"And what is that?"

"While I haven't been outright removed from the World Council" —Jav'ril rolled on the back of their heels— "my opinions are taken with a heavy dose of skepticism, given that I am responsible for the rise of two of the largest troublemakers on the planet."

"Can I trust you?" Her stern glare emphasized the punch of the blunt questioning.

"Always so solemn." They chuckled. "I had faith in you when you were a recruit, and I have faith in you now."

"That was not a direct answer to my question."

Jav'ril's smile widened, accepting the tone of her warning. "Yes, you can."

Nara paused to examine their presentation, picking through the subtleties of language beneath their jovial appearance. They were earnest enough, having no apparent gain in any of this chaos. But they were the only common figure between the old and new regimes. And the only one who could cause her the most harm.

"What is your position on this matter?" she prodded.

"We have now established a considerable presence in space." The warlord shrugged. "We need to take responsibility and ensure we get along with our neighbors who have been knocking on our door for quite some time."

"So, you would be in favor of aligning with GaPFed?" Nara tilted her head inquisitively.

"I didn't say that." Jav'ril firmly shook their head. "We should play nice with the other kids in the playground but also make sure we don't allow bullies to establish the rules."

"I see." She paused to consider their words. While she'd never understood their worldview, she appreciated how little they expected of her, letting her express her thoughts and opinions openly, never agreeing nor disagreeing with her conclusions. They were a just commander, and she wished more would see from their perspective.

The warlord's face suddenly shifted. Their smile faded to a remorseful frown. "Would you like to hear about the trial?"

Jav'ril's softened voice struck the nerves in her chest. They were a direct witness to her treatment, the chains, and the drugs. They were there when she was cast aside for *Xannat* to play with, the witness to the conclusion of her behavior. *Vanished.*

"No." Her jaw clenched tight as her fragmented recollection teased at the edges of her mind.

"As you wish." They bowed their head. "You know where to find me should you change your mind."

"Sure." Words were becoming difficult to process, her thoughts distracted by the winding trails of suspicion and remorse.

"I will bid you a good evening. And please, take care of yourself. Many look up to you." Their projection evaporated from the office floor.

Upon hearing the wish, Nara collapsed into her chair, nerves rattling across every inch of her body. She forced her eyes shut, attempting to regain control of her breath and steady the waves of nausea coursing through her guts. Wiping the sweat from her forehead, she snatched a half-empty carton of liquor, replacing the bile in her throat with the scalding concoction. She fought with her shaking fingers as she pushed it toward the increasing collection on her desk.

Get a fucking grip on yourself, she scolded, dragging her nails through the tangles of her hair.

"Hey." A voice broke through her smoldering as Garrett poked his head into the doorway. "Can I help?"

She wasn't surprised the human could detect her agitation. She must be radiating miles away. How could she even begin to compress the situation small enough so that he could provide input? She couldn't. Not now.

She would solve her problems the only way she knew how—by ignoring them.

"Congratulations. I am granting you diplomatic immunity." She stood up from her seat, cracking the pressure out of her joints. "Which doesn't mean much. They will ignore you regardless, but they will at least attempt to contact me before throwing you in jail for poking around where you shouldn't."

"I—what?" His perplexed gaze followed her down the stairs.

"I am leaving to meet with Bellanar before he comes looking for me." She punched the door control. "Entertain yourself until the translator comes for you."

"Oh—" The door snapped shut behind her, leaving him alone in the hostile domicile. "Okay."

##2.2##

THE SOFT LIGHT shining down from the stained-glass windows illuminated Nara's quest for knowledge, a glittering mimicry of the foliage surrounding the towering wooden form of the Capital Master Archive. Delicate inky washes of greens and purples danced over the words she pondered as the greenery swayed, teasing the sun with its tenuous obstruction.

This was her favored sanctuary, surrounded by the most rigid order of tomes spanning eternity, far away from prying eyes of the populace. Bookcases curled up to the ceiling, imitating the organic forms of trees, stretching out their branches to offer their wisdom to visitors. The landscape was quietly attended to by a battalion of scribes who maintained the golden rule of peace and neutrality, their fealty sworn to the books.

Nara took shelter in a hideout carved into the tower, a haven of wooden reading tables and cushions large enough to be used as seating. Murals were hand painted over the walls of the bubble, artistic interpretations of plant life that opened to scenes from history. Recreations of life before the recorded eras, how the ancient tribes managed to survive despite the hostile force of nature fighting against them with their armored minions.

She reached over to the service machine and ordered another cup of tea, taking in the warmth as the heady steam rose to her face. Once in a while, her mind could unhinge its claws on reality and pretend to relax. All it took was the right environment.

But her solace was quickly shattered by a presence hastily climbing the ladder to her refuge. Bellanar pulled himself into the grotto, sliding onto a plush cushion across from her.

"Thank you for taking the time to—"

"Out with it. Now," Nara snapped.

"Certainly. While I don't have concrete evidence" —Bellanar rotated his wrists, steeling himself for his account— "I don't think Abberon is on the planet."

"That doesn't surprise me one bit." She leaned back in her seat, watching the curious scribe fidget.

"I have a suspicion, just a small one, that they have been actively talking to GaPFed." He hesitated, wincing as he pushed the conclusion from his lips. "For decades…"

She drank in a weighted mass of air, cleansing the instinctive anger from her body. It was the most logical conclusion, and if true, it would reveal the motivations for the events that took place under her reign. And her deposition.

But what was done in the past cannot be corrected, and avoiding bloodshed now was what mattered the most. Theory had to be a certainty before she could act.

"Suspicion is a dangerous resource to tangle in, Scribe." She drummed her fingers against the gnarled wooden reading desk.

"Understood. But I've been poking through some" —Bellanar raised a finger, shifting his glance around the room— "*places* lately, and I think I am on to something."

"Officially" —she folded her arms and gave him a look of warning — "I must advise that you take no action upon your findings."

"But—"

"O–fi–cial–ly." Nara narrowed her eyes, waiting for the scribe to come to his senses.

"Yes, right. I see." Bellanar stood and bowed. "Thank you for your guidance, *Savant*."

"Safe hunting, Bellanar." She sipped her tea, watching the leaves dance around the bottom of the cup. The scribe took the hint and scurried off, leaving her in the quiet company of the tomes.

CHAPTER 3

##3.0##

Left alone with his sensibilities, Garrett pushed back the need to decrypt the entirety of his situation and focused on the singular challenge waiting for him in the bathroom.

He rubbed his chin as he glared at the control panel, swiping through the puzzling symbols and digital buttons to coerce them to reveal their secrets. A stream of contemplative noises burbled in his throat as he tried to hammer the flourished alphabet into Trade lettering. But it was no use. The languages were simply incomparable.

He passed a finger around the edge of the screen until a slider control revealed itself, a candy-bright gradient shifting between red and blue. With a tentative tap, he beckoned the cursor toward the center of the two extremes.

A cheery yet clamorous ring blared through the room, whipping his nerves to a riotous start. Garrett frantically looked around for the source of the disturbance. With a head scratch, he turned to the console questioningly. *Did I do something?*

The house belted another cry, berating his eardrums with the jaunty tone. He stepped out of the bathroom and turned toward the stairs, where the seam of the front door blinked with a gentle radiance.

Great. I'm covered in grime, I smell awful, and now there are strangers at the door. He sighed, heading back to the accursed device. *Maybe they'll go away.*

The unknown stranger persisted, sending waves of domestic summons battering against his brain. With each ring, his concentration decayed, amplifying his frustration against the tenacious puzzle.

Aw, hell. He flicked on the sink and splashed water over his face, slicking back his disheveled hair into a semblance of controlled chaos. After scrubbing dry with the tail of his shirt, he hastened down the stairs.

The door obeyed as he slapped the control, opening to reveal a bright-eyed Ara'yulthr beaming down on him. Their aura bubbled with a pervasive cheery vigor, and their unsettlingly welcoming grin radiated beyond the confines of the apartment.

"Uh. Ah, shit. I don't speak... Nar–Er... E–Elam isn't here." Garrett pointed down at the floor and shook his head vigorously, maintaining eye contact in hopes the glowing stranger would understand him.

"I am here for *you*, actually," the visitor said in fluent Trade. Their sweetened voice somehow emphasized the force of their personality. "*Loremaster* sent me here to collect you."

"Oh! Sure, right. Do forgive me. I am a little out of sorts."

"Do not apologize. What you are feeling is completely understandable." They nodded, their smile widening so far that their cheeks pushed their eyes shut. "My name is unpronounceable to human anatomy, but it roughly translates to Data Prism in Trade. But you can simply call me Prism."

"I'm sure I can—"

"Nonsense, Ambassador! Come along. *Loremaster* tells me you are very interested in learning more about our culture, and we have a lot to cover. If you could please follow me."

"Ambass—what? I think there's been a mist—" The stranger disregarded his protest, a multitude of tanzanite braids threatening to lash out at him as they sharply turned around. Their hair undulated with a gay rhythm as they retreated, brushing over their hips in time to their bouncy march. He ran to catch up with them, blindsided by their assertive friendliness.

He was led outside the compound to their vehicle, a modest craft that resembled the air cars in Arcadia, but much less flashy than what the luxury brands back home offered. And considerably more armored. As Prism approached, the craft opened its passenger door, permitting access to the dark-paneled interior. With an emphatic wave of their hand, they ushered him inside, their smile never fading as they watched him assess the craft.

"Now let's begin with the correct address of anyone you meet here." Prism hopped into the flight seat. "Despite many people speaking Trade here, it is most respectful to convert your words to conform with our practices."

"Of course—" Garrett's reply was battered aside by the flow of conversation.

"We do not have gendered pronouns in our language. Ours are solely based on our job descriptions. Though many people have adapted to Trade pronouns, you should only use them with permission. So, for example, you may refer to me in the third person as 'they,' or 'kv'ai,' since I am a scribe." Through their explanation, Prism conducted a concerto of commands at the controls of the vehicle. "If you do not know the job of an individual, you can call them 'Serr,' which literally translates to 'student' but is also known as a 'person' in the formal sense. Pronouns also work as prefixes, like Mr. in Trade and so forth."

After sending the craft into the sky, Prism swiftly rotated the pilot seat to face Garrett, lips pursed into an expectant smile. Their unblinking eyes trained on him, removing any opportunity to sneak a glance at the beauty of the landscape surrounding them.

His throat spasmed as he submitted to the implied request. "Uh. S–Ser?"

"Yes, roll the 'R' a little." They twirled a finger through the air as Garrett struggled with a second attempt. "Good!"

He squirmed in his seat, growing increasingly uncomfortable with the quirkiness of his captor, unable to discern condescension from their unflappable enthusiasm. Gathering his mettle, he hesitantly stitched pieces of logic together from the few conversations he had heard between Nara and her kindred, attempting to sound more intelligent than what his presence implied. "Qu'ol Fariem?"

"Ah! Very good!" Prism clapped their hands together. "Qu'ol Fariem is part of the science division, so qu'ol is their pronoun. There are others that describe a person's specific discipline within their field, but unless you know that ahead of time, the umbrella term is just fine."

Their impeccably vertical posture made Garrett self-aware of his own awkward position, and he abruptly corrected his seating. He remained silent as he waited for Prism to continue, folding his limbs to display his attention and a hint of irritation.

"You might be called 'Ahm'Serr." They leaned back in their seat, tilting their head curiously as they analyzed his new arrangement. "Which means 'unfamiliar,' or 'foreigner'."

Garrett nodded in affirmation, picking up a shift in their tone. Perhaps there was a nonverbal aspect to the Ara'yulthr communication methods. In the short time he had known Nara, he'd never noticed any strange nuances in her speech, but then again, he would not have known what to look for.

He made a conscious attempt to control his movement, hiding his bewilderment behind a neutral wall of pleasantry—a parlor trick he was especially skilled at from being raised in the glimmering oily seas of Arcadia's upper echelons.

"I don't think you will encounter anyone from the military regimes, but for the sake of consistency, their pronouns are 'Sci'ith' unless you are aware of their ranking." Prism gave a nod. "A little harder on the tongue, but you should be understood."

"I see." Garrett remained still, taking care not to broadcast his frazzled state.

"Ah! Here we are." They gestured to the window. "The Capital Master Archives."

The transport delicately settled at the feet of a towering monolith crafted from archaic materials akin to concrete and steel. Like its hyper-modern successors, it was artfully sculpted to imitate the surrounding forests. The porous material was etched with furrows of simulated bark tracing splintering paths around the artificial trunk.

The tower branched out in glassed walkways that gently dipped to the surrounding canopy of scintillating treetops. It was a symbiotic relationship, the foliage welcoming the artificial invader with its webbed embrace, climbing the winding structure to gain aerial advantage over its neighbors and drink in the sun's rays.

Prism escorted Garrett out of the vehicle and toward the building, stopping several meters in front of the trunk. Strands of ruby scattered from a collection of curious metal gadgets perforating the earth. With a swirl of their fingers, the tongues whipped aside, splitting to form an outline of empty air stretching just above Prism's head. They waved Garrett through the ghostly barrier, their pervasive smile broadening as they awaited his reaction.

A set of intricately carved wooden doors guarded the entrance. Reliefs of geometric leaves and vines traced the borders, seamlessly extending into the living ivy that fed on the walls. The gate slowly creaked open as the visitors approached, revealing the magnificent vault of records. Rows upon rows of wooden bookcases lined the literary haven, matching the aesthetic with their twisting, bark-coated forms.

"This is amazing," Garrett breathed. He delighted in the sound of his footsteps, the soft click of his boots over the tessellated mosaic of mint green leaves. Each tile was bordered in bronze filigree, creating a scintillating net stretching over the floor.

"These are all duplicates. The majority of information is kept in bunkers scattered all over the planet," Prism explained. "Everything has multiple redundant copies, reproduced in the five most recent digital formats, sometimes more if there are important versions in the middle of the development lifespan. Plus the originals, and a duplicate of the primary format. Analog books, for example, are often copied using traditional techniques."

"That is quite thorough."

"Yes, it's certainly a labor-intensive task to maintain." Prism nodded excitedly. "Most everything is stored on cloud servers, and should something happen to this branch, others can easily piece together any missing information."

"Has anything ever happened to the library?" His heart seized at the thought of such precious information reduced to dust.

"Not to such a catastrophic scale, but it's ingrained in our culture to protect anything we create," they pointed out. "It's a habit we developed from our ancestors. They had to contest with the wildlife to preserve settlements, and I suppose it's just something we never grew out of."

"I see." Garrett's attention wandered to a curious gathering of beings, smaller Ara'yulthr people but with a striking physical characteristic contrast to any other he had encountered. Their skin was pigmented with a muted collection of pastel colors, each individual presenting a spectrum of greens, blues, and purples, coordinating with the foliage outside. Not a single chitinous plate ruptured the surface of their smooth arms, save for a few of the larger, presumably older individuals who possessed a hint of shadow tracing over their muscles.

"Ah, class is in session!" Prism smirked at the human's curiosity.

The students sat motionless as they absorbed the lecture presented by an elder scribe who gestured at the projection screen plastered with a network of diagrams and text. Images of the world cycled through the views, displaying the landmasses in a vibrant gradient that marked the borders of each climate zone.

"I wonder what color Nara was as a child?" Garett thought out loud as he watched the lesson.

Prism suddenly froze, the human's curiosity melting the grin from their face. Their lips twitched as they stammered a reply, nervously brushing at their uniform. "Yes, well, perhaps Savant Elam could elucidate on that subject."

Garrett scrunched his face, watching Prism fervently search through the archive bookshelves. *Savant?* "Is something the matter?"

"Not at all!" They coughed, quickly pointing toward the information labyrinth. "Ah! Perhaps this would be of interest. You have simulation games in Arcadia, don't you?"

"Sure." He raised a suspicious eyebrow as he was led deeper through the archive.

"We have something similar here. It's what we do for leisure while also training ourselves for combat, since there is never any conflict that requires bloodshed." They pinched the edge of a shelf, pulling open a screen over the digital tomes. "Present circumstances notwithstanding."

The shelf glowed as the projection conjured a model of an Ara'yulthr standing with arms outstretched, a skintight material covering every inch of their flesh. Dotted arrows jabbed at the subject as words raced across the screen.

"These are the immersion suits that are worn by all players for the entire duration of the games." The annotations morphed into Trade with Prism's requesting prods. "They spend the entire campaign living inside continent-sized arenas, which work in synch with the suits to construct a hyper-realistic simulation of a battlefield scenario."

The figure dissolved on the screen, replaced by an overhead view of a bubble-like structure that surpassed the borders of a landmass. Segments of the walls broke apart in hexagonal tiles, layers of material separating to showcase the composition of the structure.

"Each clan pits against each other in a tiered tournament battle. The bracket takes one year, then another year of rest before the next tier proceeds. The winners move on while the defeated spend time training for the next war they qualify in. However, the final tier can take as long as it needs to until the objective is completed."

The perspective shifted to display the world map, now divided into thirteen brightly colored regions. In a swirling dance, the countries popped out of the map and organized themselves in a pair of parallel lines. The odd region splintered off from the screen, waiting patiently for its challenger in the next tier.

"It's quite a fascinating system, actually. Military programmers work alongside scientific researchers to ensure an accurate simulation of every aspect of war, from sickness and injuries to environmental hazards." Prism paused to flip through equipment loadouts. Fierce-looking rifles and armaments rotated over the screen. "All of which are procedurally generated to keep one side from having an advantage over the other and keep the warlords thinking on their feet."

Injuries? Garrett watched the implements of destruction move across his view. "This *is* a game, right?"

"Certainly! It's even broadcast across the planet networks for everyone to see. It's quite a popular spectacle."

"Can we watch one of the games?"

"I think I can oblige that." Prism emphatically nodded. "But since a tournament can span over years, even decades, we'll just look at some highlights and the winning end results."

"Can I see one of Elam's?"

"I suppose that would be all right." They traced a finger over a list of recordings, tapping on a title. "Oh, this was a *good* one! It's how Savant earned the invitation to participate in the World Council."

<hr />

##3.1##

AN UNSETTLING STILLNESS chilled the dimly lit corridor, amplified by the calm rhythmic gait of a uniformed official. The visitor made their way down the path of holding cells, a wry smile infecting their lips with concealed intent.

While most of the Ara'yulthr would consider the word "demon" a slur, this individual appeared to embrace it. Soot from past burned bridges stained their tousled mane, framing their cold features in a disquieting shadow. Their severe eyes lanced through the walls, an otherworldly gaze that could effortlessly excavate the universe's darkest secrets for later use.

They paid no mind to the soft pattering behind them, deliberating over obscured plots as they waited for the soldier to catch up.

"Your briefing, Lieutenant." Abberon's icy voice resonated through the chamber.

"I'm afraid the situation has grown critical, Warlord," the soldier reported, maintaining their distance behind their superior. "At even a minimal supply consumption rate, we will last two, maybe three weeks."

"Anything else?" The warlord concealed their displeasure, preferring to wait until the knife was buried and leave the victims to draw their own conclusions.

"As of now, we have lost approximately thirty percent of our forces to the opposition." The lieutenant paused to take in a weighted breath. "If we can't get the missile silos activated again, we will lose on even ground."

"Take me to the collaborators."

"At once, Warlord." The lieutenant pushed the shadow of foreboding aside and stepped ahead, leading Abberon deeper through the facility. Thoughts raced across their mind as they attempted to decipher the intent of their superior, uncertain what judgment would face the offenders. The lieutenant cleared their throat as they stopped in front of a cell door, inviting Abberon to assess the monitor with a gesture.

The warlord tapped the screen awake, revealing a camera view inside the cell. Two soldiers huddled together in the corner, holding hands and murmuring quiet assurances to each other.

"Send them into the wilderness without provisions. If they want to leave so badly, let them contest with nature first." Abberon leered at the lieutenant expectantly. "I trust you can arrange this."

The soldier averted their gaze. "Yes, Warlord."

A chirp from Abberon's wrist sliced through the atmosphere. "Warlord? The med bay is ready for you."

"Good. I will be there shortly." Abberon gave an approving nod and stepped away from the cell.

A darkness cast over the lieutenant's face as realization tore through their features. They braved a glance at the warlord's back, disbelief corrupting their tone. "You're throwing the fight."

Abberon stopped, turning back to their subordinate. "I prefer to call it 'leaving a lasting impression'."

##3.2##

"THE LATEST OPERATION WAS A SUCCESS," the lieutenant reported to a young Nara, who was barely broad enough to fill the chair she commanded from.

47

She raised an eyebrow. "You don't sound confident."

The lieutenant dropped their shoulders. "I'm just very tired, Warlord."

"It should be over soon."

"I—" They inhaled a flustered breath while their arguments processed. "Everyone's tired. Morale has been lower than ever before after uncovering the weaponry Abberon's side possesses. They're scared."

Nara displayed no concern, bringing up a screen of the battle map for analysis. "Which is why our shadow units decommissioned them."

"Suppose we can't next time? What if—"

"Pardon the intrusion, officers. We…" A shaky-voiced soldier entered the office, hesitating to clear the apprehension from their throat. "We have captured Abberon."

Nara leaned back in her chair, the weight of the report pressing down on her. She could sense the relief radiating from her lieutenant, but she did not share their enthusiasm. The news smelled rotten. Another motive was at play. "How?"

"They surrendered to us," the messenger said. "They are currently en route to this station in armored transport."

"Thank *Xannat*! We can deal with this—"

"Contain yourself, Tek." Nara raised a hand in warning. *This isn't right.*

"But, Warlord, there's no need to drag this on any further." Tek leaned forward, jabbing a finger on the desk. "The death of a warlord is the final objective. We can finish this now!"

"That's enough."

"You *know* Abberon," Tek pressed. "Our units will die by the thousands and—"

"*Enough*, Lieutenant." Nara snapped up from her seat, her cold gaze cutting off the soldier's protest. "I *do* know Abberon. Which is why we need time to consider the situation. Ensign, come with me."

"Yes, Warlord." The messenger bowed and followed Nara out of the office.

"But we don't have that time," Tek breathed.

##3.3##

NARA PARTED the vines of her cover, watching the armored truck enter the compound. She had chosen to act with caution and move away from headquarters, the abnormality of the situation flooding her nerves with itching paranoia.

Her discomfort reflected against her escort, who was examining the scene with similar apprehension. "What are you thinking, Ensign?"

"It's hard to say with Abberon." They shook their head. "Maybe they're trying to win favor with their units by making a sacrifice. Or setting an example."

From the grounds, a squad of infantry awaited the approaching vehicle, rifles raised. The driver walked around and opened the back doors, revealing the passenger with arms restrained. The squad leader ordered the smiling figure to step out of the vehicle.

The prisoner's grin leeched into the spirits of the infantry as they staggered down the loading ramp, swaying gently as they struggled to maintain composure. They strained their eyes against the light of day, revealing a sickly pallor to their complexion. But their smile persisted with a profane glow.

It's Abberon, all right. Nara fixated on the prisoner's peculiar behavior, her doubts magnifying tenfold. "They were alone?"

"Yes, Warlord," the ensign reported. "Came in from a ground vehicle near another encampment. Appeared unarmed, and the vehicle wasn't trapped."

I shouldn't be this close. "Get me through to the squad leader. I want them taken far away from headquarters until further notice."

"Warlord, look." The ensign pointed at a figure walking toward the gathering. Lieutenant Tek made their way over to question the commander while eyeing Abberon nonchalantly.

Nara's blood froze as the situation rapidly slipped from her hands. "Ensign, get me that leader now! Apprehend Tek immediately!"

Before they could make the call, Tek snatched Abberon, wrapping an arm around their throat. The warlord didn't fight back, their vile grin widening as a pistol raised to their temple. Tek ignored the shouts of the disoriented squad, ejecting three bolts of energy through the head of his captive. The light extinguished from the warlord's eyes, their victory forever etched on stretched lips.

Tek released the body, letting it fall as they wiped the blood from their face. They were granted no time to assess the weight of their consequences. The ground started to shudder beneath them. A concussive crack ruptured the air, sending violent waves of energy through the scene. Shouts from the squad were drowned out by the roar of an infernal blaze as plumes of wrath lashed across the compound.

Time slowed around Nara as she witnessed the oncoming fire. Her fist clutched the ensign by the collar. She shoved the soldier down, recoiling as the ravenous force approached. White consumed her vision and detonated into agony as her skull struck the unyielding obstruction of an ancient tree.

Pain engulfed her abdomen, nerves firing across her flesh. Then nothing. Her strength swiftly drained from her body, her lower half numb. The shouts of her ensign dissolved into a murk of blackness, her mind hiding from chaos.

##3.4##

THE CAMERA PANNED over the wake of the explosion, scanning over churning vehicle fires and the charred remnants of bodies. It zoomed into the forest to capture the painful aftermath of Nara's predicament, her body pinned to a tree by a shard of another splintering branch. She made a feeble attempt to grab the instrument invading her flesh, her fingers brushing aimlessly over the blood-slicked projectile.

>>EVENT TERMINATION - ENDGAME PHASE INITIATED

Garrett's eyes widened in horror, his mouth agape as the gruesome battle replayed in his mind. *"That* is a game!?"

"Well, yes. Loosely." Prism's face shrank with concern. "Is everything all right, Ambassador?"

Jesus Christ. His eyes could not leave the screen. *Nara was so young, barely bigger than the children here.*

"You have to consider that everything here is a simulation. But despite this, many steps are taken to ensure the mental health of each participant is protected. Severely injured vets are usually excused from the next war. When a war is over, everyone takes an extended break to spend time in counseling before going back on duty."

He barely registered the consolation. "Counseling?"

"The simulations are programmed to put the user in the most realistic situation, and as a result, certain injuries can create a traumatic impact on the individual. The brain can have a hard time convincing itself it was not injured while outside the gaming confines."

"Where do the dead… go?"

"They are placed in stasis until the end objective of the game has been declared completed."

"They're put in a coma?!?"

"That's an oversimplification of it." Prism frowned, unsure of what to do with the human's distress. "I am sorry. I have apparently troubled you with this information, Ambassador. I simply thought that—"

"Ah! Friend! Garrett, was it?" The cheery voice of Bellanar disrupted the discourse. He approached the two swiftly, waving eagerly at Garrett. "I need to ask a favor of you."

Prism's face wrinkled at the intrusion. "Scribe, this is hardly appropriate—"

"I will just be one minute, Chief." Bellanar slipped an arm around the distraught Garrett and ushered him to the side. He then leaned down to his level, lowering his voice. "You are the only one I can trust right now."

"What's the matter?" He let his discomfort slip out of his grasp as he watched the excitable man shift his eyes over the room.

"I am going out, and I cannot tell anyone where. Here." Bellanar placed a transmitter into Garrett's hands. "If this flashes, go and get Elam. Tell her it's Abberon, but from an arm's length away. She'll listen."

"I don't think I can—"

"Please." The man seized his gaze with pleading eyes. "I know I can trust you with discretion. This is vitally important."

Garrett could only nod in compliance.

"Good! Better not keep your instructor waiting." He ushered Garrett back to the judgmental glare of Prism. "Until next time, friend!"

And with that, the curious man dashed off.

"I think..." Garrett began, his senses numbing from all the excitement. "I have learned enough for one day, Prism. Would you be so kind as to drop me off back home?"

##3.5##

GARRETT QUIETLY MADE his way through the lab, evading the suspicious glances of the duo working. The weight of the transmitter tugged at his pocket, the thoughts of Bellanar's cryptic message looming over him. He had only spoken with the man briefly back on Arcadia. What was so important that he trusted him with his whereabouts? And why did he have to hide from Nara?

"Look at that the color of that one's face." Syf clicked their tongue, eyeing Garrett with feigned concern. *"You'd swear they had seen a war, that shell-shocked dimness in their eyes."*

Ki'nit uttered a pacifying grunt, disinterested in their companion's observations.

Garrett stopped in his tracks as Syf's scrutiny warmed his shoulder. He turned and pointed at his chest. "Are... are you talking to me?"

Syf smiled and slithered uncomfortably close, pensively rubbing their chin as they analyzed Garrett's expression.

"Syf," Ki'nit warned from across the room, not looking up from their research notes. *"Leave the human alone."*

"I was going to offer assistance."

"They didn't ask for any." Ki'nit rubbed their eyes irritably, the errors on the screen giving them grief. *"And for the last time this century,*

tie your hair back. I am tired of throwing out samples because of contamination."

"Yes, dear." Syf tsked, snapping an elastic off their wrist.

"Do you need something, human?" Ki'nit looked up from their work.

"No, I… no." He shook his head firmly. "My name is Garrett, by the way."

"I know."

Fariem suddenly stormed into the lab, carrying a tray of dirt with a curious specimen of flora. A thick stalky vine coiled out of the soil, coated in a scaled armored carapace. The tip of the plant was decorated with a spiral of leaf shards. From the center of the bud grew a large thick-skinned purple fruit. A sheen of gold highlighted the curvature of the orb in the light. The shiny membrane was embossed with tiny green bumps, each tipped with a single black dot.

"You two! Quit fraternizing with the human and come help me with this," Fariem ordered as they placed the tray on the table. *"It's about ripe and needs defusing."*

Ki'nit produced a pair of metal trays and held them a short distance away from the fruit as Fariem wrapped their arms around, covering it on three sides. They nodded to Syf, who slipped on protective eyewear and gathered a set of needle-like tools from storage.

Garrett utilized the distraction to slip away to the apartment.

Syf then took a tool and slipped underneath Fariem's hand, placing the point at the end of the berry. With a slow twist, they pierced through the flesh of the fruit. As they pushed deeper, the black dots on the skin began to extrude, squelching out into the open to reveal saw-edged black spines dripping with vibrant fuchsia pulp. Syf held their breath as they continued drilling through the fruit, the spines threatening their hands with their menacing barbs.

"Too much pressure on the left. Try going—"

SPLORT. *Tink-tink-tink-tink.* The plant exploded in a squish of juice, the barbs launching from their fruity enclosure, leaving a delightful sweetly sour aroma in their wake.

Fariem irritably picked spines out of their coat. *"Well, can't save them all, I suppose. There should still be enough inside the thorns to—"*

A deflating whine from behind them abruptly stopped their words. They turned to see Garrett frozen in place, staring at the pulsating projectile invading his shoulder.

He took a step back as a scorching pain began to lash through his body, an acid wash flicking across his searing skin. The sensation began to engulf his chest, impeding his breath. He reached at the jagged spine, his arm twitching as it fought with his commands.

"You've hit the human." Fariem dashed to his side, slapping his hand away. "Don't touch it. Just lie down. Ki'nit, take him…"

The room began to melt away, green flooding his vision. He couldn't hear the voices shouting orders in his direction. Hands pressed against his back, and he began to float through the air, a trail of lights dissolving across his view.

CHAPTER 4

##4.0##

It took effort to pry his eyes open, but when he finally managed, regret pummeled his senses. Lines of the ceiling tiles twisted around his vision, sending his brain through a nonconsensual coaster ride around the room. He tried to focus on a single point, only to speed up the devious force of gravity pulling his organs around.

Nausea seeped across his guts, and he scrunched his eyes shut to gain relief from the journey. A gentle, meditative slosh of liquid disrupted his focus, and he braved a glance at the source.

Nara was slumped in a seat next to him, her elbows propped on her knees as she gently rocked a carton in her hands. The clasps around her collar were undone, the flaps of fabric fluttering in time to her listless motion. Crinkled strands of hair jutted out of her braid, emphasizing her preoccupied expression as she scrutinized the ground. She looked like hell.

"Hey." He wanted to muster a more appropriate response, but his voice scratched between the sticking walls of his throat.

Her eyes snapped up to him and the carton froze in her hand. "How do you feel?"

He rotated his stiff neck from side to side. An audible *pop* relieved some of the pressure and bestowed him a sense of equilibrium. "All right. Still not sure what happened."

"You got hit with a Minefruit thorn. Fariem got the antivenom in you, so you might be a bit dizzy." Her tone crackled as she explained.

"Makes sense," he lied.

Fariem glided into the room, feigning ignorance to the conversation as they edged toward the monitoring machines next to the bed. They fidgeted with controls and settings, taking notes on a tablet as they nonchalantly shifted their glance to Nara. Their eyes softened slightly as they regarded her, a miniscule glimmer of contrition.

Nara didn't react to their admission of guilt and stood up, distractedly brushing out the creases in her uniform. "I've got to leave. Listen to Fariem."

"Sure." Garrett watched her shambling gait as she left the room. While it was nice to know she cared enough about his well-being, guilt inevitably seeped through, chastising him for distracting her from the enigmatic turmoil that pointed swords at her.

His nerves jolted as Fariem's stealthy hands undid the clasp of his bandage, and he met their irritated glare reprimanding his sudden movement. With an apologetic whimper, he relaxed his shoulders, letting them finish unwrapping the injury.

The skin beneath had no trace of a puncture wound, but the thorn had left a net of darkened veins in its wake. Swollen red streambeds bordered their pathways, forming a grisly web enveloping his shoulder.

Fariem plucked his wrist with disturbingly cold fingers and turned it over, waving a device at his palm. His hand shook in their grip, fingers twitching as the sensory beams investigated his skin. Keeping the urge to pull away at bay, he gathered scraps of courage to test the conversational waters.

"I'm sorry I got in the way."

"You did nothing wrong." Fariem dropped his hand, shaking their head as they recorded their notes.

Not the response he was expecting. "I'll, uh, head back and not trouble you any longer."

"Try it. I'm due for a laugh." They snorted, stepping back with an inviting gesture.

Garrett didn't pick up the snide tone as he pulled himself upright. His mass increased tenfold as he slid his wavering legs over the edge of the bed. Communication lines severed between his brain and his body, and he did not feel his toe touch the floor. Or Fariem diving underneath him as his shoulders dipped.

They scoffed as they gruffly rolled him back on the gurney. "Lay down."

"Okay." His brain fluttered with the attempt to carry a conversation. "So, are you Nara's... parents?"

Fariem wrinkled their face. "The human is so noisy."

"Sorry."

"And needlessly guilty."

He chewed the inside of his cheek in response.

"You should be fine in the morning to move around." They shook their head admonishingly and walked out the door.

"Thank you."

Fariem hesitated, glancing over their shoulder. They analyzed the human's tone, performing intangible calculations concealed by their stony expression. "Go to sleep."

##4.1##

"WE HAVE NOT COME to a unified conclusion." The image of the Councilor of Science shrugged at Nara from the screen. "Your unannounced arrival has stirred up possibilities that have never been accounted for, and we simply need more time to consider it."

"You wanted *Loremaster's* voice and now you have it." Pangs flicked across Nara's cheeks as she restrained a scowl.

"It's just not as simple as that, *Savant*. I am sorry." The channel went dark, giving a final response.

Nara slammed her fist on the desk, unleashing a torrent of hot air from her nostrils. It would be more effective to gain respect from a wall. If she wanted to get anywhere, she would have to do it the hard way and gain the trust of each remaining representative individually. But with Abberon and GaPFed spreading their pestilence over the planet, she did not have the luxury of time to ease into their favor.

She was about to quiet her wrath with another draught of intemperance when her computer blared with the summons. With a growl, she accepted the call, meeting the solemn expression of Fariem.

"I'll take better care of your human."

Nara waved them off. "I'm sure they'll be fine."

"Listen, I know I shouldn't be prodding, but—"

"No, you shouldn't."

Fariem pressed harder. "They are a liability."

"I am aware." Nara cracked the tab off another beverage. "I'll deal with it if it arises."

They tsked at Nara's self-destructive display. "You really need time away from this mess. Deal with all that baggage you carry."

"And when do I have time for that?"

"You've been dealing with all this political refuse for years." They folded their arms, projecting their sympathy with a frown. "And *Xannat* only knows what else from your life on a *human* planet."

Nara grumbled at the assessment, resting her head in her hand. Fariem had long been absolved of the responsibility of being her caretaker, but their insistence never ceased. It made her uncomfortable to have someone exert the effort to care beyond contractual obligation.

"Your indulgences are an impediment," Fariem chastised as they watched her gulp down the carton. "If you insist on working despite your obvious exhaustion, I could prescribe—"

She dropped her hand down on the desk. A splash of the liquor dribbled down her fingers. "Absolutely *not*."

"Fine." They sighed, letting their frustration stiffen their posture. "You should get some air to clear your thoughts, at least. Maybe find some familiarity at the training grounds."

Irritation dissolved into sorrow as Nara considered the proposal. Her feelings toward the Council were clear, but she didn't get the chance to see those under her command before her banishment. To atone. As far as everyone knew, twelve of their fellow soldiers had died because of her.

"Well, I can see you have other matters to attend to." Fariem bowed their head, aware of the distress they had caused.

"Fariem, please be courteous to Garrett. That's all I ask."

With an affirming nod, Fariem closed the channel.

"God *damn* it." She slung a torrent of curses as she stomped to her feet. After ordering another drink from the food servo, she lurched into the patio and stared out into the glittering forest.

While it wasn't fair of her to desert Garrett in this unfamiliar world, she refused to accept total responsibility. He made his choice when he stepped onto the *Armored Wake*, and he should suffer the consequences of his curiosity.

But the human considered her a friend, a title she was beyond uncomfortable carrying. This language didn't have a name for friends, only colleagues and subordinates. While some interpreted that as a liberty to be as intimate or platonic as they pleased, she preferred to keep those around her at a distance and instead fill the isolation with duty and work. It was comforting to her, a routine sense of order she could rely on.

She pressed a palm onto a pane of glass, summoning a dot of light on the material. It snapped to the side, tracing a square around her hand. The material shielding her palm disappeared with a whisper, permitting the elements to creep into the room with a cooling breeze.

She inhaled the air, letting the woodsy perfume of the earth wash away her thoughts. A gentle tinkle of the crystalline leaves danced around her ears, playing a medley of icy tones harmonious to her melancholy.

Her fickle state of ease was jolted away by an obnoxious flurry of knocks on the front door. She scrunched her face at the interruption, muttering indignantly as she stormed off to answer the summons.

Two individuals from her command greeted her as she opened the door, one her most excitable scouts, Elerick, and the other, Lieutenant Tek, standing unusually quiet and stiff.

"It's true!" Elerick repeatedly smacked Tek in the chest with a friendly back hand. "I told you!"

Nara blinked the astonishment from her face. "What are you doing here?"

"Jav'ril sent us over." Elerick's lips stretched into a devious smirk. "Or rather, I pestered him until he spilled his guts about the rumors."

"Did he, now?" Ice seized her nerves.

"Kestra's been made Warlord." They beamed and shoved Tek forward, who obliged the force. "They were doing border control when you left until trade was closed. Now they're plotting out waypoints to explore in space whenever we finally get access to the fleet."

Nara tilted her head curiously. Tek to Kestra. Eager Force to Calculated Strike. It must have taken quite a feat to have such a contrasting name change.

"Congratulations on your advancement and Renaming," Nara cautiously bade.

Kestra gave a meek shrug. "It wasn't much of an achievement."

Apprehension warmed the silence. She was looking at a recognizable character in Kestra, despite the unusual wall of caution toward her presence, the uncertainty radiating beyond their aura.

Back when she was active, Nara had longed to be Renamed. The hours spent hoping to erase *Eternal Red* from their tongues. *Sleepless* was only a minor upgrade. *Nothing* was preferred.

Elerick stepped in to break the tension, reaching for her hand. "Some infantry units made an encampment in the woods. Please come spar with us!"

"I don't think that's appropriate." She stepped back. "How many of the others know of my presence?"

"Just a handful. Jav'ril expressed the need for discretion. It's only a small gathering." They tried to beam through her concern. "Just like old times."

Old times. Her heart sank. "I—"

"Come now, the car is waiting!" Elerick flailed their wrist in her direction. "They all brought down a beast for the occasion. It should be ready by the time we arrive!"

Nara glanced at the quiet warlord, who offered a nervous smile. They were glad to see her, but their mind was reeling with questions.

It was no use. She couldn't avoid them forever. "For only a little while."

"Of course, of course!" Barely waiting for her response, Elerick pulled her along, slipping their arm around hers.

Kestra accompanied her other side, linking around her other arm, and relief began to seep into their posture.

##4.2##

THE JOURNEY WAS uncomfortable despite Elerick's attempts to keep the brevity at bay. Nara let them fill the vehicle with noise as she watched the blur of trees. The machinery pattered quietly as the treads skirted around the dense brush below, taking care not to crush the living carpet with its pronged slats.

Elerick spoke of the activities the soldiers partook in, the combat techniques they had studied reflecting her previous guidance, the games they had re-enacted. Nothing political. The upper ranks had kept them busy with idle tasks to hide the Council's indecisive quarreling. Strange, but not unexpected.

They arrived at a small clearing where prefabricated shelters and cooking arenas jutted out from living quarter cubes, hardly a scene of battle against the wilderness. Soldiers darted from station to station, performing their tasks in a display of efficiency. Some assembled containers and refrigeration units from storage in preparation for leftovers, while others cleaned dining areas for the makeshift feast.

Several people tended to a bonfire, flames licking a massive quadrupedal creature impaled through a spit. The beast was built like a living war machine, its long, lean limbs ideal for deftly skirting through the woods to spring upon its prey. Due to its infamous ferocity, it would have taken the collective effort of every soldier at the camp to bring it down without casualties. But a hunt of this size was reserved for a special occasion and the aftermath worth every struggle.

A circle of rocky scales and chitinous plating surrounded the blaze, the armor of the beast providing insulation for the earth against the inferno. Three soldiers operated the crank of the spit to rotate it over the fire, while another splashed a fatty elixir over the meat to keep it hydrated, the athletic creature possessing a scant amount of fat to insulate it against the flames. The crackles and hisses of dripping oils kept the tempo of the smoke riddled orchestra, dancing in harmony with the charred perfume wafting into the atmosphere.

Heads turned as the trio exited the vehicle, the crew chirped noises of excitement as they watched the visitors approach.

"Warlord!" A member of the infantry rushed over, soon to be followed by the others. "Welcome back!"

Aion, Dev'lin, Volma… she remembered them all.

"I…" Words protested from leaving her tongue as she examined their faces. Relief swirled with eager attention bombarded her spirits. It was as if nothing had happened. "It's *Savant* now."

Elevated gasps wisped out of glittering faces upon hearing the proclamation. She was overwhelmed with their hunger for answers, their curiosity clawing at her.

"Come! The meal is almost ready. Why don't we sit by the fire?" Elerick ushered her to the head of the dining station.

Excited chattering followed her as she slid into her seat, The gathering dispersed to make the final preparations for the meal. The warm reception flooded her skin with discomfort, a lash of shame tore into her brain.

The tension in her posture loosened slightly as she watched the plates assemble at the table. Steaming mounds of succulent meat seeped an earthy aroma into the atmosphere, the tang of bitter herbs speckling the savory perfume.

Charred vegetation began to appear, forming a structured fortification around the centerpiece. Poached fruits foraged from the neighboring trees glistened in the rigged spotlights. Stacks of preservation jars of fermented garnishes bathed in in colorful fluids, their vibrancy warning of their potency. All was flourished with gallons of fizzing berry juices to wash everything down.

The familiar smells and sounds teased her senses, something she had taken for granted when she considered this place her home. She had gained an appreciation for culinary arts from her stay on Arcadia. Taste was one of the human pleasures she could understand and even grew a fondness for.

Kestra slid to the seat at her side, a worrisome frown shading their face as they passed a plate to her. She stared down at the table, burying herself in the sounds and textures. The tide of conversation was appeased by the sound of clattering silverware and munching noises accented with grunts of enjoyment. The revelry magnified as the soldiers chatted among themselves between mouthfuls of food, some not bothering to finish chewing before continuing. Just like old times.

She poked around the plate, admiring the meal and allowing herself to soak in the casual atmosphere. Could it go back to the way it was?

Feeling more secure with everyone distracted, Nara sampled a piece of the steaming meat, letting the nature-cured meat dissolve on her tongue. The tension in her muscles relaxed as the smoky taste soothed her senses. But the sensation faded as something flickered at the corner of her vision.

As she looked up, her eyes moved to a group of three speaking in hushed voices, avoiding her gaze as they contemplated an inaudible plot. The soldier to one side nudged the center individual in the ribs, evoking a scathing glare. Nara met gaze of the trio, who shrank back into their meals.

"Is anything the matter?" Nara challenged. The soldier on the right glanced back at their two companions avoiding the question then inhaled a fortifying breath.

"Forgive me, *Savant*," they addressed her with hopeful eyes. "But we would all like to know, what happened? We were led to believe that you had died."

Silence pierced through her heart as everyone halted mid-bite. Eyes moved to the speaker and then to her. Too polite to agree but yearning to know more.

"*Rahksha*," Kestra warned with an icy glare. "*Savant* is probably overwhelmed by this meeting. Be mindful of your questions."

The soldier hung their head ashamedly. "Apologies, *Savant*."

"It's—" Nara cleared the snakes of nausea constricting her throat. "Didn't the Council tell you?"

"We've heard no word from the Council since…" Rahksha looked down in remorse. "Since you and the shadow units were reported dead."

Aches spasmed across her chest as she struggled to inhale her breath. So much for normalcy.

"Nothing is broadcast anymore," Kestra added. "Everyone's in a holding pattern until we get orders from higher up. Even I don't have enough clearance to find out more."

"We know the Council hates working with you, but to think you've been here the whole time..." another lamented. "Why didn't you come back to us?"

The plea resounded through her ears, their ignorant faces staring back at her. In all her years of command, she'd never let her guard down around them, concealing her inner turmoil. But she could no longer hold it in. She had to tell them. They deserved to know.

She covered her mouth, beating back the tremors from her voice. "They told me I killed them all."

No one moved.

"I... I don't know what happened myself." Her hesitation rattled spirits around her. "They kept me sedated for the duration of the trial. They thought I was *Fevered*. They—"

A gasp choked out her words as her throat seized shut, bile searing her tongue. Words could not illuminate the severity of her sins. She thought she had come to terms with the ordeal, but faced with the score of those she had wronged, it was no use. They needed to know.

Tar pulled at her limbs as she rose from her seat. Her fingers trembled as she fought to unbind the clasps of her uniform. She turned her back toward her observers, slipping the garment off her shoulders to reveal her final judgment.

Four plates of bone were supposed to protect her back from assailants, but a mass of scarred trenches took the place of the one that had once covered her right shoulder. It was a ritual used to mark those who were considered a danger to society, a traitor among kindred. She was forever incomplete, a reminder of her deeds literally torn from her flesh.

"I am no longer one of you." Needles prickled her skin as their eyes scanned over the crevasses of her flesh.

Her jaw clenched as she heard someone rise. Footsteps quietly approached, but she could not gather the courage to face them.

A startled gasp propelled from her lungs as the pressure of cool fingertips brushed against the mark. Their hand slithered down her back, chills sparking against her skin as they wrapped around her waist. She turned her head to find Kestra glaring at the earth with a vehement expression.

"Something is wrong." They brought her close, squeezing her hard. "We need to fix this."

The gesture clashed against her soul like the fall of a hammer. *Calculated Strike.*

For decades, she'd repressed her thoughts and emotions, hiding them from the outside world. But control slipped away from her grasp, frozen inside this alien gesture of intimacy. Tears streamed from her cheeks, her defiant eyes saturating her skin with the salted memories of the past.

The others began to approach, surrounding her with their radiance. The ones she'd fought next to, bled next to. They were so good. All she wanted was to protect them from the games the Council played. From herself.

She did not deserve this.

##4.3##

GARRETT WAS REINVIGORATED as he emerged from his dream-fueled state. He spent the newly procured energy leaping out of his skin when he met the devious eyes of Syf looming over him.

"I apologize for the startle, but I am relieved to see you doing better." They grinned and laid a tray on the table. "I brought breakfast!"

He eyed the figure suspiciously and gingerly picked up a utensil, torn between his fear of mortality and fear of offending. "I, uh, thank you."

Their eerie smile intensified as they watched the human curiously, knitting their hands under their chin.

Hairs rose on the back of his neck as he poked at the bowl of vegetables squiggling in an oily broth. "Can I... help you with anything?"

"No. Do carry on," they said through a flash of fangs.

To his relief, Fariem entered the room, snapping a finger at the leering creature. "Syf. Out."

"Yes, Serr'Maht." They winked at Garrett before obediently scurrying away.

"Pay them no mind," Fariem said as they examined the console. "They're just protective and have a habit of digging for insecurities in new people."

"It's no trouble." He tried to convince himself.

They scoffed. "There's no need to conceal your feelings for the sake of protecting mine."

Under their advice, he let his thoughts slip off his tongue. "You sound like Nara."

"I *sound* like everyone on this planet," they snapped. "Lying about your concerns wastes time and makes you look untrustworthy."

He stirred the contents of the bowl listlessly. "Is she okay? She's been acting... strange. Even more than when I met her."

Fariem turned their back to him, jotting down notes on a tablet. "That is a complicated question that I do not have consent to communicate."

"I see." He should have guessed his inquiry would hit a wall.

They pointed an authoritative palm in his direction. "Give me your hand."

Garrett obeyed, watching apprehensively as they wrapped their digits around his wrist. He bit his tongue as they pressed their finger on the back of his hand, a glimmer of metal catching his eye. With a short hum of approval, Fariem hastily left his personal space. He looked down at his hand, watching a tiny tear in his skin seal itself, not even the slightest drop of blood left to scab over.

Fariem traced a finger across a screen, following a pattern of charts and numbers. "You're fine to leave after you've finished your meal."

"Sure, thank you."

"You're a strange one, you know that?" They raised a thumb to their chin, scrunching their eyebrows tightly.

"I've been called worse." He shrugged. *By my own family, even.*

"Mmm." Fariem turned and departed, leaving Garrett with his apprehension stew.

The silence was a chilling seasoning to the neglected broth on his lap. He raised the bowl to his mouth, slurping the cold concoction. A well-balanced bitterness caressed his tongue, the earthy flavor reminding him of medicinal tea.

He picked up a vegetable with a utensil, biting into it experimentally. The fibers were simmered to a point where they were pleasant to chew, not too tough or too mushy. They added a sweetness to the brew and a salty savoriness comparable to a fragrant mushroom.

It was refreshing, the almost slushed broth going down his throat. He found a strange fortifying sensation saturating his nerves. Perhaps Syf's intent was not of malice.

When he finished, he scooted off the bed and headed toward the apartment, keeping one eye over his shoulder. No one was currently in the lab, but not wanting to push his luck in encountering Syf again, he made a hasty retreat toward the hideout. Chills ran down his spine as he pressed the door control, and he barely let the door slide apart before wedging himself through the opening.

"Hello?" Silence replied. *I guess Nara's still working. Somewhere.*

He moved up to the bedroom, giving the computer panel on the wall a venomous glare. He approached the despicable object, raising a haughty finger at the display. Recalling the sequence Prism had used, he coaxed the text into Trade and cast his own brand of wizardry at the device.

GREETINGS, GARRETT OF ARCADIA, CYTERUS SYSTEM. AWAITING INSTRUCTION.

He clapped his hands together in glee, watching as the flash of menus glittered at his disposal. A curious stream of inquiry murmured from his throat as he ran a finger around the edge of the device. His skin grazed over indentations of input ports, and he wondered if the

NetComm on his wrist would be compatible with the infernal machine.

He slid a finger over the monitor until a selection of furniture options offered their control. "Let's do something about that bed."

With his prods, the height of the mattress wall sank into itself, moving down to a more manageable height below his waist. His nail prodded at a column of slats resting on the bed frame. As he pulled it forward, the slats slid over the floor, extending into a set of small steps reaching the top edge of the frame.

"So *that's* how they do it."

The décor settings flickered deviously, inviting him to alter the aesthetics of the room. Overloaded with the responsibility of choice, he focused his attention on the walls. There, he could divide them in whatever way he wished, vertically, horizontally, even plucking out guidelines from the perimeter and bisecting them in a myriad of angles and lengths.

His eyes moved to two color wheels on the *Paint* options, one marked *Human* and the other *Ara'yulthr*. But to him, they appeared exactly the same. "Weird."

He flipped over to the *Prefab* menu and was presented with a list of environments to choose from. Forest, Mountain, Arctic, and then some nestled inside the *Domestic* tab. He plucked at the *Outsider* segment, and new worlds were revealed to him. Deep Space, Nebula, Orbit. Some civilizations of neighboring planets that were computer generated from images he assumed came from the Archives.

"Human City?" He pressed the option, and the walls shifted to a world alight with a blinding sun, no clouds to hinder its path. He pressed the weather option to Overcast and blinked away the glare in his vision.

At his feet he saw lush grasses and plants around a dirt path leading to a collection of brick structures barely touching the sky. A great bridge of wires and steel stretched over a gently murmuring ocean. A few sea craft with churning smokestacks glided along its rippling current.

"Where is this place?" It was nothing like Arcadia. For one, it still had an ecosystem.

The thought of his home wove a knot in his heart. By no means did he enjoy the bright city lights, especially knowing who controlled them. But it was familiar to him, and since he had never left his world before, he never considered that other humans might live differently.

His musings wandered toward worry as he contemplated what fate had taken Baran, his most trusted friend and caretaker. He missed the man dearly but feared the worst. If Antonin Galavantier managed to seize him in his clutches, a swift death would be a mercy.

A soft chime dispersed his sorrow, and he looked down the stairs to find the doorframe blinking again. "What now?"

Clearing his throat and stiffening his posture, he descended to the atrium. He opened the front door to the warm, wrinkled smile of *Loremaster*. They hadn't spoken since their visit in Arcadia to help arrange Nara's exodus, and it was nice to see them in a much calmer circumstance.

"Oh, hello, sir—I mean—*Serr*." He fussed with his clothing to make himself more presentable to the aged noble. "Nara hasn't returned from her duties yet."

"Well, then." The librarian's smile widened. "Then I suppose I shall visit you."

He blinked at the offer. "Oh, I wouldn't want to trouble you!"

"It's not troubling at all. I've been meaning to meet with you, anyway."

"Really? You honor me." Garrett glided to the side and raised an arm to gesture them inside. "Please come in. I would offer you some tea but… I am not sure how to use the food dispenser."

Loremaster chuckled and stepped inside. "Let's find out together."

They walked into the kitchen and leaned down to the computer, rubbing their chin pensively as they gently tapped the device awake. Garrett watched in fascination as the gentle visitor swiped through the menus, exuding elegance with every gesture.

"Hmmm." The sage's concentration intensified. "Floral, fruits, or Earth?"

"Oh. I do like a bit of floral."

"Excellent. Come this way." They waited for Garrett to lean in before poking the Trade setting. A selection of clear vials filled with colorful liquids presented themselves in an orderly grid. "What sounds good to you? I like them all."

Garrett eyed through the selection. Though he could not recognize the names of the plants included, the arsenal was broken down by flavor profiles in adjectives he could understand. A deep red concoction caught his eye with descriptions including *fresh softness, nuttiness,* and *a wisp of smoke.* Further descriptors included, *Best paired with mineral-rich waters* and *Has a sharp bite.*

"Ah. A bold choice!" *Loremaster* cooed, causing Garrett to question his safety. "Do you like sweets?"

"Certainly."

"Fantastic!" As *Loremaster* coaxed the display, the grid shifting to a selection of disc-shaped objects with stampings of presumably the flavor or contents of the confection. Chunks of dark-colored bits embedded the various shades of dough. "I'll show you a few of my favorites."

The dumbwaiter churned to life as *Loremaster* cast the order. Garrett took the initiative and went to fetch the items. He opened the cabinet to find two steaming mugs made from a plasticky material inside, accompanied by a pot of creamy liquid made from the same material as the instant food dishes from last night's dinner. A plate of cookies sealed in a sheet of transparent bouncy polymer sat in the back along with two curious clear jars and a vial of blood-red fluid.

Loremaster sat down and awaited the offerings, delicately plucking the vial and unscrewing the top. They poured several drops into each mug, and an aroma of charred wood and soft blossoms swirled into the air. They sniffed the vial and gave off a pleased smile before handing it to Garrett. "If you like it a bit stronger, feel free."

Hoping he had secured familiarity with the ritual, Garrett picked up the creamer and offered to *Loremaster*. "Do you take milk?"

They smiled and chuckled. "That is Hirapod nectar, but it does serve the same purpose. I'll take a splash."

"Oh, sure." Garrett shook his head and poured the liquid inside the mugs. It added a delicate citrus note to the brew, melding with the smoke and perfume of the flowers inside the concoction.

As he sat back down, *Loremaster* set to work preparing the sweets.

They snapped off a knifelike tool off the plate and then opened a jar containing a creamy white spread. After wafting the contents into their nose and giving an approving hum, they smeared a thin layer of the buttery substance on a cookie.

"I'll prepare one of each so you can see what they are like." They picked up a second cookie. Inside the second clear jar was a gelatinous red sludge speckled with dark orbs of what Garrett could only guess was seeds of the fruit mashed inside.

He picked up the creamed delicacy and gave it a tactful nibble. The texture of the spread was just like a soft cheese, but the flavor reminded him more of something plant based, like fresh-cut sweet grass and clovers. It had a lovely floral note binding the fragrance together that was pleasing to the senses.

The cookie had a moist, compact texture, much like a dense holiday cake. It had a soft flavor of grains mingled with crunchy dried citrus fruits. Crystals of silky sweetness separated the homogenous texture. He tried the jam, finding it akin to a sour berry with a peppery warmth. The orbs were crunchier than anticipated, leaving his molars sore after the workout of breaking them down.

Though pleasant, the confection glued traces of itself around his molars. He took a sip of the warm tea, finding a lively flavor caressing his tongue. He tasted a bouquet of wild blossoms set alight by a heady combination of cinders and ash. A nutty sweetness rolled over, softening the harsh elements.

As he looked curiously down at the mug, a strange sensation lashed across his mouth, sparking needle-like stings like the bite of a dried peppercorn combined with a tropical fruit hiding enzymes in its nectar. Numbness began to trickle over his tongue, and he pressed it on the roof of his mouth, sensation decaying as the muscle fought to detect the surrounding flesh.

"How are you adjusting?" *Loremaster's* eyebrows furrowed. "I heard you had an accident in Fariem's workroom."

His lips twitched in an awkward smile as he struggled to gain control of his tongue. "Oh, that was no trouble."

"Modest as ever."

Garrett hid his nervous smile behind his cookie, wondering where his station lay under the presence of what was considered royalty. His upbringing left him deathly afraid of tripping over an unspoken proto-col, something that took willpower to subdue.

That led into thoughts about Nara and her position. She was a warlord here, someone of utmost importance as far as he could tell. He was given an abridged version of the conditions of her expulsion, and he could not fathom what sorts of consequences she would be paying. Raised in a corporate oligarchy, he had no frame of reference for the political proceedings here. Money and influence were the only methods he knew of to advance ranks, and at least one of those did not exist here.

"Something is troubling you," *Loremaster* prodded. "Do tell."

He perked up at the inquiry, shocked by their perception. "How much trouble is Nara really in?"

Loremaster leaned back and considered their words. "This civiliza-tion is right in the midst of a cultural transition. For decades, centuries even, we have avoided involvement with the forces of power outside our world. But unfortunately, that time is nearing an end. And Elam has been thrown directly into the conflict."

"When I met her, she seemed to be just another mercenary. Gruff, no need for friends, and self-sufficient." Garrett looked at the plate. "Then we arrived here, and she's so much more important. It's strange to see the shift. I'm not even sure what she does."

"She was pretty vocal in proceedings, carrying a neutral stance that most people agreed upon, even if they did not want to admit it." They swirled the contents of their mug. "Her only opposition was bureau-cracy, which was also shifting as new issues sprang forward. And Aber-ron, but he was barred from the World Council when he repeatedly made a fool of himself just to get a rise out of her."

Garrett recalled the warlord he saw in the games video that opposed Nara. The man brought chills to his spine. "I've heard of him. Not a fan."

"You would not be the only one." They smirked as they drained their mug.

"What's his deal, anyway?"

Loremaster vented a weighted sigh. "Abberon is trying to change our Old Ways with explosive force to create a catalyst that will throw us forward into a new era of technology."

"Apart from his methods, is the intent really that bad?"

"It is perfectly acceptable to obliterate the Old Ways when they become obsolete." They nodded. "But only when the Old Ways are rigid and refuse to change. Then force is the only way forward."

"And your culture is different?"

"The problem with our Old Ways is that they are constantly changing, adapting to suit our needs. Essentially, we don't have Old Ways. Our methods can never be obsolete. What this one is doing is destroying civilization at its root by changing us into something we are not." They tapped a firm finger on the table. "We are not conquerors to force assimilation. We are innovators, explorers, creators, and most importantly, defenders."

"That's… hard for me to comprehend," Garrett admitted. Arcadia was ruled by spending tons and tons of resources crushing the opponents, a futile race to scramble up before the competition swallowed you.

Here, it was much different. The people need not want for anything. There was order, albeit room for squabbles amid a clandestine structure. People had their place and the freedom to express themselves without fear of backstabbing.

Loremaster smiled at the student. "It is a curious contrast to your standards, isn't it?"

A soft chime at the door interrupted the musing.

"Oh, excuse me." Garrett glanced over at the intrusion. "I will get that."

Loremaster chuckled and stood, holding a hand up. "Let me show you a trick." They rapped a knuckle on the tabletop, the surface shifting to a panel with a glittering button.

The door opened to reveal a sunny Prism standing inside the frame and looking studious as ever holding their tablet.

"Oh! I did not realize you were here, Serr'Maht. I was just wondering if the Ambassador was perhaps prepared for another lesson, but I can come back later."

"It's no trouble. I have lost track of time, anyway. I will not interrupt your lesson." *Loremaster* stood from their seat and politely bowed. "We shall have to do this again, Serr Garrett."

"Certainly." His heart sank as he watched the man leave, alone with this predicament and the overbearing cheeriness of his captor waiting at the door.

"So, what would you like to learn about today, Ambassador?"

CHAPTER 5

##5.0##

Gnarled, blackened trees clawed their way through the blood-red fog, their leaves long since burned away. The humid air pushed against her skin as she lumbered forward, thick, murky sludge infecting the atmosphere.

She drank in the poison, taking in the acidic fire that coated her chest. The marsh-carpeted earth began to swell and rise, erasing the path with curls of hazy muck. Thorned vines crept at her legs, cutting trails into her flesh as they twirled around her muscles. She paid them no mind, stalling her gait to let them spread up her back, the barbs caressing her mangled scars.

Her knees caved as the ground pulled her in, the soft dirt crushing her bones with its embrace. She raised her head to find a light dissipating the smog, voices calling her name. A score of them beckoned in sweetened tones.

A surge rushed up her spine, the vines lessening their grip. Fear seized her, unwilling to let her observers witness her shame. Blood splattered over the ground as she tore her arms from her confinement. A mighty bellow escaped her throat, a warning to those ahead. The ground shuddered beneath her in response to her summons. The rocks cracked and groaned.

Sludge poured into the widening chasm, the sound of water hurtling toward an inky black void. An impassable steel wall rose from the suture, splashing the refuse at her as it stretched into the sky. Its surface was carved with crude images of tormented souls, faces familiar.

The voices stopped. She turned back to the bog, wading into the muddy waters.

But then another presence disturbed the clouds above her. Cautious, silent, creeping.

She let out a gasp as it clutched her wrist, pulling her out of the mire. Her body flew out of the clutches of the trees, their branches delicately brushing her as she ascended above the crimson sky. Sound dulled around her as the force of water pulsed against her ears, blue swirls warping around her limbs. Sunlight tickled the ripples of the surface above her.

With a panicked exhale, she broke the surface, expelling liquid as a warm breeze caressed her cheek. Her body bobbed on the water's surface as the sea cradled her with a gentle swaying. She took in the strange world of color and light. The sea gently ushered her to a lush green shore, the trees dotted with vibrant birds calling out to each other in sweet song.

She saw a figure at the edge of the jungle dissolving into a cloud of shadow before her eyes. Her mind was too exhausted from the struggle. She could only focus on the grassy earth beneath her.

##5.1##

NARA WOKE with the sensation of lead weights pressing against her limbs. She pulled her eyes open to find herself lying on the ground, entangled within a pile of the sleeping bodies of her units.

They tried to commune with me. A nervous spasm lashed against her spine. *I hope they didn't see...*

Ara'yulthr didn't dream in their sleep like she did, but perhaps her mind was left open for those to enter through guided meditation. On the few occasions she did rest while on command, she kept herself far away from sight to hide her affliction. It would have demoralized them to see her weakness.

She gently slipped her arms from underneath her captors, uncurling her body upright to greet the light of day shining through the trees. Kestra was several yards ahead, sitting on a felled trunk, huddled over in contemplation. After slithering out of her entrapment, she cautiously approached the warlord.

"Can you still trust me?" Nara whispered, hugging herself. "After what has been done?"

They straightened their back, keeping their gaze on the horizon. "Jav'ril absorbed your units until I was able to take over. I wish I could say I earned that responsibility under more deserving circumstances."

Her eyebrows furrowed as she watched them closely. They sighed a shaky breath as shame shuddered their form.

"I fought against Abberon in the tournaments," Kestra began. "They implemented bio warfare against us. A voracious virus that decimated our ranks."

Their gaze intensified, their jaw protesting the recounting of the tale. Nara stood patiently as they gathered the courage to speak again. "It was horrendous and gruesome. The screams coming from the med bays are something I will never forget. I saw my comrades... Jav'ril was one of the first..."

They blinked back the tears welling around their eyes, taking a moment to recompose themself. Their voice hushed to a rasp. "Their skin cracked open, peeled away from their bodies and sloughing off in gelatinous lumps. Their plates just... fell off like they were scabs. And their eyes... their eyes just melted away into hollow bloody sockets. Seeing Jav'ril like that, I just couldn't..."

Tears disobeyed their master's command, flowing freely as they choked out Kestra's voice. They buried their face in their hands, their nails digging into their scalp.

Anger cinched Nara's jaw. It was a horrifying trick to play, but she expected no better from Abberon.

"We were able to contain it, but I was left alone to command. So I..." They hesitated, sliding a shaking fist to their mouth. "I commissioned the largest warhead known to us from alien technology, then set off on a ship of my own. Destroyed the mainframe facility. That was the objective, after all."

Nara gently slid next to them on the log while their piercing eyes stared through the trees. Moments passed as she watched them assess their memories. The breeze chimed through the leaves, the glinting movements derailing Kestra from their thoughts. They inhaled a cleansing breath to steel themselves for the account.

"It was overkill. By a gross magnitude. I did not realize it then. Nearly half the continent was absorbed in fire. After the fall, I landed on the top of the tallest hill and watched them burn. Reveled in it, even." Their knuckles faded to a bright pallor as their clenched fists trembled. "I thought Ötmarr would grant me relief. Serving the exact as they had inflicted upon us. But it was horrific. Even though I had won, I could feel Abberon's glee. And the cost…"

Nara looked at her feet, unsure of what to make of their confession. It pulled against everything she had taught them, pulled at what she thought were her principles. But it also left her wondering. Why did she feel this way?

"Thinking back to the time I served tournaments under you, I thought it fine when it was just me who died. But they suffered." They turned their mournful eyes to her. "You were right."

She inhaled heavily, digging a toe in the soil. "You did what you thought was right. And in a way, you stopped more suffering by his hand. You are also aware of the cost of your actions."

They nodded solemnly. "After the tournament, Abberon was brought to the Council to explain himself. They simply said they wanted to show us what we were up against in the outside universe. And that we needed to be prepared."

That sounds exactly like Abberon. Her molars began to grind the flesh of her cheek. "And what happened to you?"

"I withdrew myself from all activities, social, training. Everything. But despite mine and the Council's protests, Jav'ril appointed me Warlord. He said I had learned from this experience and would be a wise leader." Their voice almost mocked the assessment. "I never led a tournament during my command. I didn't miss much. They were closed soon after the dissension, anyway."

She couldn't blame him for being reserved after a game gone sour. While the tournaments were just a simulation, they had realistic consequences, shoving the burden of moral responsibility to the players. It made the leaders restrained in their actions, as the simulation had the power to leave grievous scars.

Kestra looked over at the pile of snoozing soldiers. "Like you, I kept them busy. Distracted from what was going on up high since I didn't have answers. The Council kept me at arm's reach, afraid of my association with you."

They collected their thoughts, running their fingers along the indentations of the bark they were sitting on. It was the sort of tribulation Nara wanted to protect them from. But she'd learned now that she could not bear that burden forever. No one would ever grow.

"I suppose what I am trying to say is, I let my anger guide my actions, and others paid dearly for it." They raised their head to the sky. "I know you wouldn't do anything out of malice. And for that, you have my utmost admiration."

"I appreciate the sentiment." She leaned into his shoulder. "And I understand the trial. I am sorry it had to come to that."

They shrugged. "It's something I will have to live with. The past is there. Now we have to deal with the present."

"What would you suggest?" Nara inquired.

"I don't have much experience dealing with the Council head on." They tapped a finger to their lips. "But perhaps a series of unofficial visits might leave them with fewer defenses."

"I had considered that. And right now, it's the only action I can think of." She turned to face him. "Thank you for trusting me. I hope to never disappoint."

Kestra smiled softly, then looked over to the stirring mass as the soldiers began to rise. "Perhaps you can try to speak with the Council later. We are here for a little longer. We might as well enjoy it."

Or rather hide the severity of the situation from them, Nara thought morbidly. *Some things will never change.*

##5.2##

THE CURRENT THEORY agreed upon by most Councilors of the Anthropology Division is that our kind have evolved from the Charr'Kanth approximately twenty millennia ago. Like us, the creature changes its coloration during maturity, morphing from the pastels of the grasses to the purple red tones of the trees.

The Charr'Kanth were omnivorous creatures, catching flighted insects and smaller animals in the trees as well as partaking of the fruits and leaves grown by the foliage.

The screen inside the reading corner displayed a tank-like quadrupedal creature, its back segmented in thick, rounded plates that appeared as if roughly chiseled from rock. All four legs were covered similarly, with divisions of thick, leathery skin separating its joints. It had an almost cat-like head and an elongated muzzle with a jaw filled with daggers.

While it was a large creature, it did not compare to the vast majority of the Apex predators it shared the world with. Its plating was used as a tempting decoy, either letting a hunter bite the large target of its back or tempt them to turn it over, allowing its clawed hands to slash exposed vulnerabilities.

Garrett stirred his not-so-tingly tea as he watched another creature slink into view. Its giant frame cast a looming shadow as it leaped up, snapping its jaw open wide. The hunter buried its teeth near the spine of the Charr'Kanth. It struggled with its mouth full as it attempted to heft the creature up, fangs jammed in fragments of the Charr'Kanth's plating.

Paying no mind to its predicament, the Charr'Kanth lashed out at the ankle of the hunter. Blood whipped off its claws as it severed the tendons of its captor in a messy display. A screeching yelp of pain later, the Charr'Kanth dropped to the ground with a thunderous stomp of its feet. It belted out a mighty roar as its foe limped back into the forest.

Evidence from geological examination and extraction sites have charted a progression in the development of the original creature. Fossil evidence also shows that a global migration did not occur until several stages of development.

A chart of evolutionary advancement stretched into view, lines separating gaps in a timeline spanning thousands of years between each specimen. As the creature developed, it began to lose the density of its armor, swapping out protection for mobility. Eventually, it began to stand upright and its claws and muzzle shrank into the modern Ara'yulthr.

The first of our kind were hunters and gatherers, traveling the equator of the planet since it offered everything needed from sustenance to shelters. But predators were still a major obstacle against survival, and a separate class of fighters developed a rudimentary form of martial arts to defend themselves.

A lush streambed overgrown with vines and ferns coated the moist earth. Beasts of varying pointiness grazed at the drinking hole to refresh their needs. Smaller creatures zipped through the air on leathery wings, squeaking out calls to the rest of their flock. The serenity of the scene quickly shattered as the water began to ripple.

Garrett jumped in his seat as a maw of fangs the size of swords leaped from the surface, snatching the neck of a hapless drinker. The poor victim was quickly pulled into the stream in a surge of bubbles. Those that witnessed the attack scattered, letting out whoops and cries as a warning to others.

With the numerous casualties and low birth rates, a discipline of herbalists emerged, developing medicine and practices to treat wounds and ailments. From them, their apprentices began recording remedies, since the survival of their teachers was never for certain. They used dried reeds and sap from plants to form paper, and the fruits of nearby plants made rich inks. A pictographic language developed, which quickly evolved into short-hand to expedite communication.

What could only be described as a witch's hut came into view, complete with clay campfire ovens and pots strewn all over the floor. Plants hung in neat rows all over the ceiling of the makeshift cavern, drying for future concoctions.

An herbalist walked into view, picking bits and bobs from the dried gardens and tossing them into a bubbling pot. Their acolyte sat next to the fire, meticulously recording every single action their master performed.

Relations between distant clans and families were always amenable. When they encountered each other out in the wilderness, they exchanged recipes and writing arts in addition to new tools and technologies for defense.

As the logs and records of recipes magnified, another dedicated group of individuals were required to maintain the collective. One master was tasked to be caretaker for the mobile libraries, the title now known as Loremaster. They appointed travelers to migrate between families to make sure all information was synchronized.

A traveler walked into an official's office, their backpack overflowing with scrolls and bottles. The room resembled an elegant war room, a massive carved wooden table surrounded by endless shelves of meticulously placed tomes. The librarian greeted them warmly and helped unpack the information from their guest. After the messenger's cargo was unrolled over the tabletop, the master analyzed the precious information.

With an approving nod, the master turned to select a book from the shelf, opening it to compare the two documents. They scrawled a few notes on the margin of the book, chatting with their guest amicably.

The records grew, and so did the need to settle. Farming and cultivating techniques were developed, adding yet another task for the record keepers. Information transportation advanced into more detailed processes as the continents drifted across the globe, adding new challenges to the already massive project.

Wooden ships occupied by librarians sailed across the screen, the crew hauling cases upon cases of locked chests and canvas bags brimming with parchment. The camera flew to a bird's-eye view of the craft, the ship shrinking as it soared into the sky. Land masses spread across the view as the planet shrank to a pinhead.

A seam split the earth apart as it rolled open into a flat sheet. Dashed lines traced the borders of the continents, separating the territory of thirteen clans in vibrant colors.

The librarians and scientists worked together to advance the efficiency of their needs, and the defenders morphed into crafters, the smiths and farmhands who worked with the scientists to make sure they were protected from the elements. They can be compared to a Monk class, where most of the youth and middle aged spent their time. Eventually, they developed formal combat styles to detract wandering predators, evolving into a written guide for self-improvement.

Scores of soldiers gathered at the flat plains of an outdoor arena. A perfectly symmetrical grid of observers stood in attention, watching the combatants in the sparring grounds. Combatants performed beautifully choreographed feats of agility and strength, fearlessly clashing with their opponents using a variety of wooden weaponry.

Garrett stared at the performance. He was used to seeing Nara swiftly dodge dangerous situations, but the thought of more people sharing her skills was unfathomable. A twinge of inadequacy wrinkled his lips.

Eventually, the Capital was formed, and a centralized location was chosen to house every piece of information. The Loremaster's role became the primary beacon of order and experiencer, influencing the flow of government in addition to ensuring proper record keeping.

The scientists divided their efforts, developing branches dedicated to each specific field. They developed into a governing body of their own, reporting their findings and inventing new conveniences to daily life readily accessible to every citizen.

The splendor of the capital city rose into view. Towers that mimicked the trees oversaw affairs from every aspect of the planet, land, sea, and sky. The sun rose behind the tallest pillar, cascading its brilliance around the monolith.

"That is the World Council Chambers," Prism interjected. "That is where all branches of government congregate to discuss the issues of society."

Technology developed into the backbone of production and lifestyle, eventually emerging into the societal norms of today. Knowledge skyrocketed as people from other planets began to visit. With the vast resources and medical technologies that were available to them, trade relationships flourished.

Ships from every nameable galactic civilization flew into view as the sun darkened to a star-studded sky. Engines hummed as the fleets gently glided to the twinkling buoys stretching beyond the planet's orbit.

While most traders offered weaponry and other chemicals alone, we took them graciously to understand what the galaxy outside would be like. From the need of defense arising, the three councils arose, monitoring the progress of each aspect of the planet's defense, science, and knowledge.

The projection flickered away in streaks, revealing the cozy reading hideaway.

"Well," Prism began. "That is the abridged version of our history, of course, but there are plenty of events and nuances we can discuss at a later time."

"I am sure of it." Garrett hid his snark inside his teacup.

They ignored his tone. "Was there anything you wanted further details on?"

His irritation colored his thoughts. He had dreamed of this for so long as a child, to get a glimpse of how others lived besides the superficial lights of his decadent home world. Now that he had infinite knowledge at his fingertips, he found it all overwhelming. Prism's bombastic personality didn't help, but it wasn't their fault. It was just the way they functioned.

Maybe it was because he left home in a volley of gunfire, never having the chance to tie loose ends before careening halfway through the galaxy and dumped in a new environment without any guidance or time to breathe. He never had these issues when exploring the Undercity. Was that all that was bothering him? The façade of choice?

He looked up at Prism's expectant gaze, their smile slightly dimmed in concern for the strange human's behavior. It wasn't fair to take out his bitterness on them.

"Tell me, when did Xannat and Ötmarr come into play?"

"Ahh!" Prism perked up and clapped their hands together. "What an excellent question. Let me pull up something for you!"

He restrained a whimper at the thought of watching another video but was glad to see Prism navigate through still images from across the internet.

They poked at a few examples on the screen to bring them into focus, spreading their fingertips to increase the size. "What do you know about them?"

"Elam told me that Xannat was the force of luck, and Ötmarr represented the power of the individual. Like knowledge of consequences through action. Something like that."

"Correct!" Prism dragged over an image of a bas relief carved into stone. Two Ara'yulthr at crossed blades stood in the center, inside a motif decorated with jagged flora bordering the frame. The combatants' stony, unwavering expressions displayed the force that they exerted, neither one overtaking the other.

"These stones came from older libraries, but more archaic iconography have been found on rocks and pebbles left in the middle of fields. They were most likely charms used to mark milestones, or risky choices taken by gatherers embarking on a strenuous journey, hoping to find guidance." They pulled up another image of a collection of worry stones carved with the figures. "The two characters are referenced all the way since pre-recorded times and were personified to represent the inexplicable, everything that they had no control over. Much like every culture."

Garrett examined the carving, wanting to reach up at the screen and feel the texture of the stone. He admired the artwork, the patterns and theme reflecting a similar aesthetic to the interior of the library. Seeing all the examples in their various stages let him draw conclusions about the development of the art style.

"Lots of excavations have given us knowledge on how their icons were given homage," Prism continued. "Some pictographs are carved into armor and weaponry, even on plating found in gravesites."

"I see."

"However, the mention of Xannat predated Ötmarr, according to historical record. Xannat was a centralized figure that covered anything and everything we could not comprehend at the time. Ötmarr came into view later, being the force that we can decide upon. They are often depicted at arms, and their stories often speak of long drawn-out battles that span eons. But in the end, Xannat always overcomes."

"Interesting."

"I am fascinated by the metaphor, personally." Prism hummed merrily, tracing the figures on the screen. "While the characters themselves are nondescript, it puts the struggle of life in a relatable perspective. You can choose to fight to get where you want or let destiny take the reins. But as long as you have that fight within you, you can achieve so much more."

Their words poked at Garrett's cynicism. The same sentiments could be used to describe his own worldview. But he had a hard time with Prism's description of life as a struggle. While he did grow up in a place of privilege and had his fair share of trials, he had witnessed others who did not have to struggle. And, rarely, people who did not need to use the pain of others to sustain their lifestyle. Admittedly, they were few and far between.

Now that he considered it, he could only count the number of those individuals on one hand. Maybe struggle is a necessity, keeping people from dying of boredom. Perhaps it was Nara's bitterness infecting him. She agreed with Prism's analysis of life with more pointed words, however.

"Do people still pay homage to them?" he asked.

"It depends highly on the individual." Prism shrugged. "Some speak of them as if they were living beings or deities. Some call them outside forces that influence everyday life. Others like to call them stories for entertainment. All are valid."

"Hmm. I see." His mind was drowning in existential dialogue, his eyes gazing vacantly into the distance.

"You must be tired. I think this is a good place to stop." Prism examined his face with a smile. "Was there anything else I can do for you before I take you back to your residence?"

"Huh? Oh, yes." He shook the nonsense from his head. "I wish to learn to read."

"Oh, excellent!" Prism clapped their hands excitedly. "We have a mono vocal dialect for those who don't have the anatomy to speak the language."

Garrett stared blankly. "Mono vocal... what?"

"Our kind have two separate vocal organs in our throats that help us make the sounds that compose our language." Prism traced a circle around their neck with a flutter of their hand. "Each one can be used independently of each other or at the same time. We can also adapt to mono vocal languages like Trade by using one or the other, so you may hear people speak differently depending on who they are talking to."

Huh. I've only heard Nara speak in one voice, Garrett mused. *Apart from when she's yelling at something.*

"I, uh, I think I will stick to reading for now." He furrowed his eyebrows, daunted by the size of his task.

"Certainly!" They pressed a few commands on the computer hidden beneath a cushion. "I will have a few study materials sent to your home computer."

"Thank you."

"It was nothing, Ambassador." They rose to their feet and bowed. "Please do let me know if I can be of further assistance."

"I will," he hesitantly promised.

##5.3##

After an uncomfortable trip filled with Prism's hums and inner musings, Garrett entered the lab. He crept along the border of the workroom, hoping to slip by without disturbing the trio having a silent lunch.

"*Loremaster* left something for you, Human," Fariem called to him, the summons jump starting his nerves.

"I—" Garrett looked over at them. "I have a name."

They found the contents of their salad more interesting than the timid interloper. "Mm-hmm."

Why are they like this? Their casual dismissal flushed his cheeks with irritation. *First, Prism speaking to me like a toddler, then Fariem and their crew treating me like a disobedient pet. I know I am not an invited guest, but come on now!*

He abruptly turned about-face. "All right, listen here. I may be a child in your apparently eternal perspective, but I will have you know that I am quite advanced for my age. And you should show some respect for someone from a race that has managed to stumble around the galaxy despite their shortcomings and squishy bodies."

From the back corner of the room, Syf and Ki'nit raised their heads from their meals in unison, staring blankly at the protesting human.

"My name is Garrett." He slammed a hand on the nearest desk. A grating crash of shattering glass punctuated his words as a measuring vessel bounced off the table and hit the metal floor.

The commotion caused a blob of material to blister out of the wall. An amorphous fluid formed a disc-like object that hovered over to the mess, sucking up the scintillating fragments with a tumult of clinks. With its task completed, it made its way over to the waste compressor, dumped its cargo, then melted into the countertop's surface.

"And I will replace that as soon as I figure out what that was and where to order a new one," Garrett insisted.

After a tense few seconds where he questioned his safety, Fariem snorted inside their drinking glass. The sound erupted into a cackling howl as the medic became incapacitated by laughter.

"All right, Garrett. You win." They stood and headed over to a computer, waving him over. "Come here."

"Right." Before walking over to them, he cleansed his lungs from terror with a few deep breaths. He leaned in as Fariem slowly pressed a sequence of commands, glancing in his direction every so often to confirm that he understood the directions. They selected a measuring beaker from a grid of tools and pressed the *Print* command.

The dispenser on the wall gleamed with light then slid its door open, revealing a shining new beaker inside. Fariem took it in their hands and pointed it in his direction, brandishing an amused smirk.

Remorse wailed against his spirit, the outburst rippling against his thoughts. There was probably some cultural context he was missing, and it was unfair to be so quick to judge. "Thank you, and I apologize. I don't know what came over me."

Fariem placed the beaker on the nearest table. "I will not keep you then, Garrett."

He bowed and made a swift retreat for the apartment, a victorious smile twitching across his lips.

A strobing green light pulsed next to the doorframe, assaulting his vision as he stepped inside. A hinged metal box had grown out of the wall, blinking irritatingly to demand his attention.

He walked over and flipped the lid open, having to stand on his toes to get a look at the contents. Inside he found two antiquated tomes made of leather and paper and a gilded silver metal box about the size of a cigarette case.

He took the collection into the kitchen, soaking in the material of the elegantly bound books in his fingers. Golden thread stitched together the pages, decorating the spine with curling branches. The front cover was dyed in a deep maroon, devoid of inscription yet still beautiful. He gingerly opened the cover and savored the muted green pages inside, finding them silky to the touch.

As he flipped through the book, a note slipped out and fluttered to the floor. His name was written on it in a gorgeous fluid script. He unfolded it to find that it was written by *Loremaster*.

Greetings, Garrett.

Some like to take pleasure in using antique writing instruments and journals. I thought you would appreciate the hobby as well and shared with you a few of my favorite writing utensils. Each of the inks were made using vegetation available in the wild. I have also included two books, one that is blank and one with hand-written instructions on operating the computers as well as ordering food for your enjoyment.

Take Care, and I look forward to our next discussion,

Khuul'Ren

Garrett folded the note back into the journal and picked up the other tome. The inscriptions, while written in trade, had an elegant flourish to each character. There were photos of food organized in impeccably even grids along with their descriptions in basic, understandable terms.

This must have taken hours to complete, he thought, humbled by the generous gift. He moved his attention to the metal case, brushing a finger over the swirled engraving tracing around the borders. Windswept leaves danced over the metal, circling around a blossom of innumerable pointed petals. Each flora burst into its own show of fireworks, the etchings catching every bit of light in the room.

He delicately lifted the lid open, revealing five cylindrical tools. Four of them were made of a clear plastic material, and each had metal nibs ground in different widths and angles. The last tool was slimmer than its companions and made of a solid silvery metal. The nib was sharpened to a dangerous point, and the other end was almost tacky in substance. He paused to rub a fingertip on the point, finding the utensil giving off a chalky black pigment.

The pens were filled with the most vibrant inks he had ever seen. The black was a void of nothing, almost engulfing the surrounding light. While a marvel in itself, its companions were equally gorgeous, a vibrant ocean blue, a deep blood red, and an almost neon violet.

He had only seen images that referenced this style of writing, but nothing compared to how elegant this set was. Overwhelmed with gratitude, he sat down and opened to the first blank page, selecting a stylus to use. *Now what?*

Placing the pen back into its container, he decided he did not have a proper purpose for the books just yet. He closed the book. His weariness from the day's events clouded his decision making. He flipped through the ordering menu, selecting something made with few ingredients and simple flavors, not feeling up to adventure. Bread and toasted cheese. What could go wrong?

The order came through, smelling more appetizing than what the description claimed. Yeasty grained aromas wafted through his senses as he took a bite, finding the toast thin and crispy, yet somehow dense to the tooth. Its sweetened flavor provided a nice contrast to the creamy fermented tang of the cheese. Dots of fruitiness studded the sandwich and pockets of dried berries toyed at his molars.

In addition to his full stomach, the day's events finally weighed him down. He made his way upstairs to bed, trying not to think about who will contact him tomorrow.

CHAPTER 6

##6.0##

Cold, sterile air invaded his nostrils, the acrid tang of electronics shuddering his senses awake. Bellanar opened his eyes, only to find blackness obstructing his vision. He groaned and sat up, raising an exploratory hand while his eyes warmed up to the dark.

"Ahh. You are awake. Good." A voice teased his ear from a distance. Unnervingly familiar.

What happened? Bellanar recalled. *I broke in... found a terminal... some communications... then... oh dear, nothing at all.*

"You have been lurking around my facilities for a while now, haven't you? I do not think that is in your best interest."

Abberon.

White light burst through the room with a clack, sending searing pangs to his brain. When the wave subsided, the vacant room revealed a clean white ceiling. Hexagonal black lines traced patterns of wires across its surface. The cold steel floor reflected spots of illumination, the polished chrome featureless and slick.

"You will forgive me if I do not attend to you personally, but I have an agenda with the strictest timeline." Static bleating of electric light summoned an avatar of the denounced warlord looming over him. "But before I take my leave, I require something from you.

Namely, what do you know about *Savant's* intention? You were quite familiar with them, were you not?"

He knew of Elam's return. I should have known. Bellanar kept his eyes on the blinding ground, refusing to respond.

"Is your memory failing you?" The hologram crouched to eye level, examining him curiously. "I am sure we can ignite a spark of it somewhere."

The room stirred, emitting a soft murmur as five seams split apart in the wall revealing dark corridors. Faceless humanoids coated in blackened segmented material filed into the arena, each stretching out their arms to the sky, twisting and turning their torsos to loosen their muscles.

"I am sure this scenario is familiar to you." The hologram glanced idly at their knuckles. "You see, my units would not possibly consent to more traditional means of information extraction. I have to resort to something… *unconventional.*"

The limbering rituals continued, nods exchanged as partners pulled at each other's limbs, bending and straining in a novice acrobatic performance to prepare them for their activities.

"The halt of the games has done considerable damage to morale, so we improvised with a smaller scale training ground to keep everyone in peak fighting form."

Bellanar stood up and approached one of the units, waving a hand in their face.

"They won't recognize you. Their senses are impaired. In fact, your image will be concealed from them until the game begins."

Bellanar glared at the taunting visage, reaching for the exposed clasp on one soldier's neck.

"They have already been immersed in the simulation, and I would strongly advise against releasing them from their suits," Abberon warned. "Unless you want their deaths on your conscience."

The man was not bluffing. He was well aware of the extensive grounding cycles necessary to bring a player back to reality. A sudden emergency evacuation could kill if the proper precautions were not taken. By the ex-warlord's tone, Bellanar knew there would be no assistance for them.

"I shall ask again. What is *Savant* planning?"

Bellanar closed his eyes and steeled himself, craning his neck from side to side.

"As you wish." Abberon bowed then blinked away. "Happy hunting."

The soldiers turned to Bellanar, suddenly aware of his presence. He seized what little time he had and cracked his fist against the closest person, then sprang back to distance himself from the closing circle.

An arm snaked out and snatched him as the fist of another soldier buried itself into his chest. He wheezed and lowered his stance to recover. Launching his shoulder into the side of his opponent, he twisted around, forcing them to let go of his arm as they were thrown off balance.

He lashed out a kick to the side, but the combatant anticipated and snatched his ankle mid-strike. Bracing himself against their weight, Bellanar vaulted himself up and whipped his free leg around, catching his opponent across the temple. They staggered back and released him, resting their hands on their knees as they shook the disorientation away.

Bellanar landed with a squeak of metal and bolted from the crowd, his mind reeling as he calculated his next moves. The squad pursued him in a machine-like precision, aligning themselves in a sharp wing formation, closing off his escape.

Approaching dangerously close to the boundary of the arena, Bellanar sharply strafed to one side, avoiding the oncoming claws. With momentum guiding him, he pushed his feet against the wall, bouncing on the material to elevate himself above the mob.

But his trajectory was cut short as three squad members positioned themselves around him. A synchronized performance, two took a flying leap forward and slammed their fists into his back, halting his momentum. The third acknowledged the play, catching him by the hips. With a twist of their shoulders, they hurled him to the ground.

One by one, hands pressed against his arms to pin them to his back. He flailed his shoulders and hips wildly, giving the attackers a struggle to maintain their grip. Managing to untangle a leg, he kicked around and dropped a soldier, crumpling their stance with a hit to the back of the knee. Panic flooded his muscles as his movements became more frantic, wriggling in wormlike undulations to propel himself forward.

He gained traction and managed to slide a knee up in front of him, hoisting his trunk up to stabilize himself. A swift punch to the head paralyzed his motions, and he slumped onto the cold, unforgiving floor. He shook at the dizzying motion, trying to order his unresponsive hand to wipe away the blood trickling over his eyes.

Strike upon strike burst across his flesh as he was raised into the air, his stomach exposed to the onslaught. The grainy texture of their suits left pocked abrasions against his skin. His image was programmed to appear as Ara'yulthr, and they knew where to strike, avoiding his chitinous plating to hit soft flesh, hard enough to shudder internal organs.

As each excruciating second elapsed, his nerves disintegrated to numbness, his mind brought elsewhere, looking down on him from the arena ceiling. Then, at last, he was released, his battered form dropping to the solid ground.

The group dispersed when he hit the ground, searching for their next opponent. Abberon appeared again, kneeling at his ragged frame.

"How are you feeling?"

Bellanar raised an arm to swat at the light, trying to wisp away the taunting creature.

Abberon smiled and vanished. "I see."

His body demanded air while his chest chastised him for disturbing his bruised flesh. Against his body's wishes, he pulled himself up. The warm flow of fluids trickled over his skin. He raised to one knee, bracing his movement with a shaking arm. With a final burst of defiance, he braced to a stand, swaying side to side in a vain attempt to stabilize his posture.

"Interesting," Abberon mused. "But let's see how long you can last."

A snap of pain jabbed his back, and his suffering began to subside. He dropped to his knees, left to rest in a sea of blackness that overtook his senses.

##6.1##

THE ESTATE of the Councilor of Science was the size of someone who was influential. However, most of the floor plan was occupied by the colossal greenhouse that practically consumed the miniscule living hovel attached. From outside, Nara could hear the workings of maintenance machines droning amid the artificial forestry.

She approached the steps of the house and pressed the intercom of the front door, then lowered her hands to her hips as she waited for the scrutiny of the cameras.

The outline of the door pulsed red, denying her admission. She restrained her scowl as she persisted, rapping a knuckle on the door. Another red pulse. Releasing an exasperated grumble, she slammed her fist in an agitated pace, not wavering until the door begrudgingly opened.

"In the conservatory," a voice called from the intercom.

Nara made her way around the corner, traversing through a set of translucent doors. A chill danced over her skin as the diligent environment controls performed their duty, preserving the quality of life for the green inhabitants. She could see the other quadrants isolated from this area through the steaming droplets glistening down the panes of glass.

Monitoring machines hummed and beeped, conversing with their coordinators as they zipped over impeccably organized rainbows of leaves and flowers. Reinforced steel trellises lined the back walls, providing rigorous playgrounds for vines to climb.

She made her way through the back doors, revealing a much more natural arena of greenery. Chaos was permitted to sow its havoc around the land, providing an attractive scene to the observer, most likely the councilor's personal collection.

Curtains of vine trees wept on the ground, shedding tiny barbed leaves on the plush moss-coated earth. A pond murmured in the far corner, bleeding out into a delicate stream running along the room. Buds of icy blue pads floated blissfully along the channel, too idle to open their flowers as they bounced between smooth pebbles poking out from the water's surface.

Hints of fauna buzzed around the ecosystem. Glittering insects and flamboyant scale-armored birds ran their fervent errands, jumping between vibrant blossoms to gain sustenance.

"*Savant* Elam, you certainly live up to your name." The councilor had their back turned to her, kneeling to check over a large fan-shaped leaf. "Have you not slept since we last spoke?"

She ignored the snide remark, folding her arms across her chest. "This is not a business visit. I simply want to know more about the individual I am addressing."

They stood and turned to her, revealing glittering violet eyes. Age had not quite taken a toll on their skin despite the number of years laboring the earth. The only distinguishing feature on their face was a deep crimson beauty mark beneath their eye, shaped like a crescent moon. "Hmph. Is that so?"

"I do not even know your name."

"You can pull it up in the records," they retorted. Nara stiffened her stance at their dismissal, her shoulders straightening as eyes narrowed. With a sigh, they conceded. "Torel. Head of Agriculture Science."

"Pleasure."

Torel scoffed, flipping their long navy hair over their shoulder. "I am sure of it."

Nara stood silently in the buzzing atmosphere, glaring at them expectantly.

"Fine," they grumbled and waltzed into the frigid testing room. "I cannot speak long. I am in the middle of a cycle iteration and I need to compile the results before next shift break."

"What are you working on?" She peered at the rows of steel pots, watching the numbers on the displays inquisitively.

They flashed a look of mistrust, eyeing Nara up and down. "We have been working on a way to speed up the growth cycles of essential crops, but we are running into a few obstacles."

"Like?"

"Are you sure you are not here on business?" Torel wrinkled their nose. "I find your inquiry suspect."

"I just wish to gain a perspective." She rubbed her chin pensively, fixated on the spiny trunk of a sapling. "Of what you have to gain or lose in the present discussions."

"I see."

Nara straightened and turned to them. "You don't like my involvement in the Council. Why?"

They drummed their fingers on their tablet. "Your reputation is explosive. You have no respect for order and priority. You take what has been established and undermine every command to cease. Hasty and impulsive."

Nara folded her arms, waiting as the councilor processed their analysis.

"And yet..." They ground their jaw as thoughts manifested. "You are somehow right. Anyone else acting this way would leave ruin and chaos in their wake. But you..."

"And that irritates you."

Torel closed their eyes. "It is so hard to maintain order. Just to have an upsurge like you waiting in the winds."

"Life is messy." Nara scoffed. "Order is unnatural. Surely, your experiments can affirm that."

"What my experiments tell me," their tone danced over a growl, "is that what cannot be put in order has not simply had all options exhausted. Eventually, a solution can be found."

"Tell me, do *I* have a solution?" A smirk teased at the corner of her lips. "After all, is that not why I am here? Or do you know something about me that I do not?"

"I must admit, I am surprised to see you at my door." They let out a defeated exhale. "I had not met you when you were a reigning warlord, so I hastily filled gaps that I did not witness. Perhaps you grew up in your time away. Regardless, it is none of my business what you were in the past. Just what you do in the future."

"Is that your *true* opinion?"

"Look, I do not want conflict as much as the others. What I *do* want is to be done with all of this GaPFed business so we can get back to work. It has been hard enough picking up the slack while everyone else is glued to their star-charts."

Nara leaned against a console, her head tilted curiously. "You don't feel the same way as the other scientists?"

"Yes, the aspect of space travel is exciting, but there is so much to be done to prepare. No one seems to consider what we would leave behind, the work that would amass for those who do not wish to desert the homeworld." Torel scrubbed their face in agitation. "And because of all this, we are decades behind in production. At this rate, we will need to start recruiting from the military ranks, and they won't be thrilled about that."

"I can speak with them, if you'd like."

"I don't think that would do more than delay the inevitable."

"True." Nara shrugged. "But at least you can say that you tried."

Torel did not seem to share the sentiment. They buried their nose in their notes, storming away from her. "If you will excuse me, I need to finish this report."

Nara bowed her head. "As you wish."

She removed herself from the estate and headed back to her apartment.

##6.2

Well, that didn't go so well, Nara thought as she entered her quarters. *But it did go...*

Garrett was hunched over the dining table, brows furrowed in scrutiny as he passed studious fingers between a tablet and a tradition-ally bound book. He looked up and greeted her warmly.

"Ah! You're back. I was just about to get dinner. Have you eaten at all?" He scooted out of his chair and moved to the computer in the kitchen.

"No." Food hadn't even crossed her mind, and before she knew it, her body slid into a dining chair. The scent of starch-crusted meat and pickled vegetation tickled her nose, triggering a pang of desire stabbing her abdomen.

"I hope this is all right," Garrett offered. "The description sounded good, so I figured I would try it."

"It's fine." She picked up a utensil and poked at the meal. "What have you been working on?"

"This?" He gestured at the tablet. "Oh, Scribe Prism brought me materials to learn how to read. I wanted to try and figure things out for myself first before asking anyone else."

"Ah."

He speared a morsel of the protein and inspected it. "Uh… what kind of meat is this?"

"It isn't."

"Rephrase—what is it supposed to emulate?"

Nara distracted herself with the task of cutting up the croquette in smaller than bite-size pieces. "A large raptor that hunts in trees. Eats lizards and other avian."

"Ah. A large bird."

"Snake-bird."

Garrett's eyes widened at the imagery as he took a timid bite, thankful he was on this end of the food chain. The meat was soft with a pleasant amount of chew, with a slightly sweet aftertaste of grasses and herbs. He wasn't sure if it was because of the diet of the creature or whatever they used to synthesize the proteins that offered this flavor.

The breading was crisp and airy with hints of buttery silkiness that melded with the meat. It was not the least bit soggy despite the instant preparation of the meal. The pickled vegetation was tart and fizzy, with a mellow heat that whittled away the heaviness of the main course.

"How are the lessons going?" Nara managed to scrape together the motivation to pick up a piece and take a bite.

"I, oh." The inquiry was strange to him, as if it was taking a considerable amount of effort for her to take an interest. "I think I am managing. There is a lot to take in. Your culture is very different from Arcadia's."

"Mmm."

"The script is very fluid, yet structured. It's hard to describe. Like art with a purpose."

"That's an interesting way of putting it."

"Makes it hard to decipher at times. Especially with all the new punctuation." He ran a finger across the scribbled over lines in his book. It seemed a shame to deface something so beautiful with his clumsy shorthand. But this gift was meant to be used. He rotated the book around for Nara to see. "Like here."

"*Strength is in what we bake.*" She raised an eye. "You've forgotten the *ophtet* punctuation mark above that sixth character. *See.* Not *bake.*"

"What does that do?"

"Tells a speaker when to switch vocals. You don't have that anatomy."

"Yeah, Prism told me." He scratched his forehead. "There are so many phonetics here. And they bled so smoothly. It's as if you sing instead of speak."

Nara shrugged. "I didn't invent it."

"Well, no."

The sands of time crawled through a passage too narrow for each grain as they continued their meal. Both were too frazzled to bolster each other's well-being, already grasping the dour answers. And neither wanted to pause for healing, the distractions of work providing the comforting placebo of duty.

"I think I am going to turn in," Garrett announced, clearing his plate. "I assume I won't see you when I get up?"

Nara shook her head. "Probably not."

"I see. Well, before I go, let me get you something to take on the road." He scurried to the food generator, selecting a few dry goods and nutrient rich portables. The machine wrapped it up nicely in a travel parcel, sealed with a perforated seam. He took the product and set it on the table, then headed up the stairs to his room.

"Goodnight," he called down to her.

"'Night," she managed, staring vacantly at the offering.

##6.3##

GARRETT WOKE up groggy and stiff. He pulled up a clock on his NetComm, finding he'd had a solid ten-hour nap. Jetlag still lurked its ugly head, the scale of change pressing on him with a twelve-ton weight. What time was it on Arcadia?

As much as his brain told him otherwise, it was not, in fact, a new day. Instead, it was what was referred to as Third Cycle, evening, rather, or its closest equivalent. Get up. Work. Take a nap. Work more. Take another Nap. Work, probably, though off time was implied. Then sleep fully before repeating the cycle again. And some didn't even nap when their sleep cycles where scheduled. How the hell did they manage it?

He pulled himself out of bed and shambled to the kitchen to prepare a snack. A slight smile tugged at his face as he glanced at the table, finding the parcel of food had disappeared with Nara's absence. But his attitude swiftly changed when his eyes met with the pile of books and writing instruments.

Work, and more work, he lamented as he stuffed an impeccably flaky jam-filled pastry in his mouth. *Is that all people do here? Work and sleep?*

He went back upstairs to collect himself, shrugging on a new set of uniform greys while holding the confection between his teeth. The mirror on the wall displayed a collection of crumbs over the sharply pressed suiting, and he brushed them away irritably. A tiny machine spawned from the floor, consuming the refuse before melting back into its home in the ground.

Efficiency and sterility, he sighed. *Is downtime even *in* their vocabulary? Maybe I will go and find out for myself.*

He exited the apartment, only to bump into Fariem buzzing around the lab.

"Garrett!" they barked, snapping a finger. "Can you do math?"

"Uh…" He jumped back, blindsided by the question. "That, uh, that really depends on your definition of math. I can *probably* give you the slope of a curve if I had a few minutes, but if you are looking to multiply matrices or find the derivative of an integral, I am afraid I hadn't done that in… a while."

Fariem scrunched their face and shook their hands in dismissal.

"Stop babbling. Can you count to 100?"

"Yes?"

"Good. Come with me." Fariem beckoned and led him to a counter. They poked and calibrated an electronic device, its optics focused on a singular point in the center of a white plastic tray. "Look here and you will find a white square broken up by a numbered grid. I want you to count the number of red organisms and green organisms you see in each square and record them on the computer."

"Uh, sure." *So much for downtime.* He peered inside the instrument and found hundreds of tiny spots of red and green stars flagellating in a rhythmic dance across the screen.

He settled into the task stool and began mouthing off numbers as he started from the top left corner of the grid. He moved away from the instrument to record the number on the tablet, only to look back and see the critters had shifted.

"Ah, shit." It took a while to develop an efficient method, counting the dots while writing down the numbers without glancing at the tablet, forsaking the guidelines on the pad. He began to sink into the flow of productivity until the hairs started to rise on the back of his neck.

"Aww, master likes you!" The voice of Syf lashed across his brain.

"Gah! I..." He caught his breath and glared. "Can I help you?"

Syf delicately slid a cup of steaming broth toward him. "I just thought you might want something to help you focus."

"How... thoughtful." It took every scrap of energy to suppress his irritation and startlement.

Syf lowered their eyes to his wrist. "Ooh, what is that?"

"My NetComm?" Garrett withdrew his arm. "It's a personal computer."

"Can I see it?" They shot an eager hand forward. "Pretty please? I work so far away from the borders and I don't usually get the chance to look at human technology."

Garrett hesitantly reached an arm out, only to have the cold grasp of Syf's fingers delicately pluck the clasp open.

"Oh, how fascinating!" Their eyes glittered as they pulled the device to their face, scrutinizing the interface with experimental taps.

"I…uhm."

"Syf! Let them work," Fariem scolded and shooed the scoundrel away.

Garrett watched in disbelief as they scurried off. "I'll get that back later, then."

He holstered a sigh and went back to his counting, refocusing on the rhythmic pattern—look with one eye, write with one hand, pause to refocus. He could sense Fariem nearby, chanting calculations under their breath as they went over inventories. Confident with his sense of workflow, he decided to attempt conversation and perhaps get to know their enigmatic personality.

"So… do you know how Nara and I met?" he began.

"Garrett is a master of multitasking, it seems." Fariem bit their lip and a twinge of regret wrinkled their features when they saw the human's look of dejection. "To answer your question, no."

"Are you curious?"

"Curiosity is not entitlement, Garrett." They rubbed their jaw pensively and poked at their computer. "If I wanted to know, I would not invade someone's privacy for nothing more than idle answers."

*So **that's** where she got it from,* Garrett mused. "I will keep that in mind."

Fariem uttered a noncommittal noise, disengaging from discussion.

Garrett was about to try again when a glint of silver caught his eye inside the sea of creatures. One tiny little rebel stood out from the crowd, its violet round body gently waving silver-capped flagella.

"Fariem." He paused, double-checking his observation. "Where do I put the purple ones?"

"The what?" Their head snapped to him. "Let me see that."

Garrett made way for them to sit. "There, in quadrant 12-5."

Fariem scrolled through the zoom function, taking stills of the organism and blowing them up on a projection next to the instrument. They scrutinized the image, tapping their jaw irritably. "Well if that isn't a dagger in the eye."

"Did I do something wrong?" Garrett sank in his seat.

"We've been searching for that for years, and here you come along to find it on the first try." Fariem scowled. "No wonder Elam keeps you around, *Ahm'Xant.*"

A gay aura suddenly brightened the room as Prism entered the compound, waving merrily at the scientists. "Good evening!"

"Oh, uh, Hello, Prism," Garrett managed.

"I was wondering if you would like a night lesson?" Their smiling presence tore through his concentration. "It's nice and clear, good for productivity.

"I... uh, well—"

"He's working on something pressing for me right now," Fariem cut in, sensing his discomfort.

Garrett looked back at their firm glare of disapproval aimed at the scribe. While he was appreciative of their gesture, he still felt like he was standing between an encroaching fire and a steep ravine.

"It's okay, *Serr'Maht.*" He nodded, feeling the need to excuse himself. "My eyes are starting to cross, and I don't want to miscount."

Fariem raised an eye at him. "Are you sure?"

"Yes, thank you." He bowed. However, it was nice to know he had someone batting for him. "I do appreciate it."

"As you wish." They left and resumed their work, muttering indignantly about the new discovery.

"This way, Ambassador!" Prism beamed and swooped an arm out in an inviting gesture.

"Oh, Garrett!" Syf called, gliding toward them. With a sly wink, they pressed his NetComm into his hands. "Thank you for the opportunity."

"Sure..." he cautiously slipped the device back on his wrist.

Garrett followed the scribe to their vehicle, scrubbing through every application and menu of his device, finding no obvious trace of entry. The interaction sent uneasiness coursing through his nerves, and he was unable to discern their true intention.

Syf might have been an outlier, as his most successful interactions with people were whenever he was direct, not running around flashing subtlety. Despite this, it was a challenge for him to re-train in his speech to assimilate. Human vocabulary was laced with masked intent.

The behavior wasn't logical. Relationships were founded easier speaking with sincerity. So why was it so difficult for him? Arcadia was built on a lie. A beautiful neon traced lie that maintained an artificial caste system enforced by monetary stature. It stepped on the necks of others in order to radiate in the stars. It was an expression that he always despised while living there, and he was ashamed to admit that it was suddenly comforting to him.

"And that's just about it. What do you think?" Prism looked at him, bursting the bubble of his daydream.

"Huh, what? I… oh." He blushed. They were speaking to him this entire trip. "Sorry, I seem to be elsewhere."

They emitted a soft giggle and pressed a collection of buttons on the car panel, shifting the direction of the navigation system. "Let's do something different tonight and have a field trip."

The craft murmured under the brush, shifting happily through tall grasses until it emerged at the edge of a crystal-clear lake. The surface was as if made of glass, revealing the brilliant tangles of the aquatic ecosphere. Deep vermillion mingled with strands of sunshine yellow, twirling into a flaming dance of life. Dots of opalescent creatures darted between the threads, the moonlight accenting their scintillating forms. The ecosystem glowed with verdant life, the serenity dazzling with patterns of concentric circles as creatures dipped above the surface to collect nutrients.

"I think this is an appropriate stop," Prism announced as they stepped off the vehicle, waving at Garrett to follow. They made their way to the bank, dotted with lime green fungal life that illuminated the waters.

"It is nice," he had to admit. He concentrated on a silvery serpent gliding over the shallows. It traced circles around its territory, daring to lash out at anything that would cross its path. He blinked, and the creature lunged, gnashing through the tail of a hapless amphibian passing by.

Nature is almost as brutal as humanity. He found the thought disquieting. And Nara was a survivor, for lack of a better term, more knowledgeable of nature's machinations and experienced in at least two different cultures. Though it had outward differences, was every-one's intent still the same? Survival?

"Is there something I can help you with, Ambassador?" Prism's inquiry was blended with concern, their usual glimmering smile slightly bowed.

"Tell me about Nara's scar." The words manifested without his consent.

"I… well… Oh, dear," Prism stammered, their fingers fidgeting. "Wouldn't you prefer to—"

Garett looked at her coldly. "No."

"I see." Prism settled down in the grass, their thoughts flickering as they formulated a response. "The… practice was used to mark the *Fevered*, those afflicted with a degenerative illness that causes the elderly to lose all cognitive function and become violent as a result. Back when we were hunters and gatherers, up through the times of early settlements, to assist in mortality."

"You mean Euthanasia."

"That is a simplified synonym, yes." Prism shifted their glance. "Due to our physical capabilities, the disease was immeasurably destructive to healthy individuals, causing many casualties while attempting to rehabilitate the afflicted. Drastic measures needed to be taken."

Garrett sat on a rock, arms folded firmly. "And this happens against their will?"

"Oh, absolutely not!" Prism's aghast voice elevated. "Death is a very open subject here, and people often discuss their wishes for when their time comes. Many elect either to die fighting with nature or to have a loved one assist by combat, which eventually led to the construction of holding compounds."

"Prisons?"

Prism let their disdain for the description mar their face. "Wrong. They are living quarters."

"Doesn't sound pleasant."

Prism slid their knees to their chest, staring at the ground resentfully. "Until you have witnessed the destruction one singular person could wreak without regard for their surroundings, you will understand the amount of resources needed to keep such a force in check."

That must have hit a nerve, Garrett thought remorsefully. He let his shoulders slump, softening his posture as he continued. "That doesn't explain Nara. According to your explanation, she's not nearly old enough to be *Fevered*."

"When civilization was developing, the practice expanded to those who inflicted grievous acts against the populace." Prism nervously traced a finger over their palm. "Treason, inflicting unnecessary deaths, et cetera. It phased out as we grew and hasn't been used as a punishment in centuries."

"Until now," he stated matter-of-factly.

"*Savant* is a special case." They looked down at their knee, flicking off a dried leaf. "And I do not have permission to disclose further. I am sorry."

"I see." He still had questions, but he was overstepping boundaries. It was unwise to come to rash judgments without knowing the context of everyone involved, but hearing Nara's tearful, fragmented account of what happened to her sent flares of anger through his skin.

Prism swiftly rose and approached him. "I hope you don't think less of—"

"Were you the one who tore her plate off?" His gaze never left the water.

"No, of course not!"

"Then I have nothing more to discuss." It was all too much, too different. He tried to search for parallels and similarities, but he could only find connections to the very worst of society. The practice itself was not bothersome, all things considered. It was a somewhat sympathetic approach to mortality. To give a choice for how people want to leave the world.

But what troubled him the most is that someone could slip through the cracks of normalcy and suffer the consequences of condemnation. Something did not add up.

The thought piled on to his expanding mountain of angst. The loss of a home, the disorientation from forging a new way of life. The loss of familiarity. Despite having a limited connection of friendly faces back on Arcadia, he'd never felt alone. Here, there was no one.

Frustration manifested in his eyes, and a single tear plummeted into the lake, disrupting the flight of the fish below.

"Ambassador?" Prism's hushed voice barely registered in his ears.

"I'm sorry, Prism. I can't do this right now." He turned to walk toward the trees.

"Where are you going? It is not safe—" Prism grabbed for his wrist, their warning cut off by the slippery movements of his arm. A graceful whirl of steps, and he was behind them, palm raised up in defense.

"I can find my way back." He rejected, lowering his hand as he moved to the trees. "I need air."

Prism was stupefied by the human's speed, finding the atmosphere within an acceptable concentration of oxygen and nitrogen. "I don't quite underst—"

But the human had already slipped into the foliage.

"Oh, pain." They ran for the forest, trying to collect the human's trail. They followed the sounds of softened steps pattering over the brittle earth. Prism hastened to catch up, beating back leaves and branches in the overgrowth. While they knew the territory well, the human was of considerably smaller stature and had an easier time weaving through the gaps in foliage.

"Ambassador!" Prism called out, the echoes of their voice bouncing off the vegetation. Garrett could not have gone far. *Loremaster* will not be pleased if they lose him. "This is most inappropriate! Please come out at once!"

They continued their search with vigilance, ears perked to every sound around them.

Garrett ignored their plea, plotting his stride to match with his hunter. As they took a step, so did he, masking his sounds with Prism's frantic gait and the noise of the life surrounding them. When he heard them hesitate, he dared a glance behind. Prism was out of line of sight, hidden by the thick brush. Suppressing a smirk, he took another step forward when—

"*fff-UCK!*"

The ground crumbled beneath his heel and a sharp stab flared over his legs as his body braced to catch himself, landing on his tailbone. The slick, loose earth sent him careening down a sharp incline. Zipping noises screeched across his clothing as he skimmed over every rock, bramble, and thorn. He pawed frantically at the ground, his hands sliced up by the pointed foliage blanketing the treacherous slide. His eyes snapped forward to watch his trajectory, spying a large jagged rock speeding closer, ready to receive him with its toothy embrace.

"Oh, *SHIT!*" He flipped his back around, slowing his acceleration with the change of direction. A disconcerting screech invaded his ears as the rock brushed against his shoulders. With an inelegant spin of his hindquarters, he halted his descent, landing with a full-body twirl on the softened earth. His heart barreled inside his chest as he lay wide-eyed with fingers buried into soil, ordering his lungs to force open wider than his ribs would allow. He released his shaky hand from the dirt, looking up to trace his journey down the gully.

Tree canopies obstructed the lip of the ravine, concealing him from his pursuer. A soft chortle left his throat, elevating into a devious cackle. He slowed his breathing to controlled long gasps and stood up, brushing the dirt and blood from his hands. He passed his fingers over his back, finding no trace of a scrape or cut on the formidable fabric of his clothing. Interesting.

But his celebration was cut short as the ground beneath him slithered. He jerked back, slapping his hands over his face to suppress a screech. A glistening flash bolted over his boot, and he caught a glimpse of a segmented serpentine shadow before it burrowed into the dirt. A second longer, and it was gone.

Well, I got what I wanted. He emitted a bedraggled chortle, despite the protests of his thundering heart. *What now?*

Hearing no trace of Prism around, he wandered deeper into the forest. He placed a hand against a massive trunk, examining the texture of the bark with a hesitant touch. It was a strange contrast to the crumbling wooden slats of the arboretum trees he was used to. The carapace more closely resembled composite rock, though it still yielded to the scrape of his fingernails.

He pushed weight onto the lowest branch, testing its durability. After finding a solid response, he raised himself up, cringing slightly as the bruises began to manifest on his legs. The specimen was practically born to be ascended, its plentiful boughs sturdy enough to support the force of his climb.

Easier than an Undercity high-rise. He smiled as he settled near the crown of the tree, scanning the horizon for a sense of bearings. The colony of surrounding trees glittered in the night, a soft breeze gently shifting the translucent foliage into a dance of light. Above, he could see a bubble of pink energy enveloping the sky, blockading the air from the stars as far as he could see.

The beautiful tower of the Capital Archives stretched above the trees out in the distance, strands of electricity emanating from its spire. It was a serene view. One could hardly believe that there was civilization beneath the magnificence of nature. The tension began to uncoil from his muscles and his jaw unclenched. A once in a lifetime experience, at least for a human like him.

It's all right. I'm here. I may as well enjoy it.

Hums began to creep into his spirits, and he focused on being present, observing the behavior of the flittering leaves, the chirps and squeaks of the life surrounding him, instead of letting the unfamiliarity fill him with unfathomable dread. He expanded his lungs with slow, steady breaths, the moist soil and soft, sweet flora filling a need he didn't know he had.

A sound discordant from the vivacious nature interrupted his trance. Shouting? No, laughter. Something he never thought he would encounter on this planet. Curiosity teased his senses, and he descended from his perch to investigate.

He moved toward the source, keeping a watchful eye on his surroundings. Peering out into a clearing, he spotted a gathering of people lounging around a campfire. Across the blaze, four soldiers were sparring, knocking each other senseless in a malicious dance of fisticuffs.

Even in relaxation, they fight. They train. Garett found himself creeping nearer, leaving the shelter of trees to watch the spectacle.

When a contender was pinned to a tree, the observers cheered. Before long, wooden staffs were tossed into the arena. The cracks and thwacks of wood striking wood echoed across his nerves as the playful bout continued.

"Hey!" A bark at his side sent him reeling back, and he found himself face to face with a stern Ara'yulthr soldier patrolling the camp-

site. *"Who are you? What are you doing here?"*

Garett blinked, frozen in his steps. "I—" Words would not leave his lips.

The soldier eyed him up and down, lowering a hand to their belt. *"Warlord!"*

The revelry ceased. The arena drowned with silence as everyone's eyes brushed over the peculiar human visitor. Glances were exchanged and inquisitive whispers rasped as the fire crackled.

Oh. Shit.

A formidable officer stood from their place at the fire, gliding over to Garrett with heavy suspicion. They were much broader than the other units, their frame casting a shadow over him, glaring down with an icy stare.

"Hakin, Beya. Drive us to headquarters. The Council needs to hear of this." The warlord raised a hand and beckoned to Garrett. "You are coming with me."

The deep notes of effortless Galactic Trade caught Garrett by surprise, burying him deeper in his stance. He tried to raise a shaky leg, only to frantically stamp it down to maintain balance.

The warlord nodded to their subordinates, who took Garrett by the arms and ushered him forward. He complied with their restraint, thoughts of his fate whirling around his brain. He was escorted to another ground vehicle and gently placed into a seat. The warlord stood in front of him, watching his every move while the soldiers drove off into the wilderness.

The ride was unnerving, the warlord's glare unwavering. His breath heaved in short, ragged rasps, sweat beading down his face, only to evaporate as the liquid reached the fibers of his clothing.

Oh, shit. Oh, shit. Oh, shit. Oh, *SHIT.*

"Beya, tend to their injuries," the warlord ordered.

With a bow, the soldier approached, kneeling before Garrett and offering a palm with a gesture. "May I touch your hands?"

He could only nod at the question, finding the gentle voice of the medic strangely intimidating. They delicately took his fingers, passing a scanner over his skin. With a fretful tsk, they produced an array of salves and serums from their pockets and balanced the jars on their knees. Opening a packaged cloth, they began to wipe away the dirt and fluids from his skin. Adrenaline soothed the pain from the scrapes endured from his tumble. Even the thorns embedded in his skin were unnoticeable to him. The strange discoloration of his blood did not even register until he looked down.

"You're a lucky one," they purred as they continued their ritual, dropping dots of green liquid from their portable apothecary and rubbing the ointments into his wounds. They then took out an instrument and placed it over his wrist.

With a sudden jolt, a cooling sensation flood his veins. The medic finished their work by wrapping a stretchy black tape around his hand, deftly weaving the band around his fingers, taking care to cover each piece of exposed flesh.

"Th–thank you," Garrett managed. The medic smiled and resumed their post behind him, nodding to the warlord, who was still leering.

The engine stopped with a violent halt, jerking Garrett with a start. The jaws of the door crept open, revealing a steel cavernous fortress. The warlord shifted their glance expectantly, and Garrett struggled with his gelatinous legs. One of the soldiers finally pulled him up and bolstered his exit from the vehicle.

They stood in a hangar bay, the same grim aesthetic as the internal walls of Fariem's laboratory, this time in militant navy blues. He was guided down a network of halls, his brain running around in circles as he struggled to visualize a map of the facility.

He was stopped at an imposing reinforced door, no windows revealing the contents of the room ahead. The warlord hit the control button, and the thick sheet of metal slid aside to reveal a remarkably comfortable living suite, complete with a kitchen area, lounge, bedroom, and bathroom facilities.

Garrett looked up at the soldier, who motioned him inside with a nod of their head. He eased himself into the nearest chair and attempted to release the fist in his throat or keep from passing out. The door silently closed behind him, the clicks of locks cycling shut.

The front wall warped, shifting into a transparent glasslike material. The warlord was seated on the other side, tapping the intercom control.

"What is your name?"

"G–Garrett." He flinched at the question.

"Your *full* name." The warlord's eyes narrowed.

His lips twitched as he pried the disdainful surname from his throat. "Galavantier."

"Are you a fugitive, *Serr* Galavantier?"

His cheeks flushed in both fear and ire. "How dare you assume that!" The snarl left his mouth before he could contain himself.

"Answer the question."

"No." He crossed his arms to hide his nervous shaking, praying that he recited his lie convincingly.

Moments of silence passed as the warlord eyed him over, discerning his posture. "Why are you here?"

"I–I arrived with Nara... erm. Ela..." *Shit.* He swallowed the lump in his throat. "With *Savant* Elam when she landed on the planet."

The warlord leaned back, muting the channel to speak with the other soldiers. The suspense was tearing at his body, sending his thoughts racing through tides of inescapable dread.

I should never have left Prism.

"You will remain here until either your sentence has been passed or someone can speak for you." The warlord finally spoke. "Do you understand?"

"Yes, *Serr'Maht.*" The honorific twisted over his tongue, and the warlord raised an eye at the clumsy salutation.

"There is a computer for you to summon necessities. Feel free to utilize it and the instructional guide should you need it."

"I–thank you."

The warlord gave one last scan of uncertainty before the wall shifted back to solid, leaving Garrett to simmer in his anxiety.

Oh, fuck, what do I do now? Sickly green clouds began to whirl over his vision. *Water. I need a drink.*

He peeled himself out of the chair, taking wobbling steps toward the kitchen sink. He leaned heavily on the counter and pulled himself into the basin, wrestling with the controls until a stream of cool water jetted from the faucet. He rammed his cupped hands in the stream and consumed fistful after fistful of the crisp liquid. He splashed the surplus over his face, attempting to steady himself.

Drained of all energy, he leaned into the sink, letting the swell of his brain drop into the basin. He stilled his racing mind, slowing himself down until he could afford a thought.

Nara's going to fucking kill me.

As if summoned by the forces of darkness, the front wall snapped to transparent again, revealing the smoldering glare of Nara burning through his spirits.

He inhaled and raised himself up, discovering a shred of resentment within his throat. "Diplomatic immunity, I see."

"I hadn't had the chance to inform the correct channels yet." Nara scowled. "It hasn't even been one week, and you already find yourself in jail."

He lurched toward the sofa and dropped face first into the exceedingly comfortable cushions. "No time, huh?"

Nara belted off a half growl, half sigh, rubbing her temples in aggravation. "Don't go there. I will see what I can do."

"I've been in worse prisons, I suppose," he murmured gloomily through a pillow. "At least I won't cause more trouble for you here."

"Are you being facetious?"

"Wouldn't dream of it."

"What's gotten into you?"

"I'd honestly ask the same of you."

"Not much. I'm just trying to stop a civil war, that's all. But please don't let the lives of the thousands on this planet hamper your comfort."

Garrett ground his jaw at her rebuttal.

"You're going to be here a long time." She sighed. "I have no influence over the Council yet, and you are somewhat of a security concern, given what we are facing at the moment."

"Fair enough."

"I will keep you updated with movement, but don't expect anything." The window snapped back into a wall, leaving Garrett to fester in his nausea.

CHAPTER 7

##7.0##

The sounds of the arena's warm-up cycle stirred Bellanar awake. He groaned as his muscles nagged at him. How long had he been here? Days? Weeks?

Each time, he was permitted to heal. Mostly. A residual tear of muscle here, the ache and bruises there. With each bout, his condition worsened, preventing him from performing in peak condition as each wave of gladiatorial combat whittled him down. The stabs of hunger added to the exhaustion, his fingers spasming in argumentative twitches as they strained for fuel.

"Good morning, *Tenacity*." Abberon manifested before him. "Before we begin, do you have anything you wish to share?"

Bellanar rolled his eyes and pulled himself to his feet, rocking erratically as his brain sent a rush of vertigo across his senses.

"Very well, then." As if by clockwork, the corridors opened and a new entourage filed inside. But something was different about this crowd. "My combat instructors have been a little rusty as of late. And you simply can't teach others effectively if you let your own skills dull."

The limbering rituals of the combatants displayed a much more rigorous fervor, an act that would have been considered a workout all on its own. Pairs and trios broke off to perform intimate dances of grappling plays. Arms slithered around arms, necks hidden against the attacks while each combatant bent and contorted to maintain control. Twist, bind, counter, twist, bind, counter. An immoveable stalemate that lasted for far longer than an unskilled bout ever could. They were not only masters of technique but also speed, executing maneuvers imperceivable to the outside observer.

"You were not a combat expert in your time in active duty, were you, Scribe?" Abberon commented, scrolling through a digital file. "Electronics, scouting, and sharpshooting, as far as my information tells me. Good thing I have you contained here."

Bellanar could hardly hear the taunt over the intensity of the fighting, the grunts and struggles as the teachers strained to outmaneuver one another. He could feel his nervousness sink into a churning pit in his stomach, his already fatigued muscles cringing beneath his skin.

"By yourself, you won't provide nearly a reasonable challenge." Abberon rubbed their chin pensively. "Let us have your avatar run them around for a bit."

The fighters suddenly released their grip on each other, their gazes brought to a corner of the room. Soft patters echoed in the chamber as they circled the spot, cautiously approaching an invisible foe. Like a coordinated dance, they shifted the patterns of their stance, each synchronizing to their own individual strengths. Some spread their arms wide with open palms while some kept low to the ground with softened knees, establishing their comfortable center of gravity.

In a flash of movement, the choreography commenced. Strikes flew then swiftly changed course as the target moved. Each instructor played off the act of another, bouncing off each other's shoulders and hips to aim for vital areas.

The shadow entity would take its revenge, launching the soldiers backward with an explosion of force. Shrieks of friction echoed across the shiny floor as the units swiftly righted their footing, altering their course to charge in again. The bizarre puppet show of war continued as the soldiers battled with the unseen.

"Now then, would you like to say anything?" Abberon taunted. "My ears are receiving."

Bellanar lowered his gaze, his spirits battered. He had one last chance for escape, and it was a long shot. With bated breath, he rubbed at his joints, stretching out what he could as his tendons cinched tight against his efforts.

"Very well."

The collective suddenly raised their gaze to the sky, tracing an arc around the room as their gazes centered on Bellanar.

Shit. Having played the scenario tenfold before, he had nowhere to run. He braced himself, rolling onto the balls of his feet to prepare for the confrontation.

As the mob swarmed in, he bolstered his energy and focused on evasion, mud pulling at his limbs as he dodged and swayed. Dip, weave, shove, retreat. A weakened counter to push away and steal his ground back. But the masters were honed with skill, using the tiniest amount of energy to force him where they wanted. His stamina quickly waned, and his brain fogged, unable to keep track of punch after swipe.

The chaotic patterns sent his arms flailing, his footing lost as he struggled to compete with gravity. A jab to the throat and a kick to a knee brought him face first to the cold, unforgiving ground. The soldiers pulled him to his knees. An arm wrenched his shoulder down.

His spine crackled as a boot planted on his back. Heat surged through his face as his elbow twisted behind him, the pull of tendons as his arm was forced taut. A concussive force and a *CRACK* of bone sent blazes coursing through his entire body.

He screamed as he shoved away, his searing arm dangling uselessly at his side. He dared a glance over his shoulder, only to find a pale jagged dagger poking through his flesh. A panicked gasp released from his chest as he frantically rolled over, dragging the limb behind him as it gushed vital fluid.

Sweat beaded over his face as he panted for breath, the lashes of pain overtaking his thoughts. *What will claim me first? Infection or blood loss?*

His eyes traveled to the attackers as they retreated, bolting for an illusion behind him.

"How unfortunate," Abberon taunted. "You can end this, you know."

The taunt barely registered in his mind as he felt the side of his cheek with his tongue. He took a grounding breath and clamped his teeth against the soft flesh. The quick shock of pain quickly subsided with the herbal sweetness of blood. Molars scraped against metal and plastic as he ground his jaw together. With a satisfying *CRUNCH*, mechanical fragments shattered, and he extracted a tiny device from the flesh with his teeth.

The humans make such interesting inventions. He cackled as he rolled over to spit out the refuse.

"That is a pity." Abberon shook their head. "Unfortunately, I cannot guarantee your safety for the remainder of your visitation."

Rot in whatever palace you're thriving in. Drained of energy, Bellanar once more succumbed to sleep.

##7.1##

"*When our final battle has ended, we return to nature.*" Garrett traced a finger on the line as he recited. "*The pressure of our actions pave a path behind us. We hope to guide the future, but even our greatest intention is wrecked with folly.*"

"That was perfect!" Prism clapped their hands together, the sound bouncing against the glass of the cell wall. "Your studies are proving to be quite effective."

It's not like I have anything else to do, Garrett thought. "Thank you."

He pushed away the bitterness from his tone, grateful to have visitors despite their busy schedules. Even Fariem stopped by from time to time, passing him small assignments as well as teaching him about the plant life—what to avoid, what can result in a tasty snack. They even drafted experiments for him to construct, often leading to delightful trinkets to decorate the cell. Fariem still never used his real name, consistently referring to him as *Ahm'Xant*.

He had asked Prism what the word meant, and they told him that it had roots in *Xannat*, with *Ahm* a nondescript honorific title. Loosely, it meant 'Luck Charm.'

Prism closed the menu from their tablet. "Do you have any questions?"

"Nothing I can think of." Garrett shook his head.

"Very well. Would you like an assignment, or would you prefer to continue on your own?"

"I think I can manage to get a little further."

"Absolutely!" They stood up and scooted their seat under the desk. "I will see you next time."

"Prism…"

"Yes, Ambassador?"

He hesitated, unsure of what he was trying to convey in words. "Thank you for your patience."

"It's no trouble at all." They regarded him oddly. "You are quite an adaptive learner."

"I am not speaking entirely about academics."

"I know." A smile graced their features. "*Loremaster* had told me of your trials before you arrived. You adapted to your situation to the best of your ability, and I adapted my teaching style to coincide. I think we came to a functional relationship, don't you think?"

Garrett looked at the table, knitting his hands. "My short temper was not excusable."

"Ambassador, if my skin were as thin as you imply, I would not have been made a Chief Scribe." Prism winked and bowed. "Think nothing more of it. Until next time."

"Sure."

The wall blended back to solid, dissolving the last trace of the scribe's shining smile, leaving him to simmer on the conversation.

He closed the reading applications, mind too full to focus on learning. His time imprisoned gave him ample opportunity for self-reflection, but it was not a pleasant experience. The mind was not a fruitful place to be left alone, and the house arrest made his cabin craze itch.

He started pacing about the room, tangles of his ennui brushing with loneliness. Though often incarcerated in his ivory tower whenever his antics impeded the progress of Galavantier business, it only took a few lines of code to break him free. Here, it was a near impossibility.

The attempts to crack into the Ara'yulthr network left him frazzled and defeated.

He eyed the console hungrily, forcing his will against the imaginary deities controlling the machines.

"Ah, fuck this." He flopped on the couch and raised his NetComm to his face.

Previous searches on the system let him find the console program of the security system, or at least the equivalent. But the core programming was completely foreign to him. In contrast to the fabric-like linear streams of data that worked based on yes and no switch logic, this was more fluid. It utilized phrase command switches, like speaking a recipe to the machine. Codewords and euphemisms warped around symbolism while the machine replied with nonsensical idioms.

He would love to get his hands on a dictionary that could show him the direct route to access instead of playing a haphazard game of Simon Says—where Simon changes his mind on a whim. But he was too cautious to search the libraries on his own for fear of raising suspicion, and he didn't want to get Prism or Fariem into trouble to ask.

There?... Maybe. Is this the... What the— The NetComm popped off his wrist with a snap of plastic. He furrowed his eyes, scrutinizing the tear in the band. Upon further inspection, he noticed tiny scratches wearing down the hinges of the strap. *How the hell did that happen? Great. Guess I'll figure out how to fix that... somehow.*

He resorted to holding the watch up by the undamaged strap, continuing his prodding experiments. A few strokes later, he hit a wall, no seam visible.

"Fuck," he growled, tossing the device on the couch cushion.

Just when he was about to take a pity nap, his pocket began to vibrate wildly. He fished out the foreign transponder device he had been carrying with him, glaring at it with disdain. The screen flickered red and white, each spastic light increasing in intensity. *What the hell?*

A surge of recollection jumpstarted his heart as the strange program continued its pleas. *Bellanar! Oh, shit! What do I do?! Nara's not going to answer me. Fuck!*

He ran up to the receiving window, banging frantically on the wall. "Hey! Anyone out there?" Help!"

Frantic fingers smashed keys on the intercom system, hitting the Emergency Distress signal. Upon the summons, lights flared outside, and he could hear sirens ringing against the corridor.

Moments later, the window opened, revealing a rather alarmed pair of guards staring at the distraught human in shock. One flipped the signal switch, and the clamor ceased, permitting a proper conversation.

"Are you ill?" one asked.

"I need to speak with *Savant* Elam immediately!" He took in controlled breaths to stop the rush trembling in his throat.

"If you can tell me the issue, I will forward a message—"

Garrett flailed his arms in dismissal. "Bring her here. Now. It is a matter of life and death."

"Please remain calm," the guard insisted. "I will get your message sent if you describe what the issue is."

"No. I need her here." He jabbed a finger at the desk. "Now. It's about Abberon."

The guard raised an eye in suspicion, folding their arms sternly. "Where did you hear that name from?"

He stood his ground, slamming a fist on the table. "Get her. Now. I will NOT answer any further questions."

"Savant is incredibly busy."

"I *know* that, which I why I am asking you to go get her."

"I assure you, she will be here as soon as it is convenient."

I'm not getting anywhere here. He looked around the room, frantically searching for more convincing ammunition. The only item that came to his attention was the shining tablet sitting on the desk. Drastic needs require drastic measures. "If you do not assist me at once…"

He picked up the tablet and slammed it against the desk, sending tiny shards of glass scattering across the room.

"There is no need for destruction of property," the guard assured huffily.

Garrett ignored the remark, digging his fingernails into the largest split. He wrestled with the glass until he pulled out a razor-sharp chunk. He then raised the shiv at the guards, who exchanged glances at the perceived threat. "Then tell her I will be at the hospital."

"*Ahm'Serr*, please put—"

Ignoring their words, he rammed the point into his shoulder. His hand froze as he broke through the skin, and the glass shard snapped in his grip. *Ow. Okay. Self-mutilation is hard.*

"*Stop!*" the guard barked and slammed open the door control.

This isn't convincing enough. He inhaled and ground his teeth, pushing the slice deeper, cutting into his fingertips in the process. Blood drained from his head as the pain distracted him from his task, the swirling sensation filling the void as his own mind screamed, *What the fuck are you doing!?*

He barely heard the guards rush into the cell as he collapsed, his senses numbing as he tried to stay afloat. Time flickered away from him.

When he blinked, he was in a bed with the seething face of Nara looming over him.

"You are such a shit, you know that?"

Garrett groaned and sat up, a cooling sensation caressing his shoulder. He looked over to find a patch of fabric covering the evidence of his rebellious act.

"You wouldn't have come here otherwise," he spat.

"All right then, what is so pressing that you clumsily cut a superficial wound into yourself with a broken tablet screen?"

Superficial? Well, at least I got her here. He lowered his voice and leaned in. "Bellanar is in trouble. He said to tell you it was Abberon."

Nara's eyes stopped, lit with an icy fire. Garrett leaned back at her reaction, wincing as she collected her thoughts.

"You'd better *not* be fucking with me."

"Look where I am, for fuck's sake. Does it appear like I am fucking with you?" he snarled. "I have a beacon for his location. Do you still have your NetComm?"

"Yes."

Garrett passed her a log report, revealing details of Bellanar's coordinates and general vital levels. Nara scrutinized the information, her brows furrowed in contemplation. She then swiped the display away and grabbed her temples, slinging obscenities between grumbles.

"Of *course* he is on the other side of the planet. Where else would he be?"

Garrett looked up at her. "What are you going to do?"

"There is nothing I *can* do. Not without disrupting the balance of heated temperaments in council." She heaved a sigh, her knuckles whitening with each passing second.

"You're just going to leave him there?"

"That's not what I—"

"Wow. I've never seen this side of you." He stared in disbelief. "Normally, you'd be cutting off your own limbs before abandoning someone else like that."

"It is not as simple as *that*." She flung her hands up in the air. "Look, I—"

"You what?" He glared at her accusingly.

Nara stood and turned away, unwilling to face his scrutiny. "He made his own choice when he went there against my advice."

"And he counted on you to help him out, obviously."

She started pacing about the room, shoulders hunched over as she tightened her arms around herself. "If the Council finds out what he did and I get involved…"

What is going on here? Why is she acting so weird? The solution is obvious, so why is she being so belligerent? Garrett scrunched his face in disapproval. "Who said the Council ever had to find out? I thought you were the greatest agent of espionage the Undercity could buy."

"There are different rules here."

"And apparently, no morals," he countered huffily.

"What would you have me do? I can't just break into a compound in enemy territory and risk getting captured myself."

"That is literally what you did day by day when we were together. Why are you suddenly getting cold about it?"

"Because it is not only MY life that is threatened. Or haven't you gotten that just yet, human?" She slammed a fist into the wall, shuddering the railings of the bed. "There is an entire community hanging over the edge of a precipice, and I have the power to destroy it. This isn't Arcadia. The actions of one are *not* inconsequential. You can't just stomp your way to action and expect immediate results."

Garrett sank in the bed, wounded by her words. "If you don't plan on using that power for good, then why bother acting at all?"

She didn't have an answer for him. Not one she wanted to reveal. Abberon was only part of the equation. Even if she could remove his poison from the universe, another would replace him. It was the way of life, running in a tireless cycle of maintaining order and peace.

She was exhausted. She no longer wanted to fight. Just dissolve and drift on a steady course of nothingness. But her mind would not let her, and the chance of facing Abberon again left ice in her veins. She wasn't ready. But then again, when would she ever be?

"He *trusts* you. He needs our help. No one else can. Or will, it seems." Garrett interrupted the turmoil in her thoughts. "I'll be there too."

She glanced over her shoulder. "You?"

"I assumed I was going to be hawking for you." He shrugged.

"Do you even know the systems here?" She scoffed, shaking her head admonishingly.

He sheepishly rubbed the back of his neck. "I can guess?"

"Wonderful." She sank back into her seat, glaring at the floor between her knees. Guilt nagged at her. The human was right. It was partly her fault for letting Bellanar go, even though her implications told him her hands were tied.

She was also living her most self-destructive life because of her exile. Why let those habits die on the same archaic system that had cast her aside? Mental conditioning can only reach so far.

"Fine. Let's go." She stood up and walked out of the med bay, leaving Garrett to stew over his apprehension.

##7.2##

THE VIBRATIONS of the aircraft engine countered the rattling of her nerves. It was only a few hours to travel across the globe, but Nara wished the journey were years longer.

This is it. The start of it all. She fidgeted with the armor badge in her hand, tracing every seam and facet of the jewel-like buttons with a fingertip. Every fiber of her being wanted to turn back, to flee from this fool's errand. But her guilty conscience and her ingrained sense of duty planted her there. She had a role to play in this mess, and self-pity would not absolve her from it.

She looked out the window, watching the clear oceans stretch across the horizon. Ripples of white streaked through the surface as a squadron of behemoths rose to the surface. Their giant forms elegantly stretched across the waters in an arrowhead formation, their sail-like arms fluttering beneath the currents. Jets of water quenched the air as one by one, the winged beasts breached.

Their white carapaces protected their soft bluish flesh, points of articulation that helped them skim through the icy liquid. Pointed chitinous beaks at the crest of their heads guided their flight, slashing against the curling waves. A soft melodic hum bounced between them, the calls gently kissing the aircraft with its harmonious melancholy.

Before long, the entourage slowly descended, signaling their good-byes with arcing tailfins. Off to hunt for their next feast.

Nara stared glumly at the peaceful creatures. Another complication to the choices she was forced to make. Society had been built alongside the ecosystem, the scientists striving to reduce the impact on nature, electing to cohabitate so both parties could thrive.

But she witnessed the destruction and chaos that other galactic powers enforced over what they considered home. Arcadia was an empire built on a corpse, the bulk of the surface uninhabitable by the populace. Then there was Abberon. Fighting against him always proved to end in unnecessary casualties. But not in his mind.

"They're very active this time of year, aren't they?" Kestra's voice poked through her sulking as they piloted the craft, their fingers occupied with monitoring the systems in the cockpit.

"Yeah," she responded meekly. "I can't remember the last time I saw a full wing of them together like that."

The ocean disappeared in a swirl of purple-grey fog as the aircraft headed deep into cloud coverage. Flashes of green light crackled into view as they ventured further, the control panel bleeping and ticking to compensate for the forces bombarding the hull. The inside of the craft remained steady, isolated from the battlements outside.

"I hope this escapade won't get you into trouble," Nara commented.

"Why would I ever get into trouble?" Kestra smirked. "I'm off duty, just sharing my hobby of joyriding in military-grade aircraft with a friend."

"You know I will cover for you."

"I don't think we shall need your strings, *Savant*."

Nara couldn't help but smile at them. They certainly had grown since they were under her command. It was nice to see that some of her teachings had rubbed off on them. But she had to wonder if the universe even needed more of her misguided coaching.

A jagged peak of rock broke through the clouds, signaling their destination nearing. More spikes speared the fog as they continued through the mountainous region. Soon, they began their descent, and the rocky chasms engulfed the craft.

Kestra took the ship through the maze of peaks, homing in on a lip of rock several miles from ground level. The craft rocked and dipped as they eased it down, delicately planting on the crusty shelf. As the engines wound down to a halt, the winds began to kick up, scraping bits and debris across the hull.

Kestra flipped off settings and initialized last landing checks. "The storm should provide decent cover for an hour or two, depending on how tightly their sensors are tweaked."

"If they decide to act on them at all…" She stood and placed her armor badge on her throat, pressing the center button. On her command, the liquid metal slipped around her body, coating her in its fluid embrace. Moments later, it hardened, forming a shiny metallic skin over her. She flexed and stretched inside the cloak, taking comfort in the familiarity of its weight.

"That thought had also crossed my mind." They turned their seat to face her. "Are you okay with feeding Abberon leverage?"

"I haven't been okay since I stepped on this rock," she remarked as the armor snapped over her face. "But if it doesn't happen now, it will later."

Kestra bowed their head knowingly, opening the bay door for her. "You have my contact line when you need extraction. Safe journey, *Savant.*"

"I appreciate your assistance," Nara said and stepped off the platform to the icy, unforgiving atmosphere.

The wind threatened to pummel her down the mountain, and she smacked a hand against the aircraft to maintain her footing.

COMPENSATING FOR EXTREME ENVIRONMENT, the armor chirped in her ear, the internal temperature rising inside the suit. A graphical thermometer shifted colors with the adjustments. Her boots solidified in the rocky earth as the gravity enhancers steadied her legs from the harsh gales.

She made her way forward, one labored stomp after another, until she reached the shelter of an outcropping, settling down in the powdery lavender snow gathering around her ankles. Data icons and charts manifested into view as she fidgeted settings with her HUD, poking at shield regulators and communication networks in the area.

"*Can you hear me?*"

"Barely," Garrett said from the safety of his prison cell, having been recently discharged from the hospital. "Might have to depend on speech-to-text for this one."

Despite the circumstance, he was relieved to be a hawk again. It gave him a familiar focused task, something he desperately needed for a change, plotting out maps and menus, sliding configurations selections until they are at a comfortable reach, and sliding viewports around Nara's armor to gain a perspective of her sight.

"Can you see anything yet?" He involuntarily shivered as he watched the snowstorm, the harsh beauty of the torrent bestowing him an unconscious sense of empathy.

"*Give me a second,*" Nara said and tapped a few settings.

LIDAR CAMERA ENGAGED

Just then, the world shifted to shades of red and the cloud coverage dissipated, revealing a fortress settled inside the valley. Her vision zoomed into the structure, an ice-capped monolith of metal and rivets, isolated from the main continent.

"*Odd...*"

"What is?" Garrett examined the building, finding nothing out of place.

"*This isn't a base of operations or even a prison,*" Nara muttered. "*It looks like a miniaturized gaming arena.*"

There were no military fortifications, and the only hangar bay housed a small scattering of local transportation vehicles, no munitions or even outdoor weapons grounds. A med bay and a barracks were annexed to the main training ground. The overall facility could house no more than fifty individuals.

"No one's patrolling the grounds, either," Garrett pointed out. "Either they're taking shelter from the storm or they are truly not expecting visitors."

"*Yeah.*" Nara drummed her fingers on her knee. *I don't like this one bit.*

She stared down at the mountainside, pointing her finger at the air. Dots manifested on her screen as she poked and prodded at nothing, her armor tracing out a linear path down the side of the cliff.

"So how are you going to get down the—" Before he could finish his sentence, Nara leaped off the precipice. A blast of lavender powder marked her landing, stretching across the screen as she zoomed down the face of the rock. The soles of her boots warped into slickened blades, forming shovels around her feet.

The lines of light on her HUD zipped through her vision, each waypoint passed with an authoritative bleep as she crossed it. Nara reacted quickly as the environment unfolded beneath her, hastily shifting her weight as she mapped out a new trail of waypoints to follow. Numbers skyrocketed as her acceleration increased and she became a blur of snow racing down the mountain. Faster and faster she prodded the air, the dots becoming more chaotic as she careened through the treacherous garden of spires and clefts.

Garrett clenched the arms of his chair, eyes widening as he fixated on the world speeding away.

ENGAGE DECELERATION MANUEVERS

"Yeah, yeah," Nara grumbled.

She turned her heels at a sharp angle, sweeping a leg to the side to adjust her speed. She arched her side, brushing a hand across the rock above her to gain friction against her descent.But a pang jabbed her ankle as her foot stopped short, the shovel of her boot catching a divot in the earth.

"WHOOPS! "

She was flung off her feet, arms flailing as she caught the face of a jagged outcropping square in the chest. Inertia not sated, she bounced backward, her head colliding with the ground as she landed. Gravity yanked her down as she twisted to right herself, the movement sending her tumbling down the plane.

IMPACT. IMPACT. IMPACT. The armor screamed, limbs on the miniaturized model image of her body flashing red as each bounce slammed her into a new surface.

"Shut it." She snarled as she clawed for the nearest rock, clutching onto the anchor. The muscles in her shoulder yanked against the socket as it violently stopped her, legs swinging violently back and forth. She glanced down to find the foot of the mountain taunting her from a few meters below. With an annoyed grumble, she let go and rolled into the pillow of snow.

"Ugh." Nara flipped over on her side, taking in breaths to slow the rush of adrenaline pounding through her head. *No worse than an Uppercity High-rise...*

"I am getting very uncomfortable flashbacks, I will have you know." Garrett released his grip on his chair, his jaw cramping from the tension.

"I didn't hear you offer smarter options," she shot back.

"You didn't give me the chance!"

"The network open for you?" She ignored his protesting, checking in on the connections herself.

"I... *located* it." Garrett buried his fingers in the technological goo of the code. "I have yet to determine the best way to enter it."

"So, when you said you would be helping..."

"I mostly meant moral support." He offered a timid laugh.

"Great." Nara scowled beneath her helmet as she approached the structure.

"I'll keep trying."

She hurled a sigh and a grunt, pressing her hand against the fortress's barrier. With the assistance of her armor, she hefted herself up the wall, her palms sticking against the smooth surface. Her toes padded beneath her, barely audible over the sounds of the swirling storm. She hesitated before reaching the top, peeking over to search for activity on the rooftop.

The vacancy left her anxious, and she steeled her nerves as she vaulted over the parapet. Crouching behind a ventilation generator, she toyed with her network programs to get her bearings.

Garrett followed suit, pushing and shoving against the amorphous code. Further exploration revealed familiar shapes nearing the applications, rounded lines that straightened to a singular point. With a gentle suggestion, he molded the material to a more familiar shape. His studies of the language assisted his prods, helping him make educated decisions in his quest. After a selection of actions, a viewpoint opened to him, revealing the interior views of the fortress.

A mess hall flickered into view, displaying a few members casually eating and washing up while others toyed with tablets and played war simulations for study. A few tinkered with styluses, scribbling away notes as a form of meditation. Ultimately, it was not the appearance of a rebel outpost.

"I got camera access if you need it," he announced.

"*Cameras?*" Nara stared up in vexation. *I shouldn't be surprised. Who knows what tech Abberon stole and took advantage of?* "Anything near the beacon coordinates?"

"I'll look. Everything seems to be partitioned off in their own isolated paths."

She crept over the rooftop, heading for the flashing waypoint on her view. Brushing away the ice collecting on the floor, she pressed a hand against the metal pane. Streams of code radiated from her fingers in shimmering sky-blue tendrils. A moment later, the tile of metal warped translucent, revealing the interior of the complex.

Down below, she spotted the sterile white atmosphere of a gaming arena. Seven tech-suited figures danced about in a flight of combat, all engaged with one hapless unsuited victim. The room echoed with a CRUNCH as she witnessed Bellanar's jaw whip to one side. A spray of blood splattered over the walls.

Denying them respite, she hurled another spell at the floor, dissolving the glass into nothingness. The warmth of the controlled environment kissed her sensors as she dove into the fray, her suit cushioning her fall with a soft thud. She snatched a soldier preparing for a second strike and yanked them by the shoulder, hurling them to the side.

The others seeing the flight of their comrade rushed to their aid, dropping Bellanar in the process. Nara slid to his side, catching his fall and resting him on her knees.

"Ngh... ffnd oot..." Bellanar grumbled as he struggled with his dysfunctional lips, pointing behind her.

All faces locked on her, aware of her presence. They closed in, their fists primed to deal with the intruder.

Nara dragged Bellanar and propped him to a seated position as she fumbled with functions inside her head. She slapped a hand on the wall, the data streams once again fanning out of her fingertips.

But the soldiers were insistent on keeping her here, charging forward to disrupt her retreat.

"Ah, fuck." She released the wall to lash out a jab into the attacker's throat, dodging a second oncoming strike while dipping down and slamming her shoulder into their chest.

The mob circled her, trapping her inside a tangle of grasping hands and flying knees. She ducked and weaved, meeting each strike with a counter of her own. She maintained her ground, matching their skill with restraint to conserve her energy. But they gave her no quarter, intensifying their speed to overtake her.

As she thrust one body away, another leaped on her back, snaking their arms around her throat. She sank into her weight and heaved back, slamming their back against the wall. Unleashing a roar of strain, she snapped up to her feet and smashed the top of her head into their jaw, the blow knocking their senses away. Their grip weakened, and she cast them off her with a violent shake, flinging them to the ground.

She was given no chance to savor her victory as others started to grab for her arms, weaving themselves around her like sentient vines. Meeting their traps with a web of her own, she twisted around and grabbed a pair of individuals by their elbows. With a deep inhale, she planted her footing solidly into the ground. Her breath forcibly released with a heave and she flexed her pectorals, swinging her arms inward to slam the duo into each other. She grabbed their throats and hurled them away, planting a kick into one to launch them further.

A soldier swiftly cut off her recovery and unleashed a flurry of blows, keeping themselves just barely out of her reach. She played along with their distraction, edging forward and raising her hands to engage in the playful fisticuffs, letting a second unit sidle toward her side.

The interloper chose their opening and stepped in, but Nara sensed their intent, twisting around to face them. Arcing her hand out, she lunged forward and grabbed their throat, pulling them close to her. She snaked her arm around theirs, binding them together. With a twist of a hip, she flipped them around, dropping a leg behind their ankle to throw them off balance. Seizing their shoulder, she snatched their waving arms and yanked their back against her.

The mob recouped their efforts and rushed to the aid of their friend. She was ready for them. Hoisting her victim up with a strained growl, she dangled her toy in front of their company, just high enough that their toes barely scraped the floor. She unleashed a mighty bellow and hurled her living weapon forward, chucking them into the oncoming squad. The pack stumbled in a dance of tangled feet as the body collided with them.

Nara bolted to a wall, slapping her hand on the surface to reattempt the brute force program.

"C'mon, c'mon!" she roared at the sequence of code.

With one final click, the wall behind her dissipated. She leaped into action, dragging Bellanar through the makeshift door into an empty corridor. Daring a glance back at the arena, she watched as the soldiers stopped, befuddled by the loss of their quarry. In an instant, they retreated, carried off to fight another foe as the wall re-materialized.

"Let's get you situated." She knelt down to Bellanar, wrapping his arms around her shoulders. He groaned a pittance of protest as she stood up, pulling him up to her waist so she could carry him around. *INITIATING ESCORT PROCEDURES.*

The armor melted and warped over her back, stretching out of her body in aqueous strands. Bellanar uttered a quiet moan as the material slipped around his tender flesh, coating him in its metallic embrace.

"Mmf hroh," Bellanar managed, drifting between realities as his injuries took their hold on him.

"*Shut it,*" Nara scolded as she stretched her now free arms, toying with settings in her HUD. She made her way down a corridor, creeping toward an intersection. Chattering of conversation halted her step, and she leaned out the corner to assess the situation.

MIRROR OVERLAY ACTIVATED. The armor announced as the skin warped colors, reflecting its surroundings to make Nara appear practically invisible against the interior of the facility.

She slinked around the corner, crossing over the bright lights of a mess hall where the revelry amplified. No one took notice of her presence, absorbed in their collective meals. An odd thought tickled the back of her mind.

Many times, she had played the games and fought others from another region, but at the end of the day, they were still her comrades. Still part of her community. The idea that they were now enemies left an unsavory taste in her mouth. It was hard not to demonize them for siding with such a deplorable leader. But what did he promise them? And what did he conceal from them?

Garrett watched the scene with unease, pressing the security further for more useful information. But this time, the ooze pushed back. Harder. It wriggled up to greet him, flicking a forked tongue of analytical feelers. The force seeped up his digital fingers until it coiled around his influence, gradually consuming it with voracious hunger.

"The hell…" He tried to remove himself from the system, but the machine no longer obeyed his commands. Panic began to rise as connections severed against his will. The fortress seeped further into his machinery, spreading its paralytic toxins to the core. He watched dumbfounded as it spread through his connection with Nara, trickling into her suit. "Oh, shit, NARA! I have to go! Some sort of trapdoor. Cut it off! *FUCK!*"

Paranoia forced his hands as he raised the tablet over his head. He slammed the device against the arm of the chair, snapping it in half with a spray of sparks and glass glitter. Blood seeped from his skin as he tore through the guts of the computer, shredding wires and popping chips out of the board.

He stared at the carnage, the severity of the situation dawning on him. *Shit.*

"Wait—" This silence came down on Nara like an impact hammer. A strange sensation edged closer to her, enveloping her HUD with its vile influence. She flinched as the viewscreen spasmed chaotically, her icons and graphs flashing signals sporadically. Alarms and sirens stuttered shrill cries inside her skull. Colors and shapes lashed across her vison, throwing her in an ocean of disorientation.

She staggered back, bracing one ear against the side of her helmet as the violent imagery warped, the screen cycling through every spectrum of the rainbow. Words shuddered and printed, nonsensical symbols and phrases in languages unbeknown to her, reverberating across her eyes in bright contrasting colors. Her heart raced inside her chest, her breath echoing in stifling gasps as she fought with the sensory invasion.

A second later, the surrealist jargon ceased, frozen on a still white screen.

-HELLO, ELAM.-

He knows. A familiar fire began to seep into her vision. She swatted it aside, frantically reaching for a setting in her mind, commanding the armor to obey.

With a spark and a sizzle, a jolt of electricity jabbed her in the neck. The scent of smoke teased her nostrils as the override notified her of success.

HARDWARE CONNECTION DISENGAGED. DEPLOYING SAFETY COUNTERMEASURES.

She braced Bellanar on her back as the armor peeled away from her skin, exposing her inside enemy territory. The device popped off her neck, and she grumbled as she picked it up with a hiss of a curse.

Now what? She glanced into the mess hall. No one had noticed the commotion. A sigh of irritation manifested in her throat. With her digital hacking tools out of commission, she decided to resort to social engineering, a technique she was not as versed with.

She straightened her posture and reached around the back of her neck, extracting an outer weather hood from the seam in her collar. Pulling it over her face, she sauntered ahead, adding an assertive confidence to her stride toward the hangar bay.

The compound was relatively quiet, most taking their leisure in the mess hall. Whenever she heard footsteps, she made a point of crossing a different path. Nothing unusual of note was observed while adventuring through the facility. No secret laboratories, no weapons manufacturing, no biomedical display. No prisons. It was just a normal housing facility, albeit isolated inside a harsh tundra. Abberon was exerting quite an effort to keep his plot out of their ears.

"Is everything all right, *Serr*?"

Nara looked to her left to spot a soldier regarding them with concern. Upon seeing the decommissioned Bellanar, they hastened their approach.

"Yes, thank you. I had just arrived and was off to check out the arena matches when my colleague and I embarked on a wager first." She shifted the body on her back. "Suffice to say I won that wager."

They glanced down at Bellanar, who raised a feeble thumbs-up. "They look critical. Let me help you to the med bay."

"I would rather not have you go to the trouble of cleaning up your uniform. I am afraid both *Serr* and I have indulged in a bit more liquor than advised when training." Upon cue, a gurgling noise rumbled out of Bellanar's throat. It was immediately followed by a juicy belch and chortle echoing across the corridor.

"I see." Their eyebrows wrinkled in confusion. "Well, at least permit me to alert the med bay of your arrival."

"That won't be necessary. We will be returning to the mainland to repair our pride as well as our bodies. I have a ride en route that should be arriving shortly."

"Are you sure about that? *Serr* looks a little worse for wear. I must insist that they be checked out first."

"Shall we see what they think?" Nara challenged. "Lieutenant, would you like Ensign to tend to you here?"

Bellanar raised his hands up, knitting his fingers into a succinct gesture to speak his mind. *"NO."*

"I see." She nodded with a smirk. "And where would you like to be treated?"

He signed another word. *"Home."*

Nara raised her hand in affirmation. "You see?"

"Surely, they are not in a state to speak for themselves," the soldier protested. "Even if alcohol were not involved."

"Lieutenant." She looked up at the ragged body on her shoulder. "What do you think?"

Bellanar glared at the Ensign, his gesture emphasized with sharp, terse jabs at the air. *"HOME."*

"Satisfied? Or would you like to prolong their discomfort?"

The ensign moved their glances between the two, their expression reeling with uncertainty. "If that is what they consent to. My apologies, *Officers.*"

"Then you will excuse us."

"Yes, *Officer.*" They bowed and scurried off, warily glancing over their shoulder before turning the corner.

Nara shook her head and continued her journey until she reached the hangar. Mechanics were scattered about the room tailoring their machines, oblivious to the happenings of the world. Avoiding potential eye contact, she marched forward until she reached a pile of beams stacked near the wall. She shrugged off Bellanar and gently placed him against the beams, letting him get as comfortable as possible on a cold metal floor.

"Wait here," she ordered.

A shadow of a smirk traced over his broken lips. "Mmm."

Nara brushed the creases from her clothing, then walked over to the nearest mechanic. She glared at their back, shaking her head at their disinterest in her presence. Having had enough waiting, she tapped them on the shoulder.

"Ack! What!? I—" They snapped around to meet her eyes, then calmed their tone once the startle subsided. "My apologies. I didn't expect anyone else arriving today."

"Relax, I'm off duty," she assured with a wave of a hand. "Hey, can I take one of the carts out on the mountains? I want to capture some stills of the lightning patterns and I left my card in the barracks."

They blinked. "There's a storm out. That's kind of dangerous, don't you think?"

She stared at them blankly. "Which is why I want to go out. I doubt I will get many good shots of lightning during a light breeze."

"You have a point." They cleared their throat uncomfortably. "Sorry, it has been hectic as of late."

"Oh?" Nara folded her arms, leaning against the ship they worked on. "What's been going on?"

"A lot more people have been coming in and out to use the compact arena, which is causing some resource strain." They sighed. "And the supply deliveries are having a hard time getting out here since we're so far out from HQ."

She examined their distressed posture, sensing an ulterior matter lacing their tone. "Is that *all*?"

"I, uh, well." They shook their head violently. "Besides that, just some personal issues piling up that I don't want to trouble you with."

"I'm listening." She tilted her head curiously.

"I… ah." They rubbed the back of their neck uncomfortably. "I mean, it's really nothing. Just general malaise."

"General malaise has a source, no matter how unconventional," she pressed.

"I didn't mean, oh, pain." They released a defeated sigh. "It's just… everyone around seems to be content in their life, and I don't share their feelings. And I can't really explain why."

"Sounds like you need a change of study," she remarked.

"Yeah, you aren't the first to tell me. I just can't help but feel like I am stuck. Nothing motivates me."

"Have you talked to your CO about it?"

"Yeah, and they are open to a shift change." They scrubbed their face in agitation. "I just have to tell them where *to.*"

"Others can only lend a hand. You have to be the one to take it," Nara pointed out. *Do as I say, not as I do, all right?*

"Yeah." They cleared their throat. "Anyway, sorry. I didn't mean to trouble you with my problems. Let me fire up a cruiser for you."

"I would appreciate that." The conversation felt off, as if their issues were festering inside them for the longest time, lacking the proper channels to output their thoughts. Or perhaps they were too afraid to bring it up to anyone for fear of shying away from the status quo. Then she came along, the first person to take an interest, and they were compelled to spew everything to a total stranger.

Other warlords had chastised her before about fraternizing too deeply into the personal lives of those under her command, but disassociation never brought a cohesive functioning unit in the battlefield. At least in her experience.

The mechanic led her to an all-terrain vehicle, equipped with a grid of roll bars and an articulated chassis that assisted in flipping the car back on its right side should the driver take a spill. They opened the door and reached inside, pressing a chip on the ignition switch.

"All yours," they announced with a smile and a nod.

"I appreciate that. I'll just grab my gear." Nara locked their eyes and put a hand on their shoulder. "And you take care of yourself, you hear me?"

They shifted uncomfortably. "Certainly."

"I mean it."

"Of course, Serr." A smile cracked their dour lips. "Have a safe journey. And bring it back in one piece, please."

"Will do. If I'm not back in an hour, assume I'm dead."

The mechanic chuckled and waved, returning to their spark ablutions underneath the belly of their aircraft.

When they were clear of view, Nara went back to collect Bellanar, wrapping him over her back.

"K. uld." He groaned and shifted, clearly upset by all the jostling.

"I know, I know. We're heading out." She slid him into the

passenger seat and strapped him in, pulling down the recliner so that he could rest more comfortably.

After settling into the driver side, she flipped on the control panel switch and revved the machine awake. The bay doors opened behind her, and she backed out of the hangar into the gusts of wind and snow. Cleared from the eyes of any observers, she zoomed off the paths, heading up the mountain. The bumpy ride caused Bellanar to grunt and cringe while she sped around the jagged trail.

She drove up to the drop point, meeting up with Kestra's docked aircraft. Upon her approach, the bay door opened, waiting to receive her. She parked and pulled out her battered cargo, stepping up on the ramp to the inside of the aircraft.

"Thanks for the pickup," Nara said as she laid Bellanar on a medical table bolted to the back of the flight deck. The man was long asleep.

"I saw you disconnect, and I moved in," they replied, warming up the control panel to initiate takeoff procedures. "Another half hour and I would have called for backup."

She walked over to them, gripping the paneling to steady herself. "Good thing you didn't."

"How did you manage that?" Kestra nodded at the vehicle steadily drowning in snow.

"Just waltzed in like I owned the place." She threw a shrug.

"I see. Well, let's get out of here before they realize it's gone." They hurried their calculations and ushered the plane into the air, moving from the treacherous atmosphere.

Nara settled into the passenger seat, staring vacantly as she reflected on the expedition. Carrying a bleeding body around a high security compound with no cybernetic assistance. That had to have been one of the more obnoxious stunts she had ever pulled in her career, even considering her time in active duty.

Maybe she wasn't used to the culture this side of the equator, but something about the mechanic's plight set her off. She had fought against Abberon in the battlefield but never got to engage with his soldiers off duty, never learned what they were like. She had expected them to share some of his more devastating beliefs, but then again, how many actually had the choice?

"*Savant,* there's no need to hide it from me." Kestra burst her thought bubble.

"He let me go." Nara hung her head. "He knew I would show up, eventually."

"Then come what may." Kestra shrugged, initializing the autopilot procedures. "Say the word, and my units will be at your disposal."

She sighed, staring off into the abyss of the ocean. "I had hoped it wouldn't come to that."

"Abberon hoped it would, but here is not where you prove him wrong. Here is where you accept his challenge."

Kestra had a point, but she wished anyone else could be in her place. Then again, it would be cruel for her to wish it upon someone else.

##7.3##

BACK IN PLAINCLOTHES, Nara stepped in the medical bay where Bellanar was recovering. He seemed to be in good spirits despite being covered in bandages and healing polymers. Silver metal plates lined his mandible, hinged at key points to maintain mobility. Tiny dots of colored lights sent off visual signals to indicate the healing timeline to mend flesh and bone.

His arm was similarly coated in a silver cast that assisted regeneration and maintained a healthy positioning while allowing him to perform normal daily tasks. An electronic display showed an image of the bones inside. A seam traced cleanly in the upper arm.

"Ah, *Savant.* My thanks for the extraction," Bellanar said, a slight intoxication of painkillers muddling his speech pattern.

Nara folded her arms as she took a seat next to him. "Are you well enough to debrief?"

"Perfectly. Though I did not get much." He winced as he shifted in bed. "Abberon is most definitely *not* on the planet. I caught a glimpse of several transmissions from here to GaPFed space. He's standing by right now. Waiting."

"For what?"

"Well, *you*, I would assume." The twisted smirk he emitted grated against her nerves.

I had my hopes it would be otherwise, Nara thought. Hiding under cover of Fariem's warehouse was not going to last forever. Especially if he had agents listening to the Council. This extraction most certainly sped up the process. "You called out. I would not be allowed to leave you there."

"I know. I apologize." Bellanar rubbed his forehead, at a loss for words. "I may have cost the security of the planet."

"You were only doing what you thought was right." Nara released a sigh. If anyone else had pulled this stunt, she would have believed she was being manipulated. But she was just pulled along for the ride. If Bellanar hadn't gotten the information, she most likely would have herself. "Is there anything else you have to report?"

"Nothing concrete, I'm afraid. I wasn't able to copy over the transmissions before…" His eyes glazed over.

"Yeah."

"His techniques are quite fascinating." Bellanar's feverish giggle was cut off by a sting in his neck, and it diluted into a feeble whimper. "I wonder what his true persona is like. What he *really* feels. If anything."

"That makes one of us." She stood up and brushed her knees, the question setting her off.

"For what it's worth, I do appreciate your coming to my aid." He reached a silver hand to her wrist. "I know it could not have been an easy decision, given our history."

"Save it." She turned to leave the med bay. "Don't do anything foolish until I assess the situation. Or at least until you can stand."

"Wouldn't dream of it," he whispered to the empty room, a wry smile stretching across his lips.

CHAPTER 8

##8.0##

The projection of Abberon addressed the Galactic Peace Federation Council. The fleet of the wolf-like GaPFed ships glittered behind him in the window of the Great Hall. Slick slate paneling coated the floors and walls, making the meeting room resemble a starship bridge rather than a political gathering. Cobalt blue safety lighting traced pathways splitting outside the concentric circles of the booths, providing a regal ambience to the discussions.

The cavernous chamber housed the seats of the major factions of the GaPFed parliament and various human governments and corporations, along with several other races that had influence in the trade negotiation proceedings.

"I hope this will not take long, Ambassador." The Orchestrator addressed the projection. "We still remember the last time you impressed a state of urgency."

"I assure you, Councilors, that I have the utmost intention of justifying my summons." Abberon bowed deeply. "Firstly, there has been a discovery planetside that has come to my attention. This hastens my need for support."

"May I remind you, Ambassador, that you are here as a refugee, claiming that your faction is in grave danger," a venerable councilor stated gruffly. "However, despite the tension that is displayed here, we have no reason to believe a war will take place in the near future. Given our history with your culture, we are rather hesitant to impress ourselves further on your workings without concrete evidence of an impending threat."

"And that, as of now, is here." Abberon motioned to the screen. It morphed the celestial backdrop into a still image of an armor-clad humanoid. Then the image charged ahead, engaging a heated fist fight between several members in projection suits. Audible gasps babbled from the Council as the unknown being hefted a defender in the air, then violently threw the hapless victim against their comrades in a show of vicious brutality.

The Orchestrator examined the footage with scrutiny. "What are we witnessing, Ambassador?"

"As you can see, Councilors," they began, folding their hands beneath their chin, "Warlord Elam'Mutavreh has returned. And with their presence, war is inevitable."

A murmur settled over the councilors as the group discussed the meaning behind the display.

"Some of you may be familiar with this character. An incident over thirty years ago." Text from a news article sped over the screen, and Abberon circled the display with a red light. "Please consider the amount of resources lost at the expense of conflict under their order. And also remember the hundreds of lives lost on the prison ship transporting them to a holding facility when expected to be tried for their crimes. Not to mention, a wanted criminal for a long list of atrocities committed on a GaPFed-controlled planet."

As the Council continued their discussions, the Orchestrator leaned back in their seat, ruminating over the information presented. "And what are you proposing?"

"GaPFed has wanted allegiance for decades." Abberon gestured to the Council. "As previously established, my faction agrees. We would like assistance in dealing with this aggressor, and after that, I can assure you a smooth transition into treaty discussions."

Conversation elevated with a cacophony of replies and head shakes, some amicable, hoping to tap into a new font of resources, while others did not share the sentiment. But the Orchestrator called for silence, raising their hand up to the noisy crowd.

"Ambassador Abberon, you present to us an interesting proposition." The Orchestrator nodded. "Please give us some time to consider it. We will contact you with our decisions and potential resources to offer should we reach an agreement."

"As you wish, Councilor." Abberon bowed once more. "I anticipate your reply."

"If there are no more matters to bring forward, this meeting is adjourned." Upon the Orchestrator's declaration, one by one, the councilors faded from the room, their projections lost to the void as each cut off their communication channels. The few who were physically present in the meeting hall exited in a hushed fluttering of stiffened footsteps.

"Warlord Abberon," a voice called out. A singular human entered the meeting chamber, examining Abberon curiously. He was an older individual. His creased facial features exuded an experienced player in the techno-political gaming arena. Their eyes barely hid the eagerness of an opportunity. A businessman to the core, one who would make costly sacrifices to possess exponential gain in the long run. "A word with you, if you please."

"Chairman Galavantier." Abberon smiled politely, displaying a flash of fangs. "Your absence was noted in the meeting."

"Yes, I had some matters to attend to, but I could not help but overhear your predicament." The human seated himself in one of the council member's chairs. "I think you and I have mutual interests, if you would kindly hear me out. I assure you, it will be worth your while."

Abberon tilted his head curiously. "You have my attention."

##8.1##

NARA SAT on the floor of the patio, drink already in hand. She tried to drown the ache in her muscles after the night's excursion, washing away her thoughts in the pitter patter of rain cascading down the trees.

The pieces were quickly falling into place. While it was what she wanted, she doubted her ability to maintain the pace. She was already exhausted in a multitude of ways even before she stepped on this rock, and the change of environment did not offer her respite. Abberon was at the center of all this chaos, and her focus was only concerned with reaching him. But what could she do once he finally decided to show himself?

The man was patient, yet petty. Even if he were tried and found guilty of treason, a mere title stripping would be insignificant to his plans. It was doubtful that he would even attempt to reclaim citizenship here, and he no doubt had countless contacts amid the GaPFed elite. He could easily make her life hell, chasing her around the galaxy.

Would killing him resolve it? She could live with the blood on her hands, but the peace she insatiably longed for would never come to her.

A blare of the communicator disrupted her thoughts, and she reached an arm out to reply. The miniaturized image of Councilor Torel stood near her shoulder, arms crossed stiffly at their chest.

"You wanted to speak to me?" Nara gave no effort to hide her disdain, knocking back another swig of her drink.

"I am glad to see your scribe has returned in one piece." Torel paused, shifting to a wide stance to further project their discontent. "But I am concerned about the backlash we will receive because of your actions."

"And what actions are those?"

Their eyes narrowed at her evasion. "Ordering a Scribe to gather info on your behalf."

"I did no such thing. They acted of their own volition." She pointed the carton at him. "Chief Scribe Prism can verify that. They were present when speaking to my associate."

"Be that as it may, you did not have to risk your identity pulling them from the fire."

"I wasn't going to leave them," she snapped. "You've already admitted to me how much you despise that trait in a leader, so I will hear no more of your protests."

"You know very well what this will do to negotiations."

Nara scoffed and swirled her drink around. "So do what the Council always does and use me as a scapegoat. It hasn't been the first time."

"I simply cannot believe how callously you are juggling lives down here," they snapped, their fists clenched. "We have been in discussions with the Separatists for over a decade. Nothing has come of it."

"You cannot stand in a stalemate forever," she countered. "Eventually, something will crack. That is the law of nature, Torel."

"Is that what you believe, or did you let your personal feelings risk the security of the planet again?"

She held her tongue, her back stiffening with the accusation. They weren't wrong, and she knew it, but even they had to acknowledge that time was running out. The black and white solutions to this chaos were slipping further away.

"You have a responsibility to uphold, *Savant*," Torel continued. "Your close friends are just small numbers compared to the forces that live here. I will not stand by while you are willing to risk everything for them."

Her eyes snapped to the projection. "Is that a *threat*?"

"A warning." They raised a palm at her. "If you continue to prod at the opposition without consulting the Council, I will have no choice but to overrule you."

"Fine. Enjoy your evening." Nara switched off the channel. She clamped her eyes shut and released the bellow that she had forcibly restrained inside her chest.

She knocked back the remainder of her drink and walked out of the apartment into the wilderness, hoping to have a spark of clarity to decipher the councilor's intent. She calculated the remaining threads of influence at her disposal, a limited collection of allegiance spread thinly over all three branches of government.

What would come next? Abberon wouldn't show his face, so

GaPFed will probably speak on his behalf. What demands would they make? What had he convinced them that they had? Whatever it was, she had to act quickly.

Her musing brought her back to prison, drifting aimlessly down the corridor. She stopped and slid into the visitor seat, staring blankly at the wall to Garrett's cell. What would she tell him? Goodbye? She needed to find a place for him to live. Torel wouldn't release him, but perhaps she could prod someone who would.

Ugh, there's not enough alcohol in the galaxy, she grumbled as she flipped the switch, revealing the human meticulously prodding away at his NetComm.

"Hi," she started.

He hardly heard her, concentrating on the functions of the device. "Hi. *Fuck!*" His NetComm suddenly flew out of his hands. The poor device bounced, hitting the wall with a crackle.

"The guards have obliged me to inform you that if you break another tablet, the blueprint privileges on the printing machine will be revoked." Nara raised an eye.

"I can't make head nor tails of this shit." He angrily hugged his knees to his chest. "The network doesn't function in linear logic."

"I *am* trying to have you released, you know. And it would be easier to make your case if you didn't attempt to break out."

"I am sure of it."

She pressed her fingers against her temples. "What will you do once you do get out?"

His shoulders drooped sullenly. "I hadn't thought that far. But if I wanted to be a prisoner, I would have stayed in Arcadia."

"Then go back" Nara snapped.

Garrett considered the statement. Leaving the planet seemed appealing at this rate. But how would he get there? Nara told him that all ships were drydocked, and even if that were not the case, she wouldn't be able to find someone willing to take a human elsewhere.

It wouldn't be so bad if only he knew a friendly face he could trust. But all he could find were stern overseers of a culture that reveled in death and destruction. Even their games had to remind them that they were mortal, despite their seemingly endless lifespan.

Nara had probably killed friends and family in the digital world so often that she became accustomed to it. No wonder Velonir didn't faze her. The blatant display of apathy would have been considered deplorable at home, but was it still wrong if that was the norm of another society?

He turned to her with a stone-cold expression. "I want to talk about Velonir."

"Fuck off," Nara growled.

"Now."

"No." She leaned back in her seat, disconcerted by the apprehension and anger radiating around him. "There is nothing to discuss."

"Like hell. He was *my* family. You damn well owe me an explanation."

"You chose to hide your identity from me. I don't owe you shit." She jabbed a finger of warning on the desk. "You were a danger to me in Arcadia, and now you are a danger to me here."

Garrett threw his hands up, disbelief shaking his core. "How? What did Antonin do that made you kill Velonir?"

"You cannot convince me that you have no idea what your father's business practices were like."

"I was a liability to him. He kept me away from everything." He looked down at his feet, his voice wavering at the recollection. "Even Baran kept his mouth shut."

Nara examined his face upon the utterance of the man's name. Innocence and ignorance. He clearly had no idea what that henchman was capable of. What he did to her. "What happened to Velonir was business. If I didn't pull that trigger, someone else would have. He was going to die regardless of me."

"And who would be capable of that? *Cain?*" Garrett scoffed. "There are very few mercs on the bounty boards willing to take on someone *that* high-profile and hope to succeed."

"Listen, highborn, you and your family are *not* invincible. Your father is piss in a bucket compared to the company he pissed off." She could hardly believe it herself. But when it came to the shadow corporation Paragon, no one would risk getting in their way. No one knows how the ubiquitous company established, who pulls the strings. Yet somehow, their brand of pharmaceuticals lines every shelf in the galaxy. When they decide to make a move, someone seriously fucked up.

"Who?" His anger deepened through flushed cheeks, the enigmatic account sending his brain further into a maddening rhythm of questions.

Nara hesitated. A chill ran up her spine at the recollection of the contract. "I am not about to disclose that with you."

Garrett slunk in his seat, shaking his head in disbelief. "I am not sure how I am supposed to associate with you."

"Then don't."

"That's it? That's your reply? Our time spent means nothing to you?" He slapped his hands against the armrests of his chair. "You cannot honestly expect me to believe you wouldn't regret cutting ties with me."

"If I regret every single thing I have cut out in my life, there would be nothing left of me."

"And you are perfectly content with living with yourself?" His voice quaked, the stab of betrayal picking away at his social filters. "You can't just keep drinking your problems away!"

"What do you want me to say?" Nara roared. "I was constantly under fire from YOUR ties every second we met. We didn't have *time* to get to know each other. And we already discussed what would have happened if I knew sooner."

"But we—"

"I am what I *am*, human." The chair screeched behind her as she snapped to her feet. "I do what I must to adapt to a shitty, dark universe. You *knew* this, and yet you *chose* to stay around me. I do not need your pity or your desire to change me into a good person."

Silence festered between the glass barrier as tempers began to boil over. Exhaustion fanned flames on both sides of the pot, both too tired to acknowledge the point of view of the other. Neither wanted to be having this conversation, but neither wanted the issue buried deeper.

Garrett, having nowhere to flee from the confrontation within the confines of his cell, lowered his voice to a whisper. "One of these days, you will have to face the consequences of your actions."

CRACK!

He jumped in his seat as Nara's fist smashed into the glass. Fissures spiderwebbed around her knuckles. A spray of condensation haloed around her fingers as the heat of her flesh cooled on the slick surface.

The commotion summoned a pair of guards running to her side, eyeing the spectacle in alarm. *"Is everything all right, Savant?"*

Nara slowly raised herself up, filling her lungs with air. She released it in a drawn out, steady rhythm through her mouth. Crackles pitted the air between them, the glass healing the damage in grating scrapes. *"Everything is fine. I was just leaving."*

The wall filled in with inky darkness, leaving fear flickering across Garrett's chest. He shook the feelings away, fanning the heat that scorched his cheeks. There was no use talking with her. She was hiding something from him, and it would take all the forces of nature combined to extract it.

"Fuck this." He picked up his NetComm from the floor and went back to his assault against the door controls.

The logical fluid teased his prodding, binding with the input that he fed it. The unsuccessful attempts were grinding down his patience, but he thought he was getting closer.

Upon further examination, he noticed an anomaly in the network, a strange thin patch like a piece of gum stretched to transparency. It was oddly fabricated, artificial, even. He tuned his prods, sharpening them to needle-like precision. And with a few gestures, the film burst, revealing the access commands to him. Another adjustment, scraping the edges of the goo, and suddenly, the cell door opened behind him.

He glanced around the room in disbelief, stepping toward the opening. Poking his head out, he looked both ways to watch for the guards. No one in sight. Odd. He gingerly stepped out, slinking along the wall as he crossed the hallway.

Now what?

He turned around the corner, just to collide with an Ara'yulthr individual speeding his way. He tripped on his feet and landed on his backside, the jolt sending sparks rioting through his spine. *Fuck.*

"You have been released." Their glittering violet eyes scanned him up and down, their disapproving glare shifting a crescent mark just above their cheekbone. With a disapproving hum, they cleared their throat, flipping their navy hair over their shoulder. "I have been tasked with escorting you back to your living quarters. If you will follow me."

"Sure." He kept his eyes on the strange figure, slowly raising himself up from the ground. Their regal no-nonsense aura radiated as they gestured him forward, and something in their posture made him hesitate.

"Come along, now." They turned around and glided through the hallway.

Garrett quietly pattered along as they traversed the labyrinth of the prison. His eyes darted at every seam and crevice, looking for a potential escape route if things went south. He noted the expressions of the patrols that crossed their path. Initially, they bowed in respect to the seemingly high-ranking official that led him around. But as he looked around, he met their double-takes, their curiosity of the wandering human. Shrugs met with acceptance as the patrols continued their watch. But there was something else there.

The cool air of the hangar bay met them as they walked into the mechanical chasm. His guide continued forward, marching toward an aircraft just outside the entrance.

"This way, if you please." The escort waved an inviting hand toward the open craft.

He hesitated, the situation beginning to etch at his suspicions. "Do forgive me. I have been away from the beauty of your nature for some time. I cannot help but admire the gorgeous scenery."

"Time is of the essence." They gave him a disapproving frown. "I have other pressing matters to attend to."

His legs were leaden as they moved forward. A bog pulled at each step as he climbed up the stairway, and he stared blankly at the interior of the aircraft. *Something isn't right.*

"I would like to see—" A gasp stole his words as the guide snapped a hand on his shoulder. A sharp sting penetrated his flesh, and his body lost all sense of balance. His head met metal, his eyes darkening. His body was raised and placed on a cool shelf.

Voices echoed through his brain, speeding away from him as the world around him began to fade.

"Your assistance in this matter has been appreciated, Councilor."

"Spare me. After this, I want to hear nothing more from you. I want this conflict resolved."

"As you wish."

CHAPTER 9

##9.0##

After collecting herself, Nara made her way to the lab and marched straight for Syf, who was minding their own business fiddling with calculations on their screen.

"I need you or your associated network to scrub this." She dropped the armor badge in front of them. "I would prefer not to have it restored to factory defaults, but do what you have to."

"Oh, what is this? Third-party human technology!" Syf squeed with delight, snatching the device with greedy claws. "What is the phrase? Ah! 'Voided Warranties.' Yes!"

Nara turned to head for her apartment. "Have fun. Bring it back in one piece."

Just as she raised a hand to switch the security lock, Fariem charged at her with a travel pack in tow. "Ah, good. You're on time. Come along now."

"What now?" She ejected a sigh as she rested her forehead on the door.

They disregarded her disdain, opening the satchel to count off ration parcels. "It is time for another Specimen Expedition."

"You have two lab assistants." Her head lifted slightly as her brows scrunched together. "The same two assistants you have made do with for the past thirty years."

Fariem continued shoving materials into transport packs, darting back and forth to load them on a small buggy. "But neither of them could hunt for dinner as efficiently."

"Ugh." Specimen Expedition was code for *camping*, used as an excuse to get out of the lab while still being productive. Fariem was never opposed to the idea of leisure, but they took an amusement in napping on the job. After all, it was not fun unless you were breaking rules.

Nara wordlessly turned around, brandishing a searing scowl.

"There's a good soldier," Fariem chirped, pointing at a box of equipment. "Help me with that crate there."

Defeated, Nara hefted the metal container onto the cart, letting it down with a dramatic thud. She knew what they were trying to do, and she also knew they would not accept no for an answer. No matter how many stars were threatening to collapse in their solar system.

"That should be the last of it." Fariem dusted their hands then shimmied into the driver seat of the vehicle. "Right, let's go."

Letting off another grumble laced with obscenities, Nara begrudgingly slid into the passenger seat. "One. Night. That is all."

"The world isn't going to end in one night," Fariem remarked before unleashing a sharp whistle to the pair of lab assistants who obediently filed into the machine.

Nara could only shake her head. *You sound so confident.*

The trip to the campsite was relatively calm, the gentle hum of the hovercraft drowned out by the chirps and hisses of the local ecosystem. Fariem did not instigate conversation, letting Nara stew in her mental froth.

I just stomped around in the beast's lair, and Fariem thinks it's a great time for a vacation. She ground her teeth as the storm of "*what ifs*" seeped into her mind. Plots and contingencies wove a tapestry of possibility. Would he act first, or would she have to? Who did Abberon manage to build allegiances to? How can bloodshed be avoided?

The light in her eyes warped to a pink shimmer as the vehicle glided past the safety of the warding shield covering the city. With a blink, the iridescent glaze slinked behind them, leaving them exposed to the full force of Nature's arsenal.

The swaying of the machinery lulled her into a desensitized state. She peered in the rearview to find Syf laying their head in Ki'nit's lap tinkering with her armor badge, brow furrowed in contemplation. Their partner was lost in their own world, staring out the windows while idly twirling Syf's ponytail through their fingers.

Nothing changes around here. She was jealous of their peacefulness, the nostalgia burning a hole in her spirits. Contentment to such an intimate degree was a foreign concept to her, replaced by an unrelenting sense of duty and sacrifice for the behalf of others. Though was that really different? Taking security in control over her own actions?

Fariem ushered the craft through a network of trees, navigating through the maze of stony trunks. Blurs of multi-legged creatures leaped out of the foliage, letting off cries of scorn at the mechanical disturbance. Gravity pulled at them as they crested the hill, a clearing of moss and grasses awaiting at the peak. The sun's rays danced through the branches, tickling the hull of the craft as they ventured forth.

"Ah, here we are." Fariem announced. The vehicle swirled to a whisper as it lowered to the plush carpet of moss below.

Wordlessly the group unpacked and began to set up camp. The lab assistants took the initiative and constructed shelters with miniaturized domicile cubes. Frames of triangular prisms sprouted from the ground, while a delicate thermal sheeting coated each of the faces with a glistening sheen. Once assembled, the sheeting morphed into a mesh of screen that permitted the view of the wildlife.

Nara distracted herself with the campfire, summoning a metal safety pit along with cooking devices and a few seating areas. She then gathered fallen branches and dead leaves, forming a pile in the center. The pit chirped as each offering was placed inside, reciting how long the fire would last based on the weight of the kindling.

EIGHT HOURS DURATION. IGNITING. PLEASE KEEP ALL PERSONNEL AND FLAMMABLES AT A SAFE DISTANCE, the cheery voice requested as Nara pressed the control.

Fariem oversaw the production with their eyes glued to a tablet, muttering the occasional names of species surrounding them. They made circles around the campsite, tapping controls and settings with a free hand as their mind reeled with numbers.

Before long, the barebones shelter was finalized, complete with lab tables and running water facilities.

"All right, this should be enough for now." Fariem passed a data file with a map of the area. The image was coated in colored blobs for each party member, and a key listed off each plant and fungi desired. "According to the weather charts, it should be quite a frugal hunt. Your computers should be synched, so call out if you need help."

The two assistants bowed in acknowledgement while Nara waved indifferently, poking the fire with a stick.

"Off you get. There isn't that much daylight left," Fariem chastised. "You've got the east quadrant."

"Yeah, yeah." Nara groaned and stood up, brushing fallen blossoms from her thighs.

"Ah! Before I forget…" Syf approached and delicately placed the armor badge in her hand. "It was relatively clean. Whatever was inside appeared to have self-destructed. Didn't leave much of a residue."

She raised an eyebrow. "You're sure of that?"

"Perfectly. Lots of foreign languages on it, though, but nothing I haven't seen before." Syf met her eyes with a wolfish grin. "And I may have added a thing or two in there for later use."

"I would not have expected anything else from you." She scoffed and pocketed the device. "I appreciate the time you took."

"It's always fun." A soft giggle echoed from their throat as they turned and disappeared into the foliage.

Nara dismissed their revelry and picked up a collections pack from the pile of supplies. She raised a tablet to her face, examining the territory she was assigned. A few fungus strains, several moss colonies, a flying insect or two if she could manage. Nothing too burdensome. And, of course, whatever they were planning to eat for the evening.

Walking down the hill, she increased the magnification of her view of the area until grids of species and numbers overloaded the map. Percentiles of probability, the time of year, and growth cycles gave her input to plot her journey. As she selected a few waypoints to traverse, the ground beneath her began to soften. She was nearing her target straight into marshlands.

She slipped the device in a sealed compartment of her bag and examined the landscape. Directly in front of her was a gently bubbling pond, the waters dark with plum-colored algae. Wind-etched reeds pierced through clusters of broad-clawed leaves that floated on the water, the tips of their spiked fibers adorned with shining jewels of tempting berries.

Her boots sank into the greyish-green mud as she wandered around the bank of the pond, the sickening *slorp* of suction following her with each step. She took comfort in the pull against her legs, having forgotten the last time she was this close to the wilds. Her eyes glazed over the area, watching the movement of creatures shifting beneath the mire.

She knelt down to a tangled foam-like structure. Strands of milky-blue stalks knitted into an intricate knotwork, perfectly symmetrical as if hand-illustrated by a master artist. Too perfect to form in nature. Each vine ended in a bulb of shiny black dots reflecting the scenery like a set of compound eyes.

Dream-Eye. That will do quite nicely. She took out a blade from her pocket and sliced through the base of the knot. The severed ends shifted colors, the blue flesh morphing to a vibrant fuchsia, as if reacting to the damage. She slid out a container, placing the specimen delicately inside. As she closed her satchel, a flash of movement caught her eye. A wistful smile deformed her lips.

I wonder if I still have it, she mused and rose to her feet. Hanging her satchel on the gnarled branch of a nearby tree, she rolled up the cuffs of her pants, exposing her shins to the humid air. With slow, cautious steps, she glided into the murk, letting the cool liquid caress her skin with delicate ripples.

Her breathing slowed as she neared the center, the waters buzzing with the life surrounding her. She closed her eyes and focused, cutting off the sounds of the air in her ears. Every nerve of her being became still, in harmony with the liquid, feeling the flow of the vegetation trickle over her skin.

Stillness, silence.

…and then?

A flicker, a spark of movement nearing. Curious. Closer. Yes.

The weeds stirred around her ankles. A little closer.

She inflated her lungs with air, her rhythm quiet as a shadow.

Now.

The water erupted as she lunged to her side, clawing at the shining scales of a slithering creature. She drove her nails into its skin, cinching it in her grip as it flailed violently. Tightening her hold, she steadied herself and yanked it out of the water. *Gotcha.*

The whip-like creature gnashed its pointy rows of teeth, glaring at her vehemently as it was extracted from its home. Its rippled scaled pattern weaved like the waters, a cunning disguise for its prey. *Perfect.*

But Nara did not have long to revel in her victory when something in the distance stirred behind her. A rhythmic clatter of thunder. A snapping of trees.

Fuck! She dropped her quarry with a *sploosh* and charged up the water, tearing her footfalls out of the mud with each step. Abandoning her satchel, she raced to the camp, swatting at vines and branches threatening to trip her flight.

Silence marked her path. No birds chirped. No insects chattered. Nothing stirred in the grasses.

She burst into the clearing, where her suspicions were confirmed. The booming grumble of an apex predator narrowing in on the campsite. It leered at her, disturbed by the commotion of her entrance.

The beast was massive, its trail marked by the trampled young foliage too fragile to survive its impact. It stood on four legs nearly a meter above Nara. Jagged chitinous plating spiked its wraith-like structure, and it emoted its displeasure through the *thwap* of four barbed tails. Its pointed jaw was wrapped tight with leathery maroon-tinged skin. Horned crests traced over its feral eyes, burning with a voracious emerald glow.

No one else was around. She was alone with the beast.

Something shifted in her core, a familiarity that sent pangs of discomfort across her skin. Agitation. Anger.

A fire rose in her throat, crawling through her vision. Bitterness. Her mouth opened against her will. Sound forced out of her lungs, a mighty roar that strained her chords. The trees shuddered in response, the bellow reaching beyond the campsite.

"*LEAVE.*"

The creature stopped in its tracks, craning its neck down to examine the strange, noisy humanoid. It took a step forward, hot, pungent air swirling around her as it sniffed.

But it was not moved by her attempt at intimidation, and it sank down on its haunches, its multitude of fangs bared.

The fire tore through her eyes. Her nerves seized as a furor overtook her senses. Blackness began to consume her.

"Elam!" The name barely registered in her ears, a vein of clarity washing away the ink. She stepped forward. She could not hear the machinery stir behind her, the sound of energy ramping up.

Her eyes met the creature's. She was closer than she thought. It raised a taloned paw, ready to strike. Her body moved before her brain. She dove and rolled away from the speeding claws. Her legs bolted her upright, and she leapt up to meet the creature's skull.

Another roar belted from her throat, and she felt her shoulders launch forward. Her fist swung out. The impact of bone tore through her knuckles. A discordant baying rang through her ears. Thunder echoed after as the creature reeled back. It tripped over itself in a daze, falling to the earth.

It righted itself on shaking legs, retreating into the forest with staggering steps, leaving a trail of blood behind.

"Elam!" The call repeated. Nara snapped out of her trance, looking down at shining skin of her silver-coated forearm dripping with blood. Her strike had penetrated the creature's plating, bursting through to softened flesh.

Ki'nit ran up to her side, taking her arm and ushering her to the fire.

"Are you all right, child?" Fariem hurried over.

"Yeah. I... yeah." Her eyes stared beyond the trees in a daze.

"Why didn't you back off? Syf nearly fired at you!"

Nara turned to the assistant exiting the buggy, the delicate glow of the frontal weapons battery dimming to nothingness.

"I thought I could handle it," she lied.

"What utter pain you bring to me, child." Fariem straightened their coat. They were visibly agitated. Something bothered them that they were not expressing, and Nara did not have the capacity to investigate further. "Handle it? It's four times your size!"

Nara shrugged distractedly. "It's gone now, isn't it?"

"A thousand daggers, child."

"I had dinner, but it got away," she reported, ignoring the curse.

"I've managed to catch a thing or two. Don't worry about it," Ki'nit assured, slipping their pack off their back. They opened it up and pulled out a case revealing flat, snake-like creatures with angry little jaws snapping at each other. Their oily smooth skin proved a struggle for them on dry land as they fought for personal space inside the container. "Freshwater eels should do nicely about now."

Ki'nit set to work preparing the meal. Their expertise with a knife was unmatched as they cleaned the fish. Warm spiced scents began to fill the air as they seasoned the meat, its perfume magnified by the wood smoke as the skins seared over the fire. They took great care with the delicate textures, expertly turning and adjusting until it crisped to a soft amber.

Syf went to prepare the presentation of the meal, dishing out a collection of fresh vegetables and fruits they had gathered on their venture. They took out jars of preserves from storage, their deft hands dressing the plates with colorful spiced ingredients. Several clear glass bottles of home-brewed ciders and cordials accented the setting, the warm ambers and blood reds coordinating with the warm tones of the feast.

When everything was served, they all took their place in front of the fire. Silence carried the conversation, no one wanting to address the encounter. A nagging sensation poked at Nara, something itching from the depths of her memory. She could feel the insecurity emanating from all of them, a pang of guilt, even. She knew better than to inquire. She had tried before.

The fire consumed the void, its flickering comfort emanating through their spirits. Weariness pulled at the observers as sated hunger and mild inebriation added their weight. Syf leaned on Ki'nit's shoulder, their dreamy-eyed expression tracing around the pit. Soon, the duo rose, hands on hips as they ventured into the forest.

The stillness that remained raked across Nara's mind. She reached for the half-empty bottle of cordial and poured it into her metal cup. "Is there something you wish to tell me, Fariem?"

"No." They stiffened at the inquiry.

"Very well." Liquid sloshed as she swirled her vessel around. "Despite the interruption, did you gather enough material?"

"For now, yes."

Their dismissive tone irked Nara, and she restrained a scowl from the inside of her cup. "I am fine, Fariem."

"But for how long?" Their eyes suddenly snapped to her. "You can't keep shoving back your own needs for some façade of obligation."

"My position does not permit me to—"

"Stop it already. Listen to yourself for once." Their incensed voice echoed against the trees. Ashamed that they'd let their feelings loose, they eased their tone. "If all you do is react to the present, there will be no future for you."

Nara ground her jaw in response.

"I am turning in." Fariem stood, avoiding her gaze as they headed for their tent.

Wonderful. As the fire began to die down, the chill of the night air danced over Nara's back. She was too distracted to be concerned, the morbid familiarity of the fight leaving her questioning her sanity. *Fuck it.*

She grabbed the bottle of cordial and wandered into the trees. Images of the fight tangled with her memory, the creature's expression, the sinking disconnect within her guts. And yet… she knew this experience. Arcadia? Perhaps. But even further back, something had transpired.

She stopped at the base of a craggy fruit tree, its plentiful boughs reaching toward the stars. Clutching the neck of the bottle between her teeth, she ambled up the monolith, taking comfort in every abrasion that skimmed over her skin. Her head emerged from the canopy, the splendor of the scenery meeting her senses.

Gradients of blues and greens moved across the night sky, illuminated by the stars and beacons of the drifting fleet. The cries of birds echoed in the breeze, calls of formation to their brethren. The rustle of leaves warped the air, breathing a quiet murmur of assurance. Fragrant living foliage sweetened the atmosphere in intoxicating living perfumes.

She situated herself in a natural hammock amid the tangle of branches, letting leaves cover her in a blanket of serenity. Her eyes moved with the trail of satellites, their flight distracting her from the world below. *Do I dare attempt to sleep? Perhaps for a moment.*

Her eyes drooped while her consciousness melted away.

She blinked, sensing something amiss. The primary moon had traveled slightly across the horizon. A disturbance fluttered the branches beneath her.

"*Elam!*" She heard Syf calling to her.

"What is it?"

"A, uhm. Oh, dear." They scanned over their communication device, barely addressing the tree they spoke to. "A most pressing matter needs your attention. Please come down immediately."

With a grumble, Nara slid down the pebbled carapace of the trunk, bouncing back and forth between branches until she reached a manageable height. She then leaped out of the leaves and stomped to a landing in front of Syf, glaring at them expectantly.

Their gaze never left their screen, busy fingers dancing over the interface. "It seems like your human friend is in trouble."

##9.1##

HER FIST SLAMMED the window control, revealing the void of the empty cell inside. She scanned over every detail and crevice, the open door of the bathroom. There was no life here. Her senses did not deceive.

"Guard!" Her incensed bark echoed down the corridor.

Upon her summons, a lone soldier jogged to her, eyes widened with alarm. "Yes, *Savant?*"

"Where is the prisoner?" She scowled, her lips curling over a fang. "And why was I not informed of their removal?"

Befuddled by the display of anger, the guard scrolled through their data reports. "As far as I can tell, they were released by authorized personnel."

Her eyes narrowed. "Authorized by *whom*?"

"I don't…" —their voice trailed off as they searched through the report— "have information on the signature."

Funny that. She folded her arms. "I will repeat myself. Why. Was I not. Informed?"

"I am sorry, *Savant*. I am just as perplexed." The screen multiplied in shining plates of light, illuminating their perplexed expression as they pawed through multiple levels of security. "There are no details in the report."

"Get me someone who was on duty last night."

"Right away, *Savant.*" The guard bowed and scurried off with a hand pressed to an ear, their voice disappearing as they spoke with their superior officers.

He didn't break out. Someone **let** *him out.* She paused in front of the main computer to check its status, finding nothing broken, not a single program open. *There are only a few suspects I know of, and only one of them won't tell me.*

After several laps pacing around the cell, the guard returned to her with a companion just as mystified as they were. "Apologies for the delay, *Savant.*"

Her eyes snapped to the newcomer, who took a graceful step back after feeling the heat of her irritation. "What happened?"

"I was headed over to investigate some fluctuations in the security in this quadrant." They pointed off to the distance. "I was going to issue another warning to the resident about breaking into security when I saw someone escorting them from the docking bay."

"*Someone?*" She tapped a foot expectantly.

"It was raining outside, and they had their hood up." They shrugged. "That was when I got the status change of an authorized transport, so I didn't see the need to inquire further."

Of course not. Jailbreaks don't happen here. Nara pinched the bridge of her nose and exhaled deeply. "Summon a Council chamber in the operations deck. I am issuing an emergency meeting."

"Yes, *Savant*. Follow me." They bowed and led her through the compound, escorting her up a series of metal railed stairwells. Curious eyes traveled from their stations as they traveled, a whisper of intrigue following Nara's formidable presence.

Idle screens of status reports illuminated their stroll through the hub of monitoring outposts, the clicking language of feedback accenting their echoing footsteps. They stopped in front of a solitary steel door, and the guard tapped a key into the panel, prompting a refrain of cycling locks. They pulled the massive barrier open, revealing a dark featureless room.

Detecting the motion of the two figures entering, the chamber clacked alight, revealing sleek walls of grey shielded screens. The sterility of the pristine walls was defaced by a pattern of riveted holes in various rounded shapes, communications ports stamped along the ceiling.

"Here we are, *Savant*." The guard waved her forward.

"Secure these channels and watch for potential listeners." A pedestal raised from the floor, offering Nara a shining control box of digital meters and buttons. She ran her finger down the length of a gradated bar, her caress darkening the ambience to a dull aqua hue. "I want a private conversation."

"As you wish." The guard bowed and left, the hiss of hydraulics following as the door sealed her inside.

The room warped in dull tones as the council chambers manifested. The members slowly filed in with questioning murmurs. She watched patiently for the conversation to dull, her eyes focused on the heads in attendance. When the cacophony began to bubble into a restless clamor, she let herself be known.

"Councilors." Her image flickered into their view on the main screen overlooking the arena, her severity radiating beyond the screen.

"What is the meaning of this?" Councilor Torel was the first to speak, broadcasting their displeasure with a scornful glare.

Who will reveal their intent first? Them, or me? She raised her head to address the question. "It has been thirty-seven days since I have arrived back on Homeworld. What has been done in regard to resolving the Separatist conflict?"

"As we have repeatedly informed you, we are still discussing your voice in this matter." Torel leaned into the podium, raising a finger of warning. "And your brash persistence is impacting our decision."

"And what, exactly, is there left to consider?"

"Your motivation and your allegiances, especially when a GaPFed citizen has been allowed to enter our territory." Spots of light circled the bottom of the orator's pit. Beams shot up from each scintillating point, the collection knitting into a screen. The councilors' curiosity amplified in hushed tones as the Licensing Profile of Garrett Galavantier manifested, his personal information and his image displayed for judgment, sealed with GaPFed's digital stamp.

Nara threw a dismissive shrug, raising a questioning palm. "What of it?"

"While their citizenship status is under question, harboring a fugitive is certainly not in our best interests, especially from a power that has previously threatened us." Torel jabbed a finger at the podium. "And apparently, the human you brought is unaccounted for."

Really, now? Her arms tightened across her chest. The sweet taste of blood grazed her tongue as she clamped down on the side of her cheek, restraining her temper. She straightened her back and drew a cleansing breath. "This is not the matter I wish to discuss. If you are so concerned about GaPFed, why are we not discussing their potential arrival?"

"We have no proof that they have any interest in us again. Only speculation, which is not grounds for action."

"Actually…" a voice from the Present interjected. All eyes turned to the figure who stood.

"Warlord Kestra." Torel frowned as they eyed the figure. "How interesting that you have finally decided to accept your invitation to the World Council."

Kestra ignored the snide remark. "We have been monitoring communications that have been passing through the planet. They seem to be reaching somewhere into GaPFed space from several locations planetside."

"They are interested, all right," Nara added. "You have established your presence in space, brandishing a substantially-sized fleet. Sooner or later, they will turn up with another armada."

"And if that day comes, we shall deal with it," the councilor dismissed. "We dealt with them then, and we will deal with it now."

Her ire strained against her will. She slammed a fist against the panel, her voice quaking as she uttered her refute. "*I* dealt with them then. And I assure you, my judgment will not be the same."

"Enough." The councilor's voice boomed across the chamber, and the voices of the audience silenced. All eyes watched her, waiting for her to break. To show her inability to represent her faction, buried beneath the indomitable structures of tradition.

"This is your final warning." Her voice was steady, chilled by the sheer force of her will. "They are coming, and you have no time to decide what you wish to do."

Torel cleared their throat. "Is that all, *Savant?*"

"Fine. I see I have your answer." She flicked off the channel, and the meeting room snapped back into darkness.

It was not unexpected to face this much resistance. Complacency was an infection. And why would anyone want to act? A full-scale war resulting in bloodshed had not happened in centuries. They could resolve their own conflicts with chatter, and the outside galaxy hadn't dared to cross them after the first incident with GaPFed. War was an automation, requiring little effort to keep them safe.

"*Elam.*" Syf poked their through a separate communications channel. "*I've located them.*"

The glint of a menu screen popped into her view. A rotating globe whirled around, focusing on a remote location isolated from the nearest authorities of both sides of the planet. She panned into the satellite view with the swipe of a finger, revealing a featureless patch of nature where the coordinates strobed.

"Thank you, Syf. I fear I may need more of your expertise."

"Always a pleasure to assist." The projection bowed and flickered off.

I am done. No more of this. Her fingers twitched in a flurry of strokes, a new channel of communication opening before her. The carefree image of Jav'ril stood before her, their uplifting smile a beacon of geniality.

"Do you wish to speak to me, *Savant?*"

"I will ask you one more time." She analyzed their every move, wary of the latency between their face and the projection. Nothing came to her, no malice, no deceit, not even a shred of concealment. "Can I trust you?"

They gave her a nod of affirmation. "Of course." *No hesitation.*

"Very well." Every inch of her body warned her, the sirens itching across her nerves. She had to ignore them. "There is movement on their front. Abberon is waiting for us to make the first strike. And I think we should give him the pleasure."

Their smile widened as they shifted their stance. An eager finger rubbed their chin as they considered the proposal. "What, exactly, did you have in mind?"

"Something on our own terms." She passed them a data file, the map of the Separatist continent entrapped within a meshwork of battlements and structures. "Are you interested?"

Their smile widened as they examined the proposal. While they were never one to antagonize, they were a tinkerer by nature, wanting to gently poke and prod forces to see how far they could get. Nara admired that about them while she was their subordinate. Someone fueled by the simple motive of gaining knowledge. Finding out causation with experimentation. "We can be mobile in less than a few hours."

"Good. I will be in touch."

"I will await your call." Jav'ril bowed and disconnected.

I wonder if the sky will answer. She summoned another call on the line, and to her surprise, the image of Commander Tosk appeared before her.

Nara tsked. "So this line does work."

"You had my word, *Savant,*" the commander insisted. "What do you need?"

"Do you want command of your ship again?" A devious smirk morphed her features.

They leaned back in their chair, her enigmatic words piecing together in their brain. "What are you suggesting?"

"An instigation."

Silence resonated from the channel as their piercing eyes studied her, the soft shifting of fabric breaking the stillness as the commander shifted in their seat. They folded their hands and pressed them against their lips, thoughts speeding through their mind as they considered her words.

"What you are asking for." Their discomfort resonated from the speakers. "It's treason."

"Ötmarr's Trust, Tosk," she countered with an open palm. "There is no time."

They uttered a pointed hum, and the channel went dark.

##9.2##

A DULL POUNDING ache across his entire body stirred Garret awake, sending his head reeling, his guts threatening his throat with acidic spasms. *The fuck am I?*

He opened his eyes. Black.

He closed them. And opened them. Black.

The colors did not change as he blinked rapidly, surrounded by an ever-present darkness.

Shit.

The pressure in his chest did not cease, and when he tried to turn over, he was startled to find himself immobilized. He twisted and wrenched, every part of him below his neck coated in a metallic carapace. Panic seized his nerves as he thrashed inside his confines, his heart thudding against the constricting barrier.

A bolt of white light lashed through his eyes as he smacked his head against a wall, the dizziness halting his fit.

Stop it. Stop. He forced his eyes shut, restraining his breathing to a tolerable heave. Droplets of sweat streamed down his neck, and he focused on the cooling sensation. *You've done this before. Use what is around you.*

Quieting his mind, he tuned in to the environment. The air was still over his flushed cheeks, the coolness barely stirring around him. A faint mechanical hiss disrupted the hush, a wisp of cycling air. The ambience was reminiscent of the silent processes running inside a constructed domicile cube. While alone in Nara's apartment, he would take comfort in the sounds. But now the vacancy pressed upon him like an impending doom.

At least I won't suffocate. No obstacle impeded his movement as he tilted his forehead down as far as his neck would allow. He drank in a slow breath of air, testing the capacity of his lungs against the metal. In a slow, steady stream, he slowly released it through his mouth, the stream weakening. Nothing that broke the cone of air that passed his lips. *There is room to move. Now what?*

He flexed his fingers, grasping at the smooth material trapping him. The delicate scratch of his nails sent shivers up his veins, and his nerves began to fly away from him. The futility of his situation pressed harder than the restraints, and his heart kick started once more. *I need to get out of here.*

Clouds of sickly yellow-green crawled over his vision, the air squeezed from his throat by an invisible force. His panting breaths echoed inside the chamber, the erratic pattern dissolving in the distance. Dizziness seized his brain, gravity churning his senses as he struggled to remain conscious.

A sharp sensation rumbled in his pocket, forcing him still. The tremors sent reverberating waves of warmth across his thigh. *My NetComm?*

The throbs intensified, increasing in frequency. The barrage escalated to a concussive pulse warping around him. Within an instant, a POP shuddered the room, and the pressure on his bones violently released. A gasp forced out of his lungs as he crashed, his forehead smacking against a smooth surface.

What the fuck?! He pulled himself to his feet, his hands shaking as he frantically tore at the air for any obstacles in his path. He stood up on his toes, waving an arm above him. Nothing.

He pulled his NetComm out of his pocket, taking comfort in its dull, familiar glow. With agitated fingers, he pawed through the system for an open operation, but he could find nothing except an inconsequential system check running in the background. Dazed, he raised the device in front of him, illuminating the featureless box that he was contained in.

Running his fingertips along the walls, he walked around the border of the box, the boundaries the size of a reasonable bedroom. There were no hidden seams, no panels that he could reach to extract the room's internal system.

Distracted by the puzzle of his location, he was unaware of the disturbance beneath him. He raised a foot to take another step forward and felt a leaden weight lick the bottom of his boot. Before he could pull away, the material snaked around his foot, wrapping around his ankles. He gasped as he yanked away, but his balance got the better of him.

With a yelp, he pitched to the ground, landing on the bone of a shoulder blade as he crashed. A sharp tear seared his ankle as the room maintained its grip on him. The pain intensified as he desperately struggled. His incoherent whimpers of terror filled the room while his tendons screamed for him to stop.

The voracious cold material reacted to his struggle, speeding up his legs and engulfing his calves. He pulled against the metallic mud, only to trap his hands inside the murk. His fingers seized as he scratched at the goo. It relentlessly migrated up his arms, curling around his torso. It gave him a gentle squeeze across his ribcage, making sure he knew he had no control.

A feral sense of self-preservation lashed over his skin. Shrieks of panic echoed across the chamber, his own voice deafening him. He panted for air, beating back the virulent liquid with erratic futile beats. Pops crackled over his ears as the room squeezed, a lashing pain through his heart as his bones gave way.

His screams reached a violent crescendo before his body could take no more. The air no longer sustained him. Ringing across his ears added to the cacophony, and he could no longer hear his own voice. Soon, there was nothing, a brutal tear into oblivion.

CHAPTER 10

##10.0##

"I have the report from my Shadow units," Kestra announced to the assembly. Their digital form, along with Jav'ril and a few reliable officers, gathered in a circle around Nara.

"Were any of them compromised?" she asked.

"If they were, it was not made obvious."

An orb manifested in the center of the congregation, inflating to the image of a rotating globe of the world. It slowed to a halt, a blob of red sweeping over the western hemisphere.

"If we assume by the reports of our scanning drones, the Separatist forces are centered on this continent. Given the short notice, the Shadows weren't able to gather much on the outposts, but we can assume similar training grounds as *Savant* and I had observed last week."

The projection panned in to focus on a central continent. A satellite view of the landscape displayed a scattering of fortresses throughout the mass.

"The majority of the structures are barracks, command centers, farms, and training grounds. No reports of weapons manufacturing facilities, research bunkers, or even hangar bays, save for the ground vehicle storage of reasonable size." Kestra shifted their stance. "At least on the surface. We were unable to dig further."

Nara pressed a finger over her lips, leaning into the projection. "I am willing to bet that there won't be any."

A pensive silence fell over the officers, the gentle hum of the projection acting as a soundtrack for their thoughts. Glowing yellow lines sketched over the continent, connecting each highlighted base with strands of travel possibilities.

Jav'ril swiped a finger over the globe, enabling a filter that displayed the foliage covering the earth. Green dots of glitter sprayed over the image. Population densities and colonies of the common flora illustrated the landscape. The warlord analyzed the structures, emitting a hum of intrigue. "I agree. Life signs of major forestry appear undisturbed. You know exactly what Abberon is aiming for, don't you?"

"Absolutely." Kestra nodded.

The poor, defenseless refugees need to be saved from the violent despots controlling the government. Nara let a scoff out of her nose. *Go and cry for help from bigger fish.*

"Then our priorities haven't changed," Jav'ril agreed. "Expect little resistance."

The officers in the room nodded in agreement.

"All teams are on standby," Kestra reported. "I am sending everyone signals to the secured communication channels. Team leaders will give updates on operations as needed."

"Understood." Nara fastened her armor badge on her throat, initiating the command to cover her. "Good luck to all. The first sign of trouble, evacuate. We are running on a lot of assumptions."

"Agreed. Over and out." Kestra disappeared from the congregation, along with all supporting officers. Only Jav'ril remained, looking down at Nara with expressed concern.

"You really should not be down there." Their voice hinted at a soft plea. "Far too much is at risk."

She cast the remark aside, configuring settings on her HUD. "A leader needs to provide support."

"An advisor needs to be kept out of danger," they countered, folding their arms sternly. "Or else their wisdom is lost to generations."

Nara hesitated, the warlord's caution grating against her nerves. "That is not who I am."

"I know." The warlord bowed before their avatar flickered away. "Please be careful. Jav'ril out."

The breeze caressed her cheek as she stared out beyond her modest encampment in the woods. She tried to ignore the warlord's warning while she fidgeted with the shelter, attempting to redirect her irritation with the controls. After a few choice obscenities, the tent snapped into itself, reducing to a pocket-sized card before dropping in the weed-coated earth. She fished it out from hiding and placed it in a compartment in her armor.

Her armor guided her with prickled palms as she climbed a tree to survey the horizon, taking in the fortress below her. The HUD enhanced her vision, greying out the foliage and saturating the base with amplified colors. A plain three-tiered domicile. No barricades, no obstructions, no patrols. Wide open.

Apprehension forced her to hesitate, and she dragged a finger across the screen, centering the map on a blinking waypoint nearly five thousand kilometers away. The coordinates Syf had given her. A pang of guilt teased at the back of her mind. She promptly shook it away, returning to the task at hand. *No point in dwelling on it. Come what may.*

##10.1##

KHUUL'REN STARED TOWARD THE HORIZON, watching the twinkling aircraft flutter across the sky. A sense of lacking cloaked his thoughts, dissatisfaction for his actions against the timeline. He thought he was entitled to at least a shred of vindication, but all that remained was a quiet glimmer of guilt, a numbness that overwhelmed.

A flicker lashed across his vision and a familiar heat seized his throat. And then it was gone. Like the times before. He looked at his shaking hand, squeezing it into a fist until the sensation left him. He leaned back on his desk, bracing his weight on the structure.

"*Loremaster?*" He turned to the voice, spotting Prism in the doorway, hands folded at their waist to suppress their apprehension. "Is everything all right?"

"Yes, *Chief.* I was just going over the last Council recordings before turning in." He summoned a warm smile, hoping to ease their concern.

Prism's expression turned morose, their gaze sinking. "Understood."

A sparkle of pride lifted *Loremaster's* spirits. The scribe was astute, but he should not have expected anything else from an officer personally appointed to this position.

"You do not need to worry. There is time," he assured.

They nodded meekly, raising their head to address him. "I am sorry. I do not have any more information on the human. I can't help but feel responsib—"

"Silence." He hushed softly, raising a hand. "You are not their keeper, only their teacher. We are in a tumultuous reality. Misfortune such as this is bound to happen."

"I know." Their shoulders sank and they let out a disappointed sigh.

"You should try to get some rest. There will be a lot of reports incoming this next cycle. *Savant's* work is just starting."

"Yes, *Loremaster.*" With a bow, they headed to the door. They turned to look over their shoulder, the words of well wishes dissipating from their lips as they spotted the aged librarian staring vacantly at a pair of books resting on the desk.

Prism knew the covers well, bindings ten generations old. *The Book of Immolation,* and *The Black Annals.* The only books forbidden to anyone except *Loremaster.*

Khuul'Ren met their prying eyes, and they quickly turned away, promptly leaving the aged librarian to his duty.

***

##10.2##

Mirrors melded into a liquid halo, wrapping its reflective embrace around Nara's body. She took a delicate step forward as they concealed her inside the trees, dipping her toes into a gap of leaves, taking care not to rustle the greenery. Her soft hesitation was only partially influenced by her apprehension.

The hangar bay attached to the citadel was wide open, revealing technicians performing their maintenance duties in the shining daylight. Pops of light and arcs of energy illuminated the room, showering the metal floors. Automated couriers zoomed around the warehouse, carrying components and tools to the workers on the trays on their backs.

Nara slipped into the warehouse, her gaze on the reflective surface of the floor. Light bent around her image and concealed her presence. Not even a distorted projection of her shadow matched her steps. Satisfied with her digital cloak, she traversed through the work room, listening to the shouts that competed with the mechanical hammering. Progress was nominal, commands issued to workers attuned to their tools. Empathetic care was taken when handling the machines, like a stable attended by individuals bonded to their animals.

Farewells crossed her ears from behind. A worker had finished their shift. Their nose was buried in a tablet, signing off for the night as they strolled into the locker room. Nara loomed over them, mimicking their footsteps like an invisible predator. They raised a hand to the door and yanked it open, giving her plenty of room to slither around.

Casual conversation burbled with the fall of pressurized water. Hissing steam fogged over her helmet as she tuned in. The lessons of that day's training, the new creations people had made, and how their new recruits were getting along.

Nara crept into the common grounds. Soldiers drifted idly by and discussed events from duties of the evening and their plans for the next rest cycle. Deeply personal tales of longing for their comrades beyond the neutral zone. Consolations and hopeful wishes lightened the spirits, giving a promising consolation to disheartened spirits. Assurance that these times will pass.

This is how the Ara'yulthr staged resistance. Waiting. No ill thoughts of the opposing faction, no discourse of sworn fealty. Just waiting.

"Cinder Team approaching your position, Legion Commander." The voice scratched inside her ear.

"Understood. Countermeasures at the ready." The motion of squadrons snapped her back to reality, and she found herself deeper into the complex.

This was perhaps the easiest infiltration she had ever done. No cameras, no need to hack into systems to gain access. No one on high alert. It was unnatural. Off. She was used to the technological monoliths of Arcadian research facilities, every employee trained to protect their secrets with their lives, their souls inconsequential to the cause.

Abberon functioned with similar demeanor, but he was also wise enough to not let his intent expose his morals. Everyone gave the benefit of the doubt. Greed was a foreign concept.

Her mind wandered as she climbed the stairwell to the command deck. The bright glow of the step markers brightened the metal walkways.

"Charges set, unloading in 3… 2… 1."

Tremors tore at the walls of the complex, a flash of lightning that licked through the metal in blinding tongues. Darkness engulfed the stairwell with an electronic sigh, the life signs of the station reduced to an eerie stillness.

"Communications locked down. All units reporting blackouts in all sectors."

The building blinked a dull warm glow in reaction to the interruption, emergency trails of light leading to the exits. Nara peeled herself off the wall, steadying her steps as she continued up. *And so it begins.*

Chaos took its toll on the inhabitants. A soldier burst through the doorway on the top of the stairs. She took the opportunity and leaped in, sneaking inside before the door slid shut.

Everyone was on guard, running back and forth through the complex, checking on their comrades' status and locations. Quick exchanges of concern quickly dispersed as everyone focused on their duty.

When everyone appeared calm and collected, the storm escalated.

Sunlight burst through in chaotic spotlights as sections of the hall punched open, deactivated by the strike team's brute force hacking. Soldiers swarmed inside, filing into the halls and surrounding the occupants. Shouts ordered the inhabitants, commanding calmness and to cease their flight. No weapons were raised at the defenders, and they met no resistance.

Nara crept around the commotion, sneaking through to the command center barracks, heading for the office of the local warlord. Strands of code bled through her fingertips as she pressed a hand on the door. The barrier dissolved, revealing a seated figure behind a modest computer desk.

The mirrors dissolved around her face as she stepped inside, revealing herself to them.

The warlord calmly stood, regarding the intruder with neutral temperance. "I was told to expect you."

"I am certain of that," she replied, keeping watch over their every motion, her steps slow and meticulous.

"I do not believe we have had a formal introduction," they stated. "I am Warlord Ha'kar. It is good to meet you in person."

"The same." The burn formed in her throat, an evocation of the past reeling through her brain. She forced it aside, clearing the bile with a soft cough. *There is no time for that.*

Ha'kar was part of the old regime, present in the proceedings of her banishment. While she had no recollection of their opinions, she had fought against them several times in the games. A worthy adversary. Calculated, efficient, patient. They were known for playing the long con in a test of endurance, often starving the opposition. But despite their resilience, they had never won against her.

"Area secured. Units are on standby until further notice," the legion commander reported in her network.

"Cinder team on standby. Target secured. Secondary and tertiary teams headed for next objective. No opposition."

"Torrent Team secured. Minor opposition, no casualties. Area secured."

Nine more reports flooded in. The sit-in was complete. Silence whirled between the two contenders, motive and uncertainty hiding within the void of each other's masked intent.

"It appears you have me at a disadvantage," Ha'kar finally said. "And I must say I am surprised the Council agreed with such a disruptive operation."

"The Council is not involved with this operation," she replied. There was no harm in revealing that.

They tilted their head curiously. "Is that true?"

Tremors began to shatter her bones, and a sweltering sickness pulled at her brain. She pushed it all away, focusing on the warlord's guarded movement, their impartial expression. "I am here as a separate envoy. This standstill has gone long enough."

"I am inclined to agree with you." They nodded. "*Despite* your reputation. What do you propose?"

"I am establishing a meeting in a neutral zone." She leaned against the wall, taking in the warlord's apparent amicable tone. "There I will be listening to your concerns regarding the reintegration of your parties to the community."

The warlord considered her words, stepping around their desk. They began to circle. Quiet utterances of contemplation scratched against the tense silence. After several laps, they paused and looked up at Nara, rubbing their chin pensively. "And if I refuse?"

"Then your voice in the negotiations will not be considered."

Before the warlord could formulate a response, a black shadow cast over the outside world. A magnificent nothingness swallowed the sun. The glint of the trees ceased, dulled to nothing as the shroud engulfed the horizon.

The warlord turned and peered toward the sky, watching as the magnificent form of the *Armored Wake* pierced through the orbital cloud. A cacophony of shrieks and cries resonated through the foliage as creatures burst from hiding, stampeding from the distressing shift in solar rhythm. The battleship edged forward, its nose breaching through the gas cloud to watch over the proceedings.

"Tosk here," a voice cut into Nara's helmet. *"Awaiting orders."*

"Just as resourceful as I remembered." Ha'kar smirked. "Very well. I consent to these discussions."

"I look forward to hearing your concerns." She bowed and exited the room, turning her back to the warlord. She hesitated, waiting for the officer to seize the opportunity. But nothing had struck her exposed weakness. The warlord did not move, just watched, analyzed her expressions, her posture. Their eyes remained on her as she left the room.

Cold electricity shuddered over her spine as the door slid behind her. She met the eyes of the captive soldiers, sensing apprehensive confusion laced with a soft hint of fear. They all regarded her, hushed whispers of their fate tracing pleas over the walls. Speaking about her in wary tones.

Sleepless.

Eternal Red

Fevered.

She halted in her step, turning to the averted faces that spoke of her. A chill seized her heart, a resigned numbness from the titles she carried. She could only address their concerns with a soft nod, ignoring the futility of arguing against their impressions of her. With a sigh, she removed her presence from their stares to meet with the legion commander of the strike team.

"Everything is in order here, *Savant*," they reported, checking over their communications. "What now?"

"Convene with the rest of the units. Make sure the warlords are secured," she ordered. *"Tosk, arrange transports to pick the commanding officers up. We will be arranging a meetup shortly."*

"Understood."

She switched the communication signal to text mode, the faces of the hopeful soldiers still staring at her.

>>*Make sure you stay in orbit. With the high-ranking officers on board, those on the surface will be acceptable losses. Ensure that no one can strike without getting through you.*

>>*Xannat's favor, Savant.*

* * *

##10.3##

HIS CHEST OPENED with an explosive pulse, and he voraciously consumed the chilling air in ragged gasps. Before his awareness came to him, his hands slammed against the metal floor, the rest of his body tangling in a frantic mess. Tearing pangs gnawed on every muscle, the searing intensifying with each sudden movement. He blinked rapidly inside the confinement, but only ink coated his vision.

Bolstering his mettle with a pained whimper, he slid up to one knee. When the waves of dizziness subsided to a mellow roar, he attempted to rise to his feet. But the slightest pressure on his other ankle sent him back to the ground in a crumpled mess. Bone lashed against flesh, screaming at him in agonizing twangs. Sweat beaded down his skin as his body pain lashed out.

He gritted his teeth and crawled along the floor until his fingers brushed against the cooling touch of a barrier, then pulled himself up on his good leg. With a gasp, he released the wall, a sudden terror sending chills along his arm. The sensation of the material consuming his body was still fresh in his mind.

He backed away and brushed the feeling aside, tuning in to his surroundings. The silence proved unyielding, but his persistence was desperate. A gentle hum in the distance spiked his heart rate. A shift in his surroundings raised a spasm of warning on his neck. He reached out a hand, only to brush against a wall that was not there before. Nerves shuddering against his spine, he promptly turned about-face…

And smacked into another wall.

That wasn't here. That. Wasn't. There! With his perception of reality toying with his senses, he groped his way along the barrier. A blurt of surprise left his throbbing chest when he turned again, the seam of a corner startling his timid fingers. Another wall. He took a step back and…

CRACK, his back slammed against another wall. He flailed his arms forward, the shriek of friction grazing his knuckles. The air began to heat around him as his confines shrank around him. He was trapped inside a coffin just barely large enough for him to stand.

No. No. No. No. No. No. No. Please. His panting intensified, the throngs of pain dissolving into adrenaline-induced panic. He frantically pushed against the room creeping toward him from every direction. "STOP!"

The walls softened to a viscous goo, engulfing his arms with a nauseating slurp. Having forced his strength against the constrictive barrier, he slipped and flung forward. Clouds of light burst in his head as he smacked it against the wall. The cooling sensation of blood dripped over his skin, his senses fading in a whirlwind of disorientation. With a pleading sob, he leaned back, pulling against the ravenous material. The more he fought, the tighter it sealed, swiftly calcifying around his flesh.

Sobs rang into his ears while the desperation magnified, the unyielding cold metal resisting every struggle. He could not sense the disturbance in his pocket, the reverberation clicking against the air.

POP!

An invisible orb of energy carved out a perfectly smooth hollow in the pervasive walls, relinquishing their grasp on him with a violent hiss. With a cry, he yanked his arms away, hugging himself as tears streamed down his face.

The walls crept in, threatening to consume his entire body. He flailed an arm forward, keeping his vitals safe from the vile contaminant. It greedily accepted the offering, snapping over his forearm within its unrelenting embrace. A sickening *CRUNCH* echoed inside the chamber as the material cinched closed with a snap.

A primal scream escaped his chest, resonating in his ears. His spirit floated to the ceiling, watching his body down below as it became engulfed in the murk. The ooze slid up his chest to the discordant pop and crackle of bone. The pain was distant, yet unnervingly surrounding him.

With another pulse inside his pocket, the walls violently released their hold. He rejoined his body and crumpled in a puddle of sweat, the sobs intensifying as his mortality loomed over his shivering form.

The NetComm remained vigilant, unleashing a consistent rhythm of vibrations against the creeping walls. A bubble of ethereal magic surrounded him. Tangles of code enveloped his being and functions tore at functions, classes dissolving as variables became lost in the ether. At his back he felt the stir of loose soil, the nourishing earth warming his senses.

His head swirled at the pain. How did he get here? A person. Hood. Gaunt face. Violet Eyes. Moon Scar. *Who?*

The room was spinning faster and faster. Agony seized his consciousness. A rustling clamor barely registered in his ears.

Distorted voices. Footsteps. The pounding of boots above him.

"Heh—"He attempted to cry out. "I…"

Thunder rattled his core. The bubble surrounding him swelled with a fervent tenacity, pummeling skyward. He could feel the walls strain against the force, threatening to crush him in its wake. Warm air rushed to meet him. With a final thrust, the room burst into a dull haze of soft yellow. Crumbles of earth rained down on him, pattering against his bruised flesh.

The voices intensified, shouts in languages he could not comprehend. The sky rumbled as footsteps hastened to him.

The light.

##10.4##

NARA SAT atop the highest tower of the compound, legs dangling over the edge as she gazed out to the horizon. The artificial night cast by the *Wake's* shadow blanketed the forest with an eerie calm. Even the insects took notice of the tension in the air, the stillness only disrupted by the hesitant breeze circulating over the trees.

"*Message to Savant. Direct,*" the quadrant's Legion Commander summoned in her ear.

"Send."

"*Objective secured,*" They reported. "*Heading for the nearest infirmary.*"

"Status?"

"*Critical. Unconscious, several broken bones. Fevered and delirious.*"

"Where were they?"

"*Underground in a makeshift bunker. No other personnel on site.*"

That was not a comforting thought. "Anything else to report?"

"*They were repeating a strange phrase.*"

"Which was?"

"*Moon Scar.*"

Her jaw clamped shut. *Torel.*

"*Savant?*"

"Keep me updated on status. I have something to take care of."

"*Acknowledged.*"

This ends now. She propelled off the tower, sliding an armored hand against the pillar to guide her descent. Fallen leaves flew up into the air as she landed, whisked away by the breeze. *If they know, I will find them.*

Revelry met her ears as she slipped back into the tower. The mess hall was brimming with an assortment of scents, stews and roasts charring over chemically fueled fires. Apprehension seemed to have disappeared as she traveled down the ranks, plates of food and flagons of drink passed around the collective. With the laughter and comradery clamoring above the clatter of utensils, it was hard to decipher who was on which side of the conflict.

She spied her target feasting with the crew and approached. "Commander."

"Yes, Savant?" They stood to their feet and acknowledged her with a polite bow, their smile adding to the warmth of the scenery.

"Summon a team of your best fighters and hackers and meet me in the hangar bay."

"Yes, *Savant.*" The tension elevated slightly. Faces hid inside drinking vessels while the officer hastily left to complete their task.

She could feel their unease radiating off them as they regarded her. What about her set them off? Being the figurehead of the operation? The gruesome colors their leaders had painted her? Or her questionable mental stability? Regardless, her actions mattered little to their established impressions.

The corners of her mouth raised in a gentle smile and her eyes softened as she regarded each and every one of those who displayed their apprehension. With a bow of her head, she turned and left the room, their caution fading behind her.

It doesn't matter. She let off an exhausted sigh as she headed for the hangar bay.

"Savant," Tosk hailed from her radio.

"Yes?"

"We have a problem."

She looked out the open hangar bay, the shadows covering the earth bombarded by glitches of blinking lights. In the sky, the impressive form of the *Armored Wake* was haloed with bursts of scintillating colors. Pops of light flickered on and off, setting the battleship alight with spectral fireworks.

"GaPFed ships have breached our airspace," Tosk reported.

Shit. "Who has command over the fleet?"

"As of right now, no one. Command hierarchy does not cross between battleships."

"Congratulations, you are now fleet commander." She sent them up a data file. "Keep them at bay and send transport to these coordinates. Use orbital if the other ships aren't listening. I'll be in touch when I am ready for pickup."

"Affirmative." Tosk hesitated, the silence speaking a thousand words. *"Stay safe."*

And the players begin to show their hands. Nara scowled. A party of six jogged up to greet her, and she stormed into the awaiting plane. "Squad. Inside."

The soldiers filed in as she slid into the pilot seat. She entered the coordinates to her destination into the automated pilot and sank back, letting everyone settle before guiding the craft out of the hangar.

The internal computer carried the conversation as it initialized takeoff procedures. The tension inside the cockpit heated with the fuel intake. She evaded their questioning glances, watching the bow of the *Armored Wake* migrate from view.

She was not looking for justification for her actions. After all, her personal feelings had a motivation. Exactly what they would expect out of her. Right and wrong were always shifting, and given the fluidity of motivation, she hardly had the strength to feel guilty for forcing her hand on society. She owed the world nothing, but it owed her flesh. However, she was far too exhausted to cash in. *The sooner I fix this, the sooner I leave.*

The craft eased down to the earth, hovering toward a large greenhouse. She barely let the vehicle touch the ground when she stood and marched for the opening bay doors. The crew followed behind as she jumped down to the soil, the craft exhaling a swirl of coolant around them.

Would they expect it? Probably. She pointed at the estate's front entrance. "Blackout team, secure the compound."

Two of her support units charged at the building, setting up a base at the near corners of the property. The buried instruments into the soil, calibrating their machines to the estate's primary computer. Nara did not give them the time to finish their operations and stormed to the front door.

Something stirred within her. A driving force slammed her fist into the door. The ache rocketed up through her bones, the strike grounding her for the task ahead. With a pop and a fizzle, the electronic locking system submitted to her demands, obediently sliding away to reveal Councilor Torel.

While they expected her, the sheer force of will that radiated beyond her stony expression sent them back with a jolt. Her presence boiled the atmosphere.

"*Savant.*" Torel cleared their throat, stiffening to compose themself.

"This is a Coup. You are under arrest." The strike team filed in behind Nara, fanning out to secure the entryways.

Torel inspected the troops. A faint hum of irritation expelled from their throat. "I see."

"Do you have anything you wish to say?"

"No." They folded their arms tersely. "You were going to do what you wished, no matter the opposition. Let's get this over with."

Nara nodded to two of the soldiers, who returned the gesture and walked over to the councilor. They took Torel by the arms and ushered them out of the complex, leading them up the ramp of the aircraft.

Torel paused midstep. "*Savant.*"

Bitterness kept her from replying, and she could only glare at the councilor's exposed back.

"I hope they returned to you safely. It was not my intent to bring them harm. I was naïve." Upon their admission, Torel resumed their climb and entered the vehicle.

Her skin seared as the plane ascended. The admission of guilt sent pangs through her jaw. Their hypocrisy ignited a spark that was once extinguished. She was used to dealing with human intent, and she hadn't foreseen unearthing it on home ground. But obsessing over it would do no good. Not now. The deed was done, and she had a choice to make.

A ray of light showered her from above, breaking apart the shadows of the watchful capital ship. She looked up to the transport vessel from the *Armored Wake* gliding down to meet her. With a hiss, it gently touched the surface and opened its doors, revealing Commander Tosk at its helm.

"Awaiting your entry, *Savant*."

##10.5##

THE COMMAND DECK of the *Armored Wake* was a beautifully crafted machine that projected efficiency with the highest level of modern technology. On the observation platform, Nara watched the movements of the migrating fleet, her arms folded in disdain. The viewscreen displayed the glittering backdrop of space, disrupted by the pack of GaPFed ships encroaching on their territory.

The foreign fleet drifted with a careful slink, their haunches coiled, their fangs bared. The Alpha of the pack was a sizeable capitol ship, the rigid geometric maw sniffing out the area with its numerous sensory fangs. Frigates and bombers glided within their leader's reach, their engines blazing against the starlight with a menacing glow.

"Commander," the communications officer reported from their station. "We are being hailed."

"Put them on screen," Tosk replied.

The panels of the observation post warped, colors shifting to reveal a human adorned with armored regalia, a plated uniformed suiting decorated with a vast collection of bars and badges.

"This is Admiral Rothgar of the GaPFed High Command." The officer's eyes scanned over the *Wake's* bridge crew, her uncertainty reflecting in augmented neon eyes. "We have come in aid of the refugees seeking asylum from the current government in power. Cease your assault and present the captives immediately."

"You are interrupting delicate negotiations between two factions here." Nara let her scorn slip from her tongue. "Leave our airspace at once."

The Admiral was not moved by the order. "To whom am I speaking?"

"I am *Savant* Elam'Mutavreh of the Council of the Past, current residing power over the World Council on Homeworld." She glanced down at her nails. "I believe your federation is familiar with my name."

"Indeed." Rothgar exchanged glances with her assisting commanders. "Your faction is in violation of—"

"You are disrupting peace talks between both factions." Nara cut her off. "I am not going to repeat myself again. Your presence is not needed, nor is it welcome."

"Distress signals tell me otherwise," Rothgar snapped, her lip curled into a snarl. "If you do not comply, we will have no choice but to take action."

Nara bared her fangs with a grin, shifting her stance and releasing a welcoming gesture out to the admiral. "Try me."

Tosk nodded to their technician, who turned to conduct a symphony of lights on the dashboard. The *Armored Wake's* hull warmed to a smoldering glow as a scintillating cloud of swirling teals and creams warped over the metal. The material collected at the bow, extruding into a concentrated central beam. The tip swelled into a white-hot magma orb, expanding out of the ship and threatening to consume all in its path. The ship's status alerts chimed into the command deck.

SYSTEMS REROUTING. STAND BY FOR DISCHARGE.

A devastating howl ramped within the bridge, the war cry shuddering the viewscreen as the immense flow of energy coursed through the ship. The orb outside suddenly burst apart, spreading out a net of energy spanning four times the width of the *Wake*. Swirls of energy warmed space with their protective blanket.

The neighboring ships followed suit, turning to face the oncoming GaPFed ships and launching their shields to protect their flock within their wings. Ships repositioned themselves around the planet's artificial gaseous forcefield, the edges of each net joining in glowing seams around orbit.

From within the gas cloud surrounding the habitable core, the automated systems ignited the air. Scores of glittering satellites formed their own barrier, a secondary line of defense burning just outside the atmosphere.

"*Homeworld to Wake,*" a voice announced by the coms. "*Planetary shielding initialized from surface stations. Standing by for further instruction.*"

The final layer revealed itself. Colossal beams of glowing pink burst between the corners of each net, the columns as thick as the *Wake's* main hull. It fed its energy into the fleet's shielding, amplifying its intensity and sending the web alight with fire.

A sly grin etched over Nara's face, watching the GaPFed representative's awestruck expression at the display. "Do you have anything else you wish to bring to my attention, Admiral?"

"Your instigation of violence is unwarranted," Rothgar protested, snapping her gaze back to Nara. "We will not leave until the refugees are safely within GaPFed custody."

"Then you will be waiting. Once we have established our new treaty, we will be willing to discuss matters within." Nara stepped forward, widening her stance. "A group of representatives will be in contact with a proposal of demands. Please use this time to deescalate tensions and approach us with neutral intent. We are not interested in war. Elam out."

CHAPTER 11

##11.0##

One fire at bay. For now. Nara exited the transport vehicle and headed for her apartment in the lab. *The discussion can wait a single fucking day so I can get some sleep.*

She caught Fariem's eyes as she entered. The researcher averted their gaze, sensing her displeasure and weariness. The last few nights took a toll on everyone's nerves, and she was grateful for the peace. She did not have the strength to hide her exhaustion from them, anyway.

"They're in the third room down the hall," they called to her.

She stopped in her steps, the information scrambling her mental process. The human was far away from her immediate thoughts, and she hadn't even considered him since the attack. He was dropped on Fariem's doorstep to deal with, but apparently, she was not absolved of responsibility.

"Right." She raised a hand to the security system of her apartment, only to feel a warm sensation nagging at the back of her head. The burn emanating from Fariem's judgmental glare.

"Fine. I will see if they need anything." She hurled a sigh and meandered to the infirmary.

Garrett was lying on his back in the hospital bed, his eyes fixated on the ceiling which was projecting a swirling galaxy. Millions of stars glittered above, the scene taken from reference photos that orbital drones captured.

Sensor cuffs were wrapped around his arms and legs. Strips of lights murmured the progression of cell regeneration. His chest was coated in silver bands, the cool tones contrasting against the sickly patches of bruises covering his bare skin.

"Hey." Nara leaned against the doorway, her legs starting to give her warning twangs of their depleted energy.

"Mmm," he managed to mutter, his eyes never leaving the twinkling stars of the digital display.

"Fariem been tending to you?"

He blinked and suddenly snapped his gaze to her. "Are you going to war?"

She stared at him, the words struggling to manifest in her throat. His mental state came into question, unsure of how conscious Fariem permitted him to be. "I… stoked quite a few fires. It is possible."

"Why?"

The point-blank question stabbed her with pointed knives. To have the gall to ask the galaxy to stop turning, to change people within an instant. Her anger got the better of her, voice studded with razors. "Are you *that* naïve?"

Silence responded. Not even a wince.

She clenched her knuckles, forcing her eyes shut. The torrent swirling around her brain teased at her senses, and she focused her mind on calming the storm.

"Why do you have to make the call?" His voice was vacant, soft, yet weighted. "People can take care of it."

"How *dare* you?" Pulses of her internal rhythm broke off in concussive beats. The storm raged, despite her best efforts, her nerves quaking as the human's words reverberated across her ears. "You would have had the same power if you didn't waste your time prancing around Undercity. How many lives would have been in your hands?"

"I—"

"And you *fucking ran away from it.*" She gave him no quarter in his fragile state, cutting him down to shreds. "You ask *me* how well I sleep at night, but how can you fathom shirking that responsibility? *Coward.*"

"*Leave.*" The warning hissed out of his lips, but his expression remained distant.

The violence wreaking havoc in her systems fogged her vision, her nails digging furrows of skin within her quaking fists.

"Fine." She swallowed the acid etching her throat and stormed out, slinging a venomous glare at Fariem lurking near the doorway.

When stillness had returned, Fariem stepped inside, picking at the machinery monitoring Garrett's condition.

"You heard every word," Garrett grumbled. The medic made no acknowledgement. "Well, go on. Please tell me how much of a vile creature I am."

"There is no concept of good and evil here." They ran their fingers over their tablet, checking the dosage of the herbal remedies saturating his veins. "Just people saying and doing objectionable things with varying degrees of intent."

"Really, now?"

They glided to a burner at a workstation. "Tea?"

"You going to poison it?" He eyed them suspiciously.

"Don't tempt me, meat bag," they scolded as they prepared a healing concoction, souring the atmosphere with the scent of bitter herbs. After pouring the steaming pale broth into a drinking vessel, they opened a collection of jars, spooning in an assortment of syrups and gelatinous blobs. With the elixir complete, they handed the vessel to him.

What does Elam see in this individual? They watched intently as the human examined the mixture, tilting their head curiously.

Garrett furrowed his brow at the scrutiny. "Is there something I can help you with?"

"*Just as stubborn as Elam,*" Fariem murmured with a smirk.

"Pardon?"

"Do you want something to help you sleep?" they offered, pulling out more jars from the cabinet. "Perhaps something to clarify your thoughts when you wake up?"

Garret exhaled, feeling the pull of the medical garments against his skin. "Sure. Just fuck me up."

"Therapeutic fornication is not my field of study," Fariem chastised, setting a tray down with a collection of salves and gauzes. "Neither is it recommended in your condition.

"That's not—"

"I *am* aware." They let a smirk shine through and rolled a stool next to the bed.

A tenuous solace began to waft the tension from the room, dotted by the clicks and sloshes of Fariem's diligent hands picking through their concoctions. They let the human settle and set to work on a pain management regimen, mixing a rainbow of oils inside a small dish.

Satisfied with the texture, they added a clear balm into the mixture, binding it to a useable paste. They took a dry cloth and dipped the material in, then began to brush the human's affected areas. No reaction from their work, no jolts or winces from the pain.

"Fariem?" His voice was gentle yet lacked a spirit at the core.

"Yes, Garrett?"

"What does it all mean?"

They ceased their work, cleaning up the materials and setting them aside. The human was distraught, their world shattered before them. It was cruel to feed into their despair, no matter their opinions of them. "Go to sleep, Ahm'Xant."

"Yes, Fariem."

The medic dimmed the lights to a soothing warm glow before exiting the room, pausing to regard the human. With a head shake, they left to return to their duties.

A soft hum of wind protected Garrett from the thoughts of isolation, the artificial ambience a comfort. Pain from his shattered bones had subsided thanks to Fariem's treatment, but the events had left a mark over him. Alone in the dark. No doors, no windows. Entombed in the earth for only the Fates knew what purpose.

He picked up the gaseous froth Fariem set aside for him, taking a delicate sip. It was a sharp, fruity tang, the effervescence scraping against his taste buds. It was easy to swallow despite the conglomeration of textures, the soft herbs dancing in a melody of citrusy delight.

The experience of his internment was difficult to process. Motivation was an enigma. Human logic did not apply here. Nara was right. He was a sheltered individual. The thought of war terrified him, but he had to admit, he could not comprehend what the word truly meant.

He was protected from the struggles of Under and Uppercity, the terrorist strikes a thousand miles away. But the news reports always framed them the same way. Bodies and fires smoking in the lowest pits of civilization. Articles proclaimed a hopeless future. The actions and lives taken could not have been avoided.

The war games played here reflected a similar theme. Bombs exploding, people suffering in grievous conditions. He was terrified at how close he was to this magnitude of destruction. And yet, reality was different here, an almost overbearing sense of empathy that kept them from destroying populations with a single button press.

He could feel the concoction stir inside him, pulling his brain into a slog. His eyelids began to weigh down on him.

Does any of it even matter?

He blinked, the glow of the nightlights saturating his brain. The descent of gravity toyed with his body while the inebriation pulled him down. Shadows played inside his vision, a presence creeping up to his side. Quiet.

Ice pressed against his wrist, a fluttering of fingers. His slurred mind grasped at the familiar shape of his NetComm, attached to his wrist with a pristine new band. He blinked, trying to mold the light into something comprehensible.

"You…" His brain refused to connect to his voice.

The invader hesitated, regarding him with a familiar devious smile. With a blink, they were gone.

##11.1##

BLOOD BOILED UNDER HER SKIN, the day's events crushing her beneath a boulder of futility. Her knuckles were sheet white as she cinched the carton in her hands, the liquid violently sloshing as she paced back and forth across her office.

No one gets to choose the die they are cast, she seethed. *Why should he?*

She tossed her head back and drained the carton, the liquid quenching the furnace inside her throat. With a snap of an arm, she launched the container at the wall, the degradable material hitting the metal with a dissatisfying *thwap.*

Another was awaiting her on the desk, one of many already consumed. She had lost count. Her habitual consumption from Arcadia bled into her subconscious. But she saw no need to stop, tearing off the seal of another with a fervent claw, then downing the contents in one ragged gulp.

She leaned against the desk, her unsteady hands braced against the surface. Despite the inebriation taunting her senses, her mood had not improved. Hatred began to seep in, destruction, resolution nowhere in sight.

The chemicals assailed her legs as she staggered toward the window, her ire amplified with each decaying step. She paused after three steps, the sensation in her muscles flickering with needles. Her foot met the ground, her pathetic fingers clawing at the air to catch her. The room swirled around her, lights fading with each slowed breath.

Her ankle caved beneath her as the floor tilted sharply. She made no attempt to catch herself, letting the lightning flash in her brain where her head landed.

Thunder pounded in her skull, threatening to drown her in a sea of hopelessness. She watched a glimmer of liquid stream out in front of her view. Red slowly dissolved into grey, the atmosphere pressing down on her.

What the fuck is the point?

##11.2##

GARRETT AWOKE FROM A DEEP, invigorating sleep, the last few hours of tumult outside his mental reach. A calming energy coursed through his muscles, the ache of his capture subsiding. He flexed his arms experimentally, finding the twang of movement had left him.

Huh. He carefully slid around, rising to a seated position. *Still nothing.*

Draping his legs over the gurney, he examined his ribs for evidence of the damage. With an awkward scooch, he lowered his leg until a toe scraped over the floor. Filling his lungs with a bracing draught of air, he gently shifted his weight on the damaged foot. He lifted his backside off the bed, releasing his breath as he took to his feet.

Vitality swelled around his body. An otherworldly sense of confidence filled him with determination. *I need to make amends.*

He walked through the complex and headed for the apartment, taking slow, meticulous steps to avoid additional damage to unhealed ligaments. The lab was quiet, no one around to inquire of his well-being or chastise him for moving.

He approached the apartment door, and an overbearing sense of dread tingled his scalp. There was a stillness inside, not unexpected. Nara thrived in silence. It was almost impossible to discern whether she was even at home.

But it wasn't the quiet that bothered him. A sensation. Warning alarms inside his subconscious.

He opened the door. The stillness magnified.

"Nara?" he called out. Nothing. *Perhaps she isn't here.*

He warily climbed the stairs, discovering the door to Nara's office open. Bumps manifested on his skin as he neared. A trail of cartons traced a path deeper into the den. His eyes followed to find Nara's body, cold and listless, sprawled over the floor. Her eyes were open, staring listlessly ahead of her, a puddle of blood clinging to the cool metal ground.

"Nara!" He scrambled to her side, clawing at her unresponsive arm. "Hey, can you hear me?"

He waved a palm above her nostrils. She wasn't breathing. *SHIT! Oh, gods, No!*

"FARIEM!!!" Electricity jolted his heart as the situation dawned on him. He bolted to his feet and raced down the stairs, nearly tripping over himself as he sped into the lab. "FARIEM!!! HELP!"

The medic appeared through the hangar bay with a basket of freshly picked flowers. "Why is the squishy making so much noise?"

"Nara! It's—" His mind reeled at the possibilities jabbed at him. "Help, she's—"

"Where is she?"

He waved his hands frantically as he turned back, ushering Fariem through the apartment. They took one look at Nara's unresponsive form and sighed, extracting a device from their pocket.

"Old habits die hard." They shook their head, placing a metal plate over Nara's chest. With a snap, the device sprung coils of needles into her flesh. Fariem fidgeted with settings, the grids on the square display on its face fluctuating madly as it attempted to normalize her.

Nara's ribcage began to inflate, her eyelids flickering as the machine injected life force inside her. But her engine refused to catch, her breath a stagnant pattern of commands. The machine pulled the entire weight, sustaining her with air.

From behind, the two assistants entered the room, eyes wide with exasperation.

"Serr, if you please," Fariem ordered the duo, who obediently carried her off. Garrett followed closely while they settled her into a new medical room. He watched intently as they hooked machinery and computers into her skin. Barbs and pipes invaded every space of exposed flesh, some injecting liquids, some removing. The sounds rattled his nerves, mechanical energy replacing the very essence of life itself.

Fariem extracted a silver-barbed tube from a computer, placing it on Nara's forearm. The object burst apart in a multitude of springs, snaking its way into her veins. The machine warbled in a hum as toxicity reports streamed from the interface monitor.

"Should have expected that again, sooner or later," Fariem tsked.

"Is she—" He did not dare finish the thought.

They dismissed his concern with a hum. "That is entirely up to her. She's been through a lot, and it is only a matter of time before it consumes her."

The last words with her were those of ire. Guilt began to overwhelm him. *Not like this.*

"You have psychiatrists here, don't you?" The words were almost pleading. "Can't you do anything about her mental state?"

"Not without her permission."

"Surely, you can—"

"*OUT OF THE QUESTION.*" The medic's snarl jolted Garrett back. They saw the fear in the human's eyes, sheer panic racing across their thoughts. Embarrassed by the show of aggression, Fariem cleared their throat. "I am sorry. But that is not how it works here. All we can do is wait."

"I don't..." But before he could finish his plea, Fariem and the assistants wordlessly left him alone. He looked back at Nara's body, wanting to leap out of his skin to try to send a piece of his own soul to save her. Perhaps he had asked for too much.

It is only a matter of time.

CHAPTER 12

##12.0##

Eons have passed. Her flesh had been taken over by the warming embrace of the rocky soil, her armor melded with the fossils that existed before her. Blossoms kissed her form, swaying gently in the breeze as they reached up to drink in the sun's healing glow. She was calm, but she could feel the storm approach.

The Wind and Rain appeared before her, a dance of civility whirling in the sky. Back and forth they clashed, blades glittering against the clouds. It was nearing. As time passed, the strife intensified, strikes craving more violent prizes.

Rain had been corrupted, darkened by an incomprehensible desire. Their cloak shifted to deep shadowy reds, enveloping the sky with its burning ambition. The earth mourned, the blossoms igniting in puffs of flame. Searing waves of heat rose to meet the sky. The soul of the world charred, dissipating from the bedrock below.

She watched as the ground became saturated with tears, salt eroding her skin. The heat bubbled away the remnants of her flesh, her nerves numb to the tremors beneath her. The sky was obstructed by plumes of smoke, smoldering orange cinders swirling within the clouds.

The noise intensified, escalating to a seismic clamor as the earth strained against its own torment. Cracks split in her ears, the earth writhing as it tore around her. The rock yawned, sending streams of emptiness in widening chasms speeding toward her. She was at the epicenter, the sutures pulling her apart until her bones separated. She watched the pieces drift out of sight, leaving her in a vacuum of space.

The cinders settled, cooling into a platter of pale starlight. The globe quaked and shifted, indiscernible voices rasping the air with heated intent. She watched as the world cracked, a jagged mouth splitting apart as tensions soared. Divides split the world asunder, each half repulsed by the other. Chunks of rock plummeted into the atmosphere as the struggle continued, steadily wasting the planet away.

Her fingers tore into the furrows, every mote of energy focused on her one true desire. She pulled the rock apart, letting the voices scream their protests as the stone shrieked. Magma vomited from the chasm, the bubbling froth spilling onto her flesh. Rock fragments melted through the stream, morphing into gaping holes, vacant eyes and mouths that voiced their malice. Her flesh melted away as the flow slithered up to her throat.

Her mouth spewed forth a bellow of malice. Her muscles strained as she heaved. With one final *CRACK* she tore the globe asunder. She hurled the pieces aside, letting them disappear into oblivion. A cackle echoed in the distance, a distorted mimicry of her own voice. Soon, it would be over.

##12.1##

LIGHT SEARED her brain as her crusted eyelids slowly peeled apart. Pain cinched them shut, waiting for the waves of ache to subside before allowing her to try again. The fragmented image her brain grasped told her she was in Fariem's infirmary. *Fucking hell.*

Her eyes moved to the ragged form of Garrett, his pallid face staring holes through the floor.

"You fucking snitch," she rumbled. With a groan, she turned her back to him, the electrolyte pumps bouncing playfully above her as she moved.

The movement startled him in his seat. "Nara! You're—"

"I'm *what?*" Her lip curled over her fangs. "*Alive?* Great. Wonderful."

Garrett slumped back in the chair, her icy tone filling him with despair. "I'm—"

"Spare me." She was in no condition to deal with the human's limited facets. Aches tampered with her mental state, her body bruised as if hit by a carrier truck. She was drained of all material fuel. And fucks to give.

But Fate was not willing to grant respite, the gentle chime of a call piercing through the torrent in her brain. She flicked the answer with a limp wrist, answering the summons with a suppressed growl.

"Tosk here. Are you well?"

She refrained from honesty. "Given the circumstances."

"I know you don't want to hear this, but Rothgar has been hailing us nonstop since your departure."

Of course she has. She winced as she sat up in the bed, plucking out each instrument from her skin. After dropping the bloody tangles over the side of the bed, she scrubbed her face, attempting to shake off the sickness clutching her guts. "I will be up shortly."

"Understood. Tosk out."

She slid off the gurney, never once meeting the human's pleading eyes. Her fingers rebelled against her as she walked over to the computer terminal to order a clean uniform from the servo. She tried her best to hide the wavering in her step, leaning heavily against the bedpost as she fidgeted with the clasps.

Breathing became a struggle, her muscles weakened by the struggle of keeping them inflated. She drank in several cleansing breaths, concentrating on her stance. When the fury pounding her head settled to a distant moan, she faced Garrett with piercing eyes.

"You are coming with me. You will make a decision about your future along the way."

##12.2##

G ARRETT LURKED BEHIND the closed door to the command center, listening to the proceeding through his NetComm. He did not have the time to enjoy the travel to the *Armored Wake*. The foreboding tones and unnerving silence left him trembling in a clutter of possibilities. A world was about to evolve violently, and he was an impartial observer to its transformation.

"Admiral Rothgar, I must protest at your insistence." Nara addressed the viewscreen, her posture rigid, her voice unshakable. "The delegation proceedings are currently in session. I have already told you we will speak once our internal treaties have been established."

The representative had no interest in her words, flashing a document on the screen for the *Wake's* crew to analyze. An arrest order from GaPFed High Command. "While the High Council is understanding of the situation on your planet, they are by no means willing to accept peace talks from a wanted war criminal. You are hereby ordered to surrender and answer for yourself at a designated GaPFed facility."

Garrett's eyes widened at the proclamation. *They can't possibly mean the incident on Arcadia?*

He examined Nara's expression, but the threat did not move her. The two leaders stared at each other, stoking fires of uncertainty between the two worlds. Finally, she raised her head, addressing the Admiral with a flat tone. "If I do, will you leave our airspace?"

There was hesitation on the Admiral's side. She searched through Nara's stony demeanor through a wary lens. "Fine. But only until discussions have been concluded. GaPFed will not tolerate terrorists running freely in our galaxy."

Your galaxy? *Arrogant cur.* It was a proposition meant to trap her. GaPFed's thirst for conquest was infamous even to Homeworld. Even if they were true to their word, who knew where she would land? But she was pursued by these forces every waking moment, if not from bounty hunters and governing warmongers, it was her own personal demons pressing her on. *I am so fucking tired.*

"Very well. I surrender to these terms." Her knees began to falter beneath her, and she raised a steadying hand to the control panel. "I will be alone on a transport. Send an escort to rendezvous at the coordinates of your choice. Elam out."

Wait, what? Garrett blinked, unsure his ears discerned what she had said. The screen went black as the channel disengaged, denying him access to the remainder of the conversation.

Inside the bridge, Nara walked over to Tosk. "I delegate you to supervise the negotiations. If you are not comfortable speaking, call for the Past to bring a Scribe to engage on your behalf. Tell them it is ordered by me."

They regarded her solemnly, certain that she would not listen to protests. Only a soft wish, a disquieting sendoff. *"Xannat's* Favor, *Savant."*

"And to you." She nodded and departed the bridge. The door slid open, revealing Garrett's panicked befuddlement staring back at her. Wordlessly, she passed him by, heading down to the hangar bay.

He bolted up and sprinted at her heels, barely able to keep pace as the world around him started to crumble. "What is going on?"

She did not stop to address him, calling out to the air. "Tosk will assist your departure. He knows Trade, but if you prefer someone familiar to interpret, Prism or Bellanar should be available by NetComm."

A vessel awaited her with open jaws. The stammering mental process of the human behind. She didn't know what she was about to do, and in the end, she didn't care. The fight was long and devastating. It would be a relief to see it end.

She stepped up the ramp of the vehicle, only to be stopped by a stifled sob. She closed her eyes. Breathe in, breathe out. The wisps centered her focus. Everything would be fine. She turned to address Garrett, a sardonic smirk twitching a corner of her mouth. "Guess those consequences caught up to me."

"Wait, you can't just... how long are you..." The vehicle door raised, sealing the answers behind its cold grasp. A hiss of steam swallowed his form as the ship elevated, gliding toward the bay doors.

His mind reeled as his world crumbled around him, heart aching with the indescribable loss. Something inside him snapped, and he found himself gasping for air. He chased after the transport, watching in disbelief as the craft sped out into the stars, a boom of engine wash shuddering across the deck. *She's gone. I can't just... someone help. Anyone. This can't be happening.*

Translators. Two choices. Who would possibly help?

He raised his wrist to his face, frantically pressing buttons until the signal connected. The reception barely registered before he shouted into the speaker. "Bellanar! Are you there? I need you."

"Of course, Garrett. What is the matter?" The sound of his voice sent reassuring waves across the channel.

"It's Nara. She's been captured by GaPFed and—" The admission choked out his words. He pushed back the tears with a chain of sharp inhalations. "And I don't know if she is coming back."

"Understood. It's going to take me a minute to get the ship back." He slung a string of obscenities, the sound of clattering metal behind him. "It's been impounded."

"We don't have a—"

Bangs drowned out his response, the noise ceasing with an agreeable electronic beep. A whirr of wakening machinery replaced the clamor. "Oop! There we go. Heading your way."

Please hurry, Garrett pleaded. *I don't know what I will do without her.*

CHAPTER 13

##13.0##

Guns were fixed on her from the very moment she stepped on the transport, her wrists bound by manacles. The expedition to the prison ship was grueling, fire creeping closer around the edges of her vision. The cold blinding white walls were no match for the churning inferno inside her. Concentration decayed as she was led down the corridor. Unable to keep track of her location, she could only focus on walking, one foot in front of the other.

Voices of the guards crackled around her, but the sounds did not knit into words. The flames licked at her ears.

"Why—security? Aren't they...."

"Can't take..." The corridor stretched out to oblivion, twisting before her eyes. An endless march to an unknown end. *"...explosions. Lots of lives—"*

Sickness swirled her senses, the waves of nausea magnifying with each second of her resistance. She had been here before. The shackles, the collar. The anger.

"... holding—for..... wait.....—xecution..."

Breathe.

"Sir...?" In. Out. In. Out. *"What should we—"*

The shackles tightened around her wrists, a jolt of static chastising her hesitation. Her jaw clamped shut, the blaze coursing through her veins. An insatiable hunger tore at its restraints.

"Hah." A jagged grin contorted her lips, the light flickering between a spectrum of emotion. Her mind was slipping away. Losing control. She clawed at her consciousness, grasping at the fleeting sensation of her body.

I can't. Not here.

A cackle shattered across the halls. The scent of prey released fear into the atmosphere. Three hearts. *Blood.*

Is this where you want to end? Are you willing to…

… juST….Let iT…….ALL…

…*BURN…*

##13.1##

"Do you have something with human tech on it?" Garrett's fingers were a blur of taps as he set up his hawking system over the NetComm. "I haven't learned enough of your systems to do anything useful."

"How about this?" Bellanar stepped out wearing the full uniform of a GaPFed security enforcer. Intimidation was certainly an aspect of the sleek design, but the man's stature amplified it tenfold. By Ara'yulthr standards, he was not a particularly strong individual, but the uniform demanded respect and exuded power.

Garrett eyed him up and down, startled by Bellanar's resourcefulness. "Where did you get that uniform?"

"Don't ask incriminating questions." He tsked, brushing the sleeves of his uniform. "I should be able to get a connection to the helmet."

The GaPFed prison ship rumbled beneath them, the engines of the behemoth churning with a course correction. They sat comfortably inside the pilot fish craft they requisitioned, docking clamps sunk into the hull to hitch alongside.

"You sure they can't see us?" Garrett scanned the viewscreen nervously, watching the bay door of the GaPFed ship.

Bellanar nodded emphatically. "They have no idea we are here."

"If that is the case, how did you get caught?"

"I ran out of battery and couldn't put the shield back up." The man scratched his neck sheepishly.

Garret rubbed his forehead and walked toward the cockpit, checking the fuel cell levels. *Now would not be a good time for that to happen again.*

"Don't worry, we will be fine! Trust me!" Bellanar flipped his helmet over his face, sealing himself from the air around him. *"Off I go!"*

He sauntered off to the airlock, leaving Garrett with an astonished expression. A jaunty tune frolicked inside the helmet, joined in by the hiss of air pressure cycling. The hatch peeled open, and he emerged from the belly of the ship, his boots clamping down on the GaPFed ship's hull with a magnetized clunk. After checking the status of his artificial environment, he climbed up to the prison ship's escape hatch, toying with the settings of the key panel.

A beep of delight prodded his ear. *"Ah! There you are! So glad you worked it out."*

"Yeah. It's just a matter of refreshing my memory." Garrett connected his feed to the helmet's sensors.

"You should give yourself more credit." The door slid open, and Bellanar glided inside the ship's hold.

"Sure." He didn't know how to take the strange person's peppy outlook. He was used to Nara's bitter cynicism. The interaction made him slightly uncomfortable. "So, what's the plan?"

"Oh, nothing special." Bellanar checked the map he'd slyly coaxed out from the security system. *"Just act like I own the place."*

"I see."

Garrett watched the camera view as Bellanar passed the intersection. A glimmer of the man's reflection danced on the wall. The carefree bounce of the man's normal gait had disappeared, a blend of an officer's stiffened gait and a relaxed stroll replacing his movement. Soldiers passed him without alarm, a casual nod here, a salute there. Bellanar displayed his knowledge of human formalities, a perfect chameleon of espionage.

"Now." Bellanar paused and leaned against a wall, flipping through the map. *"If I were holding a high-priority prisoner, where would I put them?"*

"Somewhere with either constant surveillance," Garrett answered the rhetorical question, "Or something away from other prisoners."

"You guessed it!" A multitude of conversations popped into Bellanar's helmet, various security officers exchanging shifts and ordering resupplies. Several layers of treacherous signals tempted his prodding digits, a high-level administrator account required for access. With careful extraction, the barriers dissolved, revealing a particularly important notice from the Chief of Security to a select three senior officers:

>> *NOTICE OF HIGH PRIORITY. IMMEDIATE ACTION REQUIRED.*

>> *To: Senior Officers W. Truce, M. Acklar, V. Mesrin:*

>>*High-Profile Terrorist is en route to this station. Identity is on a need-to-know basis. You are to attend to them personally and rendezvous to the drop-off point.*

>> *Once secured, you and you alone are to put them in Special Containment Quadrant 3893B. Assume Code 67 to ensure no unauthorized personnel contacts prisoner. Failure to comply with these orders will result in immediate demotion and court martial.*

>> *X. Thorat, CoS*

BELLANAR HUMMED a pensive tune and tapped a finger at a void of space in the aft of the ship. A few strokes of tinkering later and leads from the encrypted messages procured, he acquired the proper credentials to reveal the containment center. *"Let us go the back way, shall we?"*

He made his way to the nearest service elevator and stepped inside. Another individual clad in similar armor quickly followed behind, sliding in before he could reach the call buttons. They exchanged a nod, and the guest looked at him expectantly. "Foundry."

The guard pressed the command along with their own destination, and the doors silently sealed them together. Uncertainty of protocol directed the conversation, the silence interrupted by soft shuffles of fabric as the two shifted in their steps.

"Uhh…" Garrett vocalized his nervousness, the proximity to an enemy person a foreign concept to him.

"*Don't fret over it.*" Bellanar turned to meet the guard's inquisitive scrutiny. "It is very rude to stare, my friend."

"How much did those lifts run you?" they blurted, unmoved by his remark.

"Beg pardon?"

"Those bio-lifts." They pointed a finger at his legs. "I bet you can reach the top valves with those."

"If I had a credit…" His tone salted with a sigh. "I was hired because of them. Back when I had insurance."

"That a fact?" They let out a chortle. "Like hell I would have expected GaPFed to pay for 'em. I've been on calls back and forth between twenty providers to replace my debunked kidneys. But there's always something, isn't there?"

"For sure." Bellanar shook his head empathetically. "I wish you a swift solution to your health problems."

The elevator slid open, the same sterile white walls as the floor above presented before them. "Ha! Here's hoping. You have a good one." They waved and exited, leaving his comrade behind.

"That could have gone a lot worse," Garrett said.

"*All you need is a little faith in Fate.*" Bellanar smirked. "*If you don't start anything, there won't be anything.*"

His journey came to a gliding halt as the elevator hurled out a chime. A gust of humid air curled inside the chamber as the elevator doors peeled open. Inside was an inferno of bustling machines, their mechanical chants illuminated by an ominous red glow. The environment of the entire ship depended on the clanging chorus, the hollow drone of the boiling engines adding their voice in the symphony of astrophysics.

"*There has to be some sort of access line,*" Bellanar chimed as he began to walk a perimeter around the room. He passed his fingertips over piping and insulated electrical lines, digging through a key of symbols draped over the map. *"Ah!"*

He looked above to find a service hatch situated above his head. The walls offered him a convenient set of footholds, and he climbed up to investigate the porthole. He clasped his fingers around the crank wheel, giving it a good yank. Nothing except the metallic clicks of the locking mechanism bashing against its confinement.

"Oh, dear." He examined the circumference of the hats, passing a finger around the seams. *"No access here. That's inconvenient."*

"There's a command station behind you," Garret pointed out, sending a signal to his map.

Bellanar turned to glance at the flickering beacon, tracing his eyes over a grid of catwalks above him. They led to an observation deck coated in reinforced glass, technicians dutifully watching the settings of the boiler room through a set of glowing green monitors.

"Excellent!" Bellanar praised. *"Let's go say hello!"*

"I don't think—" Before Garrett could finish his protest, Bellanar had already patched through the communication line.

"Unit 56A to station." Bellanar perked up. "Need access to pressure valve 0794."

One of the techs raised their head to look over the facility, spotting Bellanar waving enthusiastically at them.

"We haven't had any reports of an interruption there," the technician replied.

"Are you sure about that?" Bellanar folded his arms, tapping a foot impatiently. "Foreman's been on my ass about sealants here and asked me to check it out. But if you want to explain that to him, be my guest."

The technician rolled their eyes, shaking their head as they pressed a command into their computer. "All right, all right. Give me a second."

Bellanar beamed and turned away. "I appreciate you!"

"Shove it."

"Have you done this before?" Garrett asked, the conversation shrouding him in disbelief.

"I have warned you about incriminating questions." Bellanar climbed

to the hatch and turned the crank. *"Besides, it's a prison ship. Who would be aboard that shouldn't be?"*

"I suppose you have a point there."

The hatch opened and burped a gust of hot air. Unphased by the temperature shift, Bellanar pulled himself through the portal, clambering into an uncomfortably narrow shaft of wires and fuel lines. *"Ooh, toasty!"*

"Will you be all right?" The bars of the temperature monitor flickered deviously in Garrett's view.

"Perfectly!" Power lines vibrated beneath him as he traversed on hands and knees, the lifeforce of the ship coursing through the channel. He verified his location on the map, selecting a quiet place to emerge. Pausing in front of an exit hatch, he switched filters on his view, summoning a collective of cone-shaped beams waving back and forth along the hallway above. *"Well, that simply won't do."*

With a tap of a finger, he highlighted the security camera shining down on his position. A few strands of commands later, and the beacon stopped moving, giving him the opportunity to sneak through. *"Much better."*

Delicate fingers traced the seams of the panel, and with a tiny shove, the sheet of metal popped out, sliding on the floor with a modest rattle. Bellanar rolled out of the opening, standing up to stretch out his limbs. He yawned softly and headed for a heavy reinforced door at the end of the hall. A sharp *ting* rippled through the air as he rapped a knuckle on the material, analyzing the thickness of the barrier.

"All right, that was the easy part," he hummed, pawing through his computer. *"Now I just need to break through—"*

CLANG!

A heavy thump whapped in front of him, the noise dampened by the bulkhead obstructing his path. Muffled shouts of distress bounced over paneling and panicked orders barked through the discharge of weaponry. A moment later, there was nothing but silence.

"What was that?" Garrett locked his eyes to the monitor.

"If I were to guess..." Bellanar deserted the thought, furiously

unlatching the seals of the barrier through his interface. A familiar sickly sweetness tickled his nostrils as the panes slowly slid apart.

"Oh, *shit.*" Garrett caught a glimpse of the source, the slumped body of a security guard lying on the floor. Blood saturated their clothes, splatters streaking down the walls where they fell. Their distant glassy eyes were frozen in an expression of sheer horror, mouth slackened after releasing their final cries to the world. A smoking gun rested in their lap, fingers tightly wound around the handle.

Taking a cautious step back, he slid a hand to his helmet, feeling for a setting in his communicator. *They don't need to see this.*

"Hey!" Garrett protested. "What are you—" With a click, the human's presence evaporated.

Bellanar rested a hand on the wall, bracing himself, and slowly turned the corner, silence tapping the base of his spine. There he found Nara, covered in blood, unnervingly still. The manacles that had bound her wrists were severed, the sharp fragments chafing at her skin. Her clothing was torn with numerous gunshot holes, but the skin beneath them was immaculate, fresh, and youthful.

At her feet lay the remains of two other humans, their uniforms covered in a warm blanket of their own viscera. The eye of one had been gouged out, their skull cracked open by what appeared to be furrows of claws.

"Elam," Bellanar softly called out to her. "Are you okay?"

He caught her eyes, the light inside flickering flames. Her body was unearthly still, her lifeforce concealed from him. Only emptiness remained, her mind completely blank. Unreachable.

He was alone with this predator, cut off from any help inside dangerous territory. The ubiquitous chill of the unknown washed over him in unrelenting waves.

"Elam? Can you hear me?" No reaction, not even a breath. "I am going to approach you."

He crept forward and reached out a hand, ice consuming his arm as his trepidation surged.

Nara snapped her head toward him, staring down at the quaking extremity. She tilted her head, perplexed by the gesture.

"Come along," he beckoned with deliberate waves. "I have a means of esc—"

A storm of clacks interrupted his statement, and the lights extinguished. Sirens erupted through the hallway, screeches of warning sirens strobing with pulses of vicious red light. Behind him, Bellanar could hear a flood of boot stomps headed their way.

SECURITY ALERT. ALL PERSONNEL REPORT TO ALL CELL FACILITIES. ALL STATIONS ON LOCKDOWN.

"Hold it right there!" a voice shouted, the glint of a multitude of gun barrels pointed at him. "Who are you?"

Before Bellanar could muster a response, Nara turned to the command, bared fangs shimmering behind a crooked smile. A low rumble reverberated across the chamber. Her threatening growl set the nerves of the assault squad on edge. Their guns lowered as they watched her unshakeable form begin to approach, her steady gait animated by machines, methodical, calculated.

"Stop at once," the squad commander warned. "We will use lethal force."

"Elam, wait." Bellanar tried to usher her away, but his words fell on unresponsive ears.

Clicks echoed across the corridor as the squad raised their weapons. Shrill cries of energy fueled up their charges. But before they could acknowledge the order to fire, Nara hurled out an earth-shattering bellow. Frozen by the outburst, the assault squad just stared as she rushed at them.

Static blooms of laser fire burst through the darkness, a fragment of the team firing in reaction to the attack. Their wild shots illuminated the slaughter of their compatriots, the shrieks of their weaponry drowned out by terrified screams. The commander's orders trailed off in a half-breath, their voice stolen from their throat.

Amid the chaos, Bellanar stood stunned by the carnage. A flash of light jolted him back to reality and a searing warmth lashed across his skin. The sight clicked into his brain, and not knowing what else to do, he dove back around the corner to take cover. He dared a glance at the fight, his contingency plans slowly dissipating from his brain.

Round upon round perforated Nara's skin, but she was unmoved by the pain. Her mind was hyper-focused on the retreating beings, her arms coiling around any extremity within her reach. The last unit standing slipped on the blood-slickened flooring, crashing headfirst into the body of their fallen commander. They met the lifeless eyes and let out their terror in a nerve-rending screech. The sound was cut short, replaced with the sunder of flesh and pop of bone. After a moment, the carnage ceased, leaving only the sirens wailing in its wake.

Bellanar stood immobile at the sight, watching Nara's panting form normalize to slow, steady breaths. Her skin glistened, her exposed muscles binding and fusing back into place. She craned her neck from side to side, the bone crunching back into place. She turned to face him, the gashes across her cheeks melding back to their original state.

"Elam…" he whispered. "*Please come back.*"

CRACK

Lightning consumed the corridor in vivacious pink tongues. The lights exploded with a *POP*, leaving him in darkness. The sirens dissolved with a winding moan and an eerie stillness filled the void. The ship no longer possessed a heartbeat.

The emergency power cycled on, radiating a warm yellow glow to illuminate the area. Now he was alone. Nara was nowhere to be seen.

He frantically switched back his communications feed. "*Garrett, are you still there?*"

"Are you all right? What happened!?"

"You tell me."

"Tosk is here with a fleet. They disabled the prison ship." The sounds of flustered pounding of control panels were heard in the background as Garrett spoke. "And us with it. I can't seem to get the ship's controls to work."

"*Find the shield settings. You should be able to disengage from its influence through there.*"

Outside, Garrett and the scouter ship were cocooned by a swirling pink glow, the web stretching around the GaPFed ship. The *Armored*

Wake exhaled its breath weapon, the beam of light swallowing its hapless prey, edging closer to feast.

Behind the battleship, a battalion of cruisers emerged. Whorls of blues and greens bled into the void, tearing apart reality through flashes of hyperspace.

"Where's Nara?" Garrett demanded, keeping his eyes glued to the viewscreen.

"I don't—" Bellanar's reply was cut off by shouts in the distance. *"Damn it. I've got to go. Try to hail Tosk."*

"Don't leave—"

Bellanar bolted down the corridor, following a trail of bodies. He halted when he met Nara around a corner, a gasping victim in her grasp.

"Elam, please," he implored, reaching out to her. "I have you now. We can leave."

She hesitated, staring through the human as she considered the words. The guard's eyes bugged out of their sockets as they futilely clawed at her hand, the grip of stone cinching their throat. Her arm slid down to her side, releasing her quarry in a whimpering mass. As they scrambled away, Nara sank to her knees. Fired faded from her eyes, leaving cold embers behind.

"Hell!" Bellanar dove to her aid, catching her as she slumped to one side. With a grunt, he slung her over his shoulder, pulling himself up to his feet. He braced himself along the wall as he dragged her out of the fight. The scent of death overwhelmed his nostrils, and he did not dare to look back.

"Come along. I've got you now." His attention moved to the beacon of the scouter ship inside his HUD, hovering to their position. *Ah! Perfect!*

A spark of light ignited on the adjacent wall, the sizzle of metal burning against the ship's hull. The glow traced a perfectly round circle into the material, the white light cooling into an inviting orange warmth. With a clatter, the chunk of metal popped onto the floor, revealing the inside of the scouter ship.

"Inside, now!" Garrett shouted from the cockpit.

Bellanar did not hesitate, pushing the unresponsive body of Nara into the ship. A small cheer trailed him as he rolled in behind, flopping onto the main hold.

Magma began to leech out of the scouter. A bubbling mess of liquid metal poured out of the laser cutter. A blast of cooled air cured the material, fusing with the hull of the prison ship. When the hole was fully sealed, the scouter disengaged, shooting off into the vacuum of space.

"You figured it out!" Bellanar praised. "Great work!"

Garrett shrugged then input tasks for the navigation system. "Not really. There's a lot of computer brains available to tell me what to do."

"Well, it was a good show, regardless." He slid over to Garrett's side. "I can take over if you like."

"I....sure." He stepped out of the pilot seat and regarded Nara's unconscious form. There was blood everywhere, caked and dried over her shredded clothing. "What happened in there?"

Bellanar hesitated, busying himself in the controls of the ship. "I don't really know. It was difficult to see with the emergency lighting."

Even Garrett could tell he was lying. His evasive tone and nervousness percolated with each button press. He was about to address the matter when Bellanar charged the acceleration, forcing him back as the craft zipped over the disabling beam weapon to reach the battlecruiser. When he was fully braced, Bellanar opened a channel of communication

"*Scribe 1* to *Armored Wake*," he hailed. "I have *Savant* in custody."

"*You have clearance to land. All hands at Cargo hold 1 ready to assist.*"

The scouter eased into the gravity shield, making a gentle landing onto the first open platform. Chaos erupted as crewmembers stormed in. They snatched Nara and placed her on a medical carrier, placing instruments and metal plates all over her body.

Garrett was about to follow behind when an announcement thundered over the ship-wide intercom:

HYPERSPACE DRIVE INITIALIZED. ALL UNITS PREPARE FOR EMERGENCY JUMP.

The GaPFed prison ship shrank to nothing as the *Armored Wake* accelerated. A low rumble tore through the artificial atmosphere, jittering his eardrums. Space tore apart with a piercing whine, a craggy bolt slicing through the stars. The seam opened into a violent torrent of blinding green and purple clouds, and the *Wake* willingly entered the ravenous maw, letting itself be consumed by the energetic blanket of hyperspace.

In a flash, the *Wake* returned home, only to find another score of guests awaiting them.

CHAPTER 14

##14.0##

Homeworld was being assaulted by an unknown force, a school of predatory creatures zipping in by the droves. Their flat faces and jagged teeth gnashed across the night sky, shining scales of choppy geometric shapes lit up with the pulse of ion weaponry. Predatory sensors homed in on their desires, the pack diving straight for the planet's core. But the Ara'yulthr fleet remained steadfast.

A greedy cruiser dared too close to the surface, speeding straight for the orbital shielding. The planet reacted to the unwelcome guest, hurling tendrils of sticky light from its mass. The crackling web ensnared the frigate in its sweetened embrace, immobilizing their prey with its venomous tangle of energy. Others soon suffered the same fate, the carnivorous planet feasting upon the cells of its newfound food source. Specks of glittering explosions brightened the scene as the enemy fighters launched missile salvos against the shields, attempting to free their comrades from the sap.

Squadrons of Ara'yulthr capital ships folded their wings, speeding toward destroyers distracted by the plight of their brethren. Cones of static pulsed from their mouths, their breath speaking words of silence to the piranha ships. The enemy could not sustain their attack, drifting aimlessly as their engines choked out.

The largest of the capital ships swooped in and towed them away, pulling them out of reach of Homeworld.

"Tosk to Main Fleet," the commander hailed from the bridge of the *Wake*. "What is your status?"

"Minimal casualties, energy stores optimal."

Tosk examined the conflict, scrolling through reports of resource consumption. "Who are they?"

"Definitely not GaPFed. Records show closest build and technology to be Charon Clan pirate fleet. Onboard scribes are verifying flags."

"Board who you can and get answers."

"Affirmat—"

The void screamed a mournful wail, interrupting the communication with a surge of energy. Blackness extinguished the stars, swallowing their fires beneath its dark influence. The scream intensified to an ominous drone. The scene blistered apart in a scar of bruised light. Blood reds, violent purples, and sickly yellows swirled open, the infection spreading to a massive scale.

The visceral storm bellowed, and out from the shadowy clouds emerged three black-barbed spires. Time slowed as the mammoth ship emerged into Ara'yulthr territory, the vile beast dominating the space. The gruesome construct diminished the *Armored Wake's* stature, its spiked carapace radiating an aura of power. Its engines belched an ocean of noxious venom, marking its path with pollution as it glided with a dreadful elegance.

"Flags confirmed. Charon Clan," the Homeworld station reported. *"Known planet killers in the GaPFed archives."*

"What are they doing here?"

Gravity churned around the behemoth, interrupting the conversation with a torrential inferno of vicious red light. The spiked fangs of the ship glowed, metal scalding inside a coil of jagged energy. The energy expanded to a head, molten light collecting in a pustule of fire. An abyssal war cry ejected from the monster, sending shredding waves of noise rippling out through space. The sound climaxed, and the growth burst into a concentrated flow of seething energy.

The core of discharge hurtled toward Homeworld, threatening to consume everything within its path. It radiated with the light of three suns, the refuse scorching the atmosphere as it sped toward its mark.

"*Wake* to *Guarded Cloak*," Tosk yelled into the comms. "Evasive maneuvers at once!"

Engine fire exploded from the battleship as it turned its massive hulk, burning into overdrive to avoid the corrosive energy. But their flight was swiftly cut short. The acidic fire of the insatiable monolith lanced through the ship's hull, warping and bending it as if made of clay. Unfazed by the obstruction, the malignant beam emerged from the other side, carving a hole through the ship's belly. Support beams of the carcass melted, the heat twisting them out from out from the flesh of its hull.

Groans from the rending metal rang out the *Guarded Cloak's* death throes. The bow peeled apart from its other half, the last strands of vertebra snapping under the pressure. Engines still burned at the aft, sending the mass on a collision course with its head. The gash widened as it traveled, the repulsive beam unmoved by the spectacle.

Fuel cells detonated with the excess heat, engulfing the magnificent creature in an unquenchable blaze. A concussive *PWANG* shattered space, a ring of fire launched from the decaying battleship. A moment later, the fires consumed their fuel sources and extinguished, leaving behind a melted husk drifting through the orbit of Homeworld.

The loathsome weapon raced on, its insatiable hunger tearing through the Ara'yulthr fleet. Searing plasma intensified at the head, planting itself on the edges of the orbital shield. The planet was engulfed with white as the weapon bared its full weight. Swirling storms of conflicting energies singed through the power generators.

The pink influence weakened with the strike, its vibrancy flickering as each second passed. Forced to relinquish its hold on the ships imprisoned within its grasp, the shielding righted itself, focusing on dissolving the corruption eroding away at its lifeforce. With the redirected fuel sources, the shield compensated, healing its flesh as the pestilence dissipated. A moment later, the poison vanished, leaving its scar on the guardian.

The bridge crew of the *Wake* stared in awe at the destruction. The impact of kindred lost resonated through their spirits.

Tosk could not afford to hesitate further. "Homeworld, status!"

"Shields holding, need to recharge," The planet responded. *"Several power stations disabled. We won't be able take another hit like that."*

"All units, deploy Carrion squadrons! Take that ship out *now.*"

Friendly battleships released their brood at the fanged creature. Gnashing teeth rotated around implements of destruction, the squadrons sizing up their hunt. They traced geometric shapes in space, calculating the most efficient pattern to take on the beast.

The blistering giant recoiled, weary from the spent energy. It savored the attack, gliding nearer to the planet while it recuperated. Red tendrils began to wrap around the spires, charging up for another strike. It grinned as it anticipated the interceptors speeding toward it, hacking out a cloud of mines at the oncoming carrion feeders.

Hunger fought against hunger, the carrion ships proving their agility as they weaved through the spined countermeasures. The behemoth was not impressed, igniting the mines with its own weapons batteries. Bubbles of light pocked the battleship as it downed as many carrion ships as it could.

But the carrion feeders craved more, tearing through the defenses for a taste of flesh. One by one, the feeders sank their teeth into the hull of the mammoth. Screeches of tearing metal rippled through waves of sparks, the squadrons masticating the flesh with greedy delight. Their work started on the spires, each consuming, tearing. Devouring.

Pieces of the behemoth began to break apart, the weaponry rendered useless. Once the carrions had their fill of this structure, they moved on to other delicacies, ripping through weapons and communications arrays. Flesh stripped from bone, crumbs trailing from the feast into the beyond.

A tear in space interrupted the meal. Fleet Admiral Rothgar and her entourage entered the battlefield, her eyes set on the *Armored Wake.*

"Rothgar to all Ara'yulthr ships. You are to cease all activities and surrender at once."

Tosk responded to the hail, letting their fury saturate their tone. "Call off your attack squad then."

"They are not under our orders."

They were through with her demands, having seen enough of GaPFed's idea of alliance. "Then you have two choices. Leave at once. Or join them."

Rothgar watched as the eviscerated planet killer floated away. The carrion feeders finished their meal and headed to the aid of the *Wake*. She held her ground, jabbing a hand at Tosk. "GaPFed will not tolerate threats upon their citizens, nor the tampering of high-profile security ships."

"So be it." The *Wake* turned to Rothgar's ship, the point of the bow crackling with violent energy. "This is your final warning. Leave at once."

Rothgar ground her jaw, not wanting to show weakness to an uncooperative force. But she was not a fool either, and she had to accept her disadvantage. "This is not the last you will hear from us."

"And when you change your tone," Tosk added, "we just *might* consider your voice."

They cut the channel, not interested in witnessing GaPFed's retreat to their higher powers. There was so much to recover from.

##14.1##

IT HAD ONLY BEEN a few weeks since he landed on this planet, but Garrett felt as if he had aged several years. Despite how slow this civilization naturally ran, they reacted with such swiftness when forced under pressure.

He looked at Nara on the medical bed, the chimes and whispers of her status a poor mimicry of her presence. She had been asleep for days now, and he feared the worst. Guilt overwhelmed him. He had no context for what she was going through, but the glimpse of violence he had witnessed on the battlefield gave him enough to piece together a fragment of context. He would never be able to understand who she is, but if he were given time, perhaps they could find common ground.

Bellanar quietly approached the side of the bed. His pensive stare spoke volumes of what he was thinking. But the flickers of his mind were too fast for Garrett to keep up with. "Are you all right?"

The man hesitated, taking in a deep breath of air, savoring it, then releasing it in a meditative stream. "We have always been told to fear those afflicted by *Fever*." He reached out and brushed a finger over Nara's hand. "They cannot recognize reality, cannot distinguish friend from foe. They can never return. Though I have never witnessed it firsthand."

Garrett looked at the ground, memories of a previous conversation with Nara echoing in his mind. "I am not sure I understand." But he had an idea. A terrible, dreadful idea.

Bellanar continued, his posture disengaged as if he were conversing with himself, detached from Garrett's addition to the conversation. "It is unheard of for one so young to experience it. They had said she was afflicted. And yet... it just cannot be. There is something else going on."

The man's implications pained Garrett. He had nearly lost her several times before. He would be beside himself if he were to lose her again.

Bellanar snapped back to reality, brows furrowed with concern as he watched Garrett's reaction. "I... I am sorry. I should not trouble you so." With a bow, he departed, leaving a hollow emptiness behind.

He sank into the guest seat, his head weighing him down. It wasn't fair. No one deserved to feel this way, least of all her. The enigma of Bellanar's words rippled through his mind, summoning tears against his will. A sob escaped his clutches as he struggled to maintain his composure. The ache in his chest swelled to an agonizing throb.

Please. I can't do this again.

From the other side of the med bay observation glass, Tosk regarded the interaction, still uncertain about their actions against the GaPFed fleet. History morphed by these moments, the voice of one altering the path of another.

The commander had maintained the flow of status quo for their entire career, the cost of breaking the chains of stagnation far too unsavory. But if one is to lean on Fate to draw the road, to remain an observer while the universe moved around them, someone else will seize their choices away.

Tosk stepped away from the observation room, setting off to resume their duties on the bridge. Resolution would be a long, arduous journey.

"Ötmarr's trust, Savant."

EPILOGUE

ADDENDUM

*P*resent Date: Era 0987
With the events of the conflict involving Homeworld, GaPFed, and the unsanctioned Charon fleets, a new charter regarding the development of the star fleet has been established.

The main screen in the Council Chamber Hall slowly scrolled with words, the neutral tone of the text-to-speech functionality reading the document out loud.

Terms of the New Galactic Accord are as follows:

—Due to the unestablished power shift of the naval fleet, discussions with GaPFed or any other galactic power are hereby withheld until internal structures are solidified.

—The primary purpose of the naval fleet is for planetary defense, therefore, at least seventy percent of the force is to remain on Homeworld.

—With this and the potential threats of outside forces increasing, the other thirty percent is to be dedicated to exploration and intelligence gathering.

—Control of the fleet is to be divided thusly:

—The Council of the Future maintains control of the ships and maintenance for further research.

—The Council of the Present is in charge of crew and strategies regarding planetary defense.

—The Council of the Past is in charge of all exploration missions, and all new information is to be reported to them with the highest priority.

—This structure will remain until it has been proven that a new branch is required.

—No disciplinary action will be taken against the Separatist movement. However, since personnel planning is the responsibility of the Present, it is under the current regime's discretion to integrate the Separatists into the new fleet with formal training in ship functionality.

—The terms of this treaty are to last 100 years, where the New Galactic Accord is to be reassessed for potential weakness in policy.

"Since this is a Global Priority issue, a decision cannot be made until we are all at a consensus." Prism addressed the crowd with a firm gesture, the flutter of their braids emphasizing punctuation. "With that said, the New Galactic Accord is written to be amended at any given notice, presuming the movement to amend is voted upon. Now as it stands, do we all accept the terms of this treaty?"

The conversation dulled to a contemplative murmur. Green lights began to spark over each councilor's seat. A peaceful emerald glow overtook the chambers, reflecting in the eyes of all participants. It was decided.

"Excellent. Let us now move on to our next subject, the memorializing of those lost as a result of this conflict."

It was easy for her to slip off the *Armored Wake*. A ship that size was riddled with pathways. She could have left then, seizing the opportunity as the planet recovered from the wreckage. But there were loose ends to tie off, obligations to perform the formalities.

Nara soaked in the sounds of her footsteps over the marble-like floor, evoking memories of quiet times reading during her youth. Gilded vines curled around the carved stone trees that supported *Lore-*

master's estate. One of the oldest buildings was created from traditional materials, a monument to tranquility in the pursuit of knowledge. Stained glass domes sheltered the building from the elements, a watercolor gradient of leaves glimmering with the sunlight.

Warm light followed her as she moved up the coiling bloom of the stairwell. She used to consider these walls a sanctuary, instilling a sense of tenuous peace inside the beauty of the structure. But now she was unwelcome, trespassing through foreign territory.

The floral webbed gate to *Loremaster's* office was open, and he sat behind his desk with a tea tray prepared. He regarded her warmly, a steady wisp of steam tracing over his smile. "Greetings, child."

"I have come to rescind my title," she announced.

"Of course. But..." He averted his eyes, the shame in his voice creeping through. "There may be a problem."

"*What?*" Her heart seized, her suspicions firing inside her brain.

"*Loremaster* must be of sound mind to relinquish that post. And as of late... that has come into question."

She clamped her jaw shut, grinding her molars as she contemplated the implication. She should have known better. It always ended up this way.

"You withdraw this plague you have infected me with." Her voice was a hiss, her severe eyes slinging venom.

He raised a hand up and exhaled, barely able to contain his voice. "I wish I could, child. But..."

Enough. "I am leaving. And you will not stop me." She turned her back to him, heading for the door.

"I understand." His voice wavered, a thousand pleas scarring his words. "But please return soon. There is not much time left."

She glared at him over her shoulder. *Did he plan this the entire time? This deceit was far beneath him.*

He swiveled around in his seat, staring off into the horizon, watching the oceans ebb and flow. "Farewell, Lev'anet." *Catalyst. Earthshatterer.* A force of nature resulting in violent, but necessary, change.

She froze at the title, her fists clenched until they were quaking. She did not want this. She did not ask for this. All she wanted was peace. To be left alone. Pain lashed at her insides as she restrained her fury, departing from the accursed ivory palace.

THE CELL WINDOW dissolved to transparency, the former Councilor of the Present inside tending to their small cultivation plot. Nara slid into the visitor's chair, waiting for the questions to formulate in her brain.

After Torel checked the irrigation system, they switched the device off then lowered into their own seat.

"Good evening, *Savant.*" The greeting was flat. Neither disdain nor contentment shone through.

"I trust your facility has been taken care of?" Small talk was not her strongest skill, but she was hoping to buy herself more time until she determined what her goal was for this visit.

"Yes, I have several students relaying the experiment data to me. And while they maintain the grounds, I am able to continue my small-scale work here." They shifted, tightening their posture with folded limbs. "I have no complaints."

"Mmm." It was no use. No matter the circumstance, she would never be prepared to hear the motivation behind their actions. She stewed in contemplation, beating back the inquiries as they bubbled to the surface.

"This.... engagement." Torel derailed her thoughts. "It leaves the future to be seen, doesn't it? Or rather, we *have* a future now."

Behind the hopeful words lay a graveyard of remorse. And it was something Nara did not have the energy to recover, nor the interest.

"Was it all worth it?" They brought their gaze to her. "All those who died for this new era. I don't deny my responsibility in starting the conflict, but was it the best possible outcome?"

Why don't you take your nose out of the weeds once in a while and take a look around? Don't ask me these deep philosophical questions and expect answers where there are none. She kept the bile inside, not having the energy for discourse.

"Death amid the stars is a different experience for the living." A dismal sigh left Torel's throat. "No one around to witness their final moments, no connection. Gone in the blink of an eye from unfathomable distance."

Why am I even here? Nara stood up and turned away, anger beginning to rise.

"I am not asking for absolution, but perhaps one day, I will have the ability to make amends." Torel's admission cracked through her spirits. "I just wanted the people to move on. Stagnation is no match for chaos."

Numbness seeped through her mind. Their admission didn't make the situation any better. But revenge was a foreign concept and something she had never desired. All she wanted was to stop feeling so bitter, to recover from all the damage she had been subjected to. And to ensure it never happened again.

"Spare me." Her voice flickered through a growl, and she left the prison more battered than when she started.

SHOULD BE enough supplies to reach a station in the next solar system. Nara passed a hand over a tablet, counting the supply manifesto. *I'd hate to have to hit Arcadia again. If I could even reach the border.*

She recited the items on the list, tracing over the screen with a stylus. "Thirteen crates of medgel, twenty-nine fuel cell rods, thirty-two reams of solar sheeting..."

How did I get off that ship?

The invasive question tore through her barriers, her grip on the stylus threatened to snap the device in half. With a blink, her eyes refocused, the distracted scrawling desecrating the tablet. She huffed and erased the marks, continuing her task.

"Forty-two vegetation seed pods..." She absentmindedly ran her tongue over her teeth as she counted.

That taste. Blood. Unforgettable...How did I get here?

"Wait!" The voice tore her away from an unsettling internal discourse. She looked over to find Garrett running toward the dock.

"What are you doing here?" She let out an exasperated sigh upon spotting Bellanar coming up the rear. "Oh."

"You're leaving?"

"My contract is completed." She tossed a container in the open cargo bay with a heave. "And I am cashing out."

"I… I am glad to know that you are okay."

She dusted her hands together, setting off to retrieve another crate. "Mmmhmm."

Her casual dismissal stole his breath. A crackling plea ejected from his throat. "Where will I go…" *Without you?* He couldn't bring himself to speak his mind, the stony figure casting him aside.

"I have given you options." She paced back to the supply cache, sorting through the labels with a trace of a finger. "That choice is up to you."

"I see." He gazed at the ground, clouds of sorrow raining on him. She left scars on him, literal wounds, and a storm of questions that still remained unanswered. They had spent so much time together, yet the tumultuous demons behind circumstance had never allowed them to understand each other fully. Ultimately, he was losing a friend… again.

Nara let out a grumble as the human's turmoil curdled inside him. *Melodramatic little shit.*

She had to admit, it was unfair of her to desert him on an unfamiliar world. And only gods knew what would happen if he were to set off on his own. Even though she was convinced it was not her responsibility. "Fine. I will teach you how to run a ship so that when the opportunity comes, you will be able to make a living for yourself somewhere else."

"I… oh. Sure." The offer bounced off him, relief far away from his reach. Exhaustion from the mental roller coaster of the season's events took a toll on him. Without prompting, he approached the pile of crates and hefted one over his shoulder, pushing back the nagging half-thoughts clouding his perception.

A cough disrupted the conversation, prompting another grumble from Nara. "What do you *want*, Bellanar?"

"I, oh, well, are you taking *that* ship?" He pointed at the sleek falcon nestled in its docking bay.

"Yes. It is mine. Tosk commandeered it as compensation for my service." She slammed another crate down. "Problem?"

"Oh, well, It's just..." Bellanar fidgeted, knitting his fingers into undulating patterns. "I was so used to the controls. And there isn't another one on queue for construction for at least another—"

"Uuuuuuuuugh." Nara stopped her tracks and leaned back, glaring up at the sky.

"I mean, it *is* a ten-person ship." He shrugged and shook his head. "I don't know what you would do with all that extra space."

"Run a mobile brothel known for decadent hedonism." Nara scrubbed her face agitatedly. "What's it to you?"

"I–I–I... did not expect that from—" Bellanar cleared his throat. "Well, regardless, you'll need a scribe for your travels, and—"

She cleared her throat, audibly inhaling a deep draught of air. "You have *three. Hours.* To pack your shit and staple your mouth shut."

"Ah! I see." The man scurried off, disappearing from the docks.

Nara shook her head, meeting the eyes of the forlorn human. *I am going to regret this.*

CLOUDS OF STEAM curled around his legs as he exited the recovery chamber. He settled into the plush seat of the grandiose black marble adorned suite, taking in his reflection on the window, accented by the view of the planet beneath him. Vibrant neon eyes flickered, summoning a hologram of a video channel.

"I hope my hospitality is to your liking, Warlord," Galavantier greeted.

"Yes, you are quite accommodating, Chairman." Abberon flexed his fingers, feeling the rush of sensation speeding through the candescent veins tracing over his knuckles. "You have quite an interesting regard for life, creating a commodity of exploration that has yet to be exploited to its fullest potential."

"You flatter us, Warlord. And I must commend you on your constitution. I hope your discomfort was not too great."

Abberon unfurled a smirk from his lips. "Quite the opposite, I must admit. Forgive me for my insistence on using my native pharmaceuticals. I have an allergy to many sedatives back home, and I did not want to risk an unfortunate accident."

"Of course." The lie did not faze the businessman. "I hope you are acclimating to Federation life."

"Indeed. I must say your concept of currency is quite fascinating." *And simple.*

"And there are plenty of ways to obtain it, especially for one as influential as yourself."

"You flatter me, Chairman."

"I assure you, this is a territory of opportunity. You will have no problems here." Galavantier poured himself a drink from an elegantly crafted glass decanter. "The skirmish between GaPFed and your home world were startling. I hope you are not too troubled by the results."

Abberon summoned a news report of the incident. Recordings of the unknown ships and the destruction they wrought looped through his eyes. "Losses will happen. A fleet like that cannot be expected to avoid confrontation from foreign forces. Especially a force as *uncontrollable* as pirates."

"I quite agree." Galavantier brandished a knowing smirk. "This looks to be the start of a profitable relationship."

"I look forward to seeing what our combined resources can bring to the galaxy." Abberon nodded his head. "I await your next proposal."

"We will be in contact." The screen snapped off, revealing the serenity of the starlight in his view.

His smile widened. A soft snicker disrupted the silence. "We shall see."

END TRANSMISSION

LANGUAGE APPENDIX

The Ara'yulthr language is based off two different independent functioning vocal cords. Punctuation at the beginning of a word, sentence, or phrase denotes which cord to use, and even to use both at the same time. Another indicator denotes switching of chords mid word or phrase.

Many have adapted a unique way of speaking in mono-vocal languages such as Trade. Using one organ or the other as a sort of signature. Occasionally, an individual may use both as an intimidation tactic, or to display offence.

Another key factor in the language is also semi-psychic, focusing on expression and projected emotions, as well as body language. There is also a gesture component to accommodate non-vocal individuals

The sound of the Ara'yulthr language is described as guttural purrs seamlessly blended with almost lyrical harmonics. Akin to throat singing.

Non-augmented humans can speak phonetically and will be understood with context.

Personal Pronouns

Here, pronouns do not refer to gender identity. Instead, they are markers of status or career function.

Commonly used pronouns:

Serr = Peer, honored, formal
Serr'kahn = student, youngling
Serr'Maht Aged, venerable, teacher
Ahm'Serr = Unfamiliar, respectable
K'vai = Member of the Scribes
K'vai'tem = Inner Circle scribe
K'vai'Luut = Loremaster
Qu'ol = Member of Science
Sci'ith = soldier, ranks have unique titles

There may be more specific pronouns to denote ranking or fields of study in the Science and Military divisions, or authorization tiers from the Scribes.

Some have adopted human pronouns whether for convenience, or they identify more closely with human characteristics.

Swearing

Instead of variations of sexual activities and bodily functions, Ara'yulthr expletives are basically different ways to say "OW." This stems from a severe familiarity with pain, either from suffering casualties in nature, or years spent in the gaming arenas. Different words and adjectives are used to imply depth of annoyance.

Name calling can vary from endearing to spiteful based on the descriptors used. The more damage is described, the harsher the obscenity. "Stabbing" versus "putting a dagger in (body part)"

Categories of swearing can include:

Household objects – implying unitaskers, having one purpose. i.e calling someone a chair or a tool of some kind.

Objects with conflicting adjectives – Something that is meant for one purpose being used for something else "You are trying very hard sweetie, but it just isn't working out." i.e a bent needle, screwdriver with a hex nut.

Diseases are the utmost offensive, as they describe nothing but malicious intent:

Parasite – You are causing harm to benefit yourself.
Pestilence – You are causing harm for the fun of it.

Now that her contract is completed, what is next for Nara and her companions? Will she find peace in the stars, or will the demons lurking in the galaxy come for her? There are still so many loose ends to tie, and so many more new adventures to unlock! Stay tuned for the next chapter in the Sleepless Flame saga!

Did you enjoy seeing Nara's home planet? Let Odin know and leave a review on Amazon!

Want More Nara? Be sure to check out https://www. odinsmusings.com/ and sign up for email updates on the next saga installments. Get exclusive access to unreleased content, sample chapters, and more of the Sleepless Flame galaxy.

And if you need some ambiance while reading, take a look at these Soundtracks inspired by the world and main characters:

Spotify
YouTube

Find the rest of the Sleepless Flame Universe on Amazon!

Do you work in a Local Library or own an independent book, comic, or gaming shop? Would you like to offer the Sleepless Flame Universe to your readers?

Feel free to contact Odin about getting copies!
odins.musings@gmail.com

ALSO BY ODIN V OXTHORN

Sleepless Flame

Mourning Ember

ANTHOLOGIES ODIN HAS BEEN FEATURED:

"The Weight of the Lotus"

Crash Code – Blood Bound Books

https://www.bloodgutsandstory.com

ABOUT THE AUTHOR

A chronically bored spooky creature, Odin dabbles in a strange array of interests to keep their wandering brain in check. When not writing under the influence of caffeinated drinks and sugary snacks, Odin can be found escaping reality with video games or getting their fingers tangled in a mess of threads and needles. Provided their cats do not scatter the contents of their workspace across oblivion, Odin also creates beaded jewelry and video lessons on YouTube.

Be sure to find Odin around the Interwebs and see more of their works:

https://www.odinsmusings.com/

Jewelry Persona Odin's Bead Hall:
http://odinsbeadhall.com/

facebook.com/OdinsMusings

twitter.com/OdinsMusings

instagram.com/odinsmusings

youtube.com/odinsmusings

goodreads.com/odinsmusings

bookbub.com/authors/odin-oxthorn

www.ingramcontent.com/pod-product-compliance
Lightning Source LLC
Chambersburg PA
CBHW072220170626
46813CB00003B/1024